www.southdublinlibraries.ie
South Dublin Libraries

D1610266

FINDING THE WAY

Wayne Ng

Finding the Way

By Wayne Ng

ISBN-13: 978-988-8422-78-4

Cover design: Jason Wong

FICTION / Historical

EB099

Published by Earnshaw Books Ltd. (Hong Kong)

To Trish, for showing me the way.

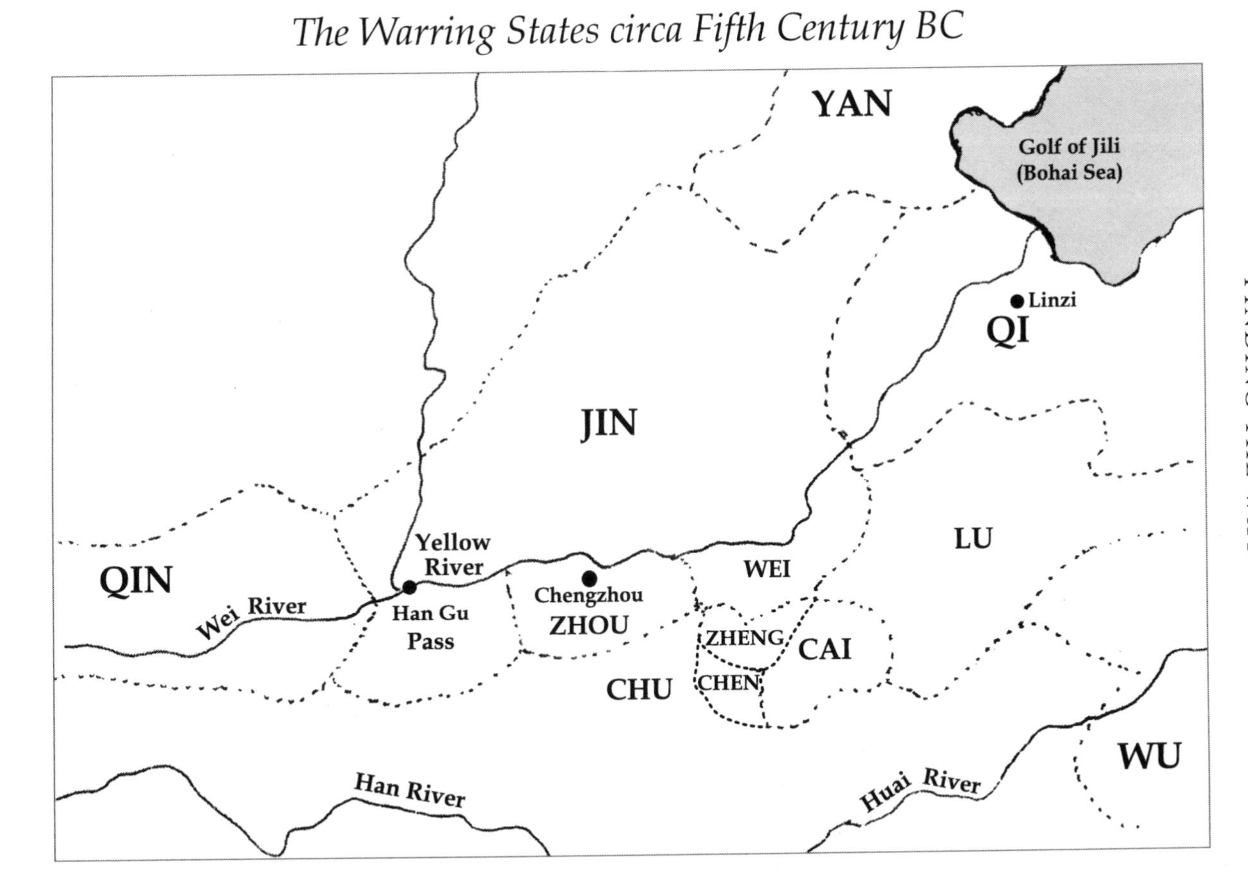
The Warring States circa Fifth Century BC
YAN
Golf of Jili
(Bohai Sea)
Linzi
QI
JIN
LU
QIN
Yellow River
Wei River
Han Gu Pass
Chengzhou
ZHOU
WEI
ZHENG
CAI
CHEN
CHU
WU
Han River
Huai River

Contents

Historical Note viii

1. Han Gu Pass 1

2. Father's Way 9

3. Bitten Peach 23

4. Alone, Alas 41

5. The Road to Chengzhou 54

6. The Forbidden Royal Palace 67

7. The Royal Archives 78

8. Mei 90

9. Prince Meng 99

10. Prince Chao 117

11. Nature's Sorrow 128

12. Confucius 147

13. The Royal Hunt 161

14. Royal Defilement 179

15. Aura of Doubt 193

16. Pawns of War 212

17. Madness Revealed 235

18. Finding the Way 254

Historical Note

The founder of Taoism, China's only indigenous religion and a philosophical cornerstone of Chinese culture for over two thousand years, is reputed to have been Lao Tzu. The historical records are inexact, but it is said that he worked in the Royal Archives of the court of the Zhou dynasty and that he and Confucius crossed paths there. It is conceivable that they met during the reign of King Jing (544-520 B.C), who supposedly had two sons, Prince Meng and Prince Chao, one of whom, according to the stories handed down, killed the other.

In the first century B.C., the historian Sima Qian referred to Lao Tzu as being disillusioned towards the end of his life. He told of how Lao Tzu mounted a water buffalo and set off to die, traveling at least as far as the Han Gu Pass, where he was stopped by a border guard named Yin Xi. This work of fiction picks up the legend from that moment.

1

Han Gu Pass

Shielding his eyes from a blinding sandstorm, Captain Yin Xi spied a figure approaching from the east. He instinctively tightened his grip on his sword and sought a better vantage point, climbing atop the ramparts of the crumbling fort which secured the Han Gu Pass.

A break in the wind allowed him to adjust his gaze east into the Royal territory he was tasked with guarding. Because of the distance he could not be certain, but as the figure approached, he was able to discern the outline of what appeared to be a man astride a water buffalo, lurching from side to side.

He imagined that both the beast and the man would be parched and exhausted as they navigated through the dry, rocky wasteland interspersed with the scattered bones of soldiers from the many states that had once been brothers under the Zhou dynasty. Not long before, it had offered a contrast to the western bleakness—lush with fertile soil, bountiful farms, meandering streams and prosperous villages. Now, it mattered little which way the Captain's eyes turned. Swaths of barrenness stretched in all directions. Unending war had ravaged the land and dispersed its people. It seemed as if Nature herself had turned on the inhabitants who had shown her such contempt.

As the lone figure edged closer, the Captain saw the man's

mane of white hair flailing in the wind. His appearance contrasted with the soldiers of the neighboring states of Jin or Chu, or worse still, marauding bandits, both of whom often strayed into Royal territory. He was thankful that his lonely outpost had seen no such threat in several months as his platoon was composed of newly-recruited peasants, barely older than children. Most had only ever unsheathed their swords to trim back bushes. He understood they were nothing more than glorified gatekeepers. Yet they were the frontline fodder of King Yuan's pitiful army, an army that had once, generations ago, protected most of the civilized world.

Now, few were left who could resist the major states such as Jin, Qin, Qi, Wu and Chu. The neighboring realms made no secret of their desire to control not only the territory of the Zhou capital, but also all the central states together, as well as the lesser states within them. An edict today from one state declaring another to be a sworn enemy could be replaced tomorrow with a new edict declaring them to be blood brothers. Such was life in a world starved for peace yet too fretful to contemplate it. A world that had witnessed profound military and economic changes, but also a golden age of great thinkers with timeless ideas who had entwined themselves with the nobility and the ambitions of governments. A world that the Captain was aware of, but felt he had missed out on.

Yin knew from the fire of the sun that it was midday. As the sandstorm subsided further, he could now plainly see there was indeed an old man on the buffalo. He loosened his grip on his weapon and shouted down from the tower to alert his lieutenant, more for the exercise than out of any real sense of danger. Each step the beast took appeared as though it could be its last, and the man riding it looked ready to accompany the beast to its death.

The Captain's guards shook off their lethargy and emerged

from the shadows of the gate. Their armor of small, overlapping stitched leather plates was caked in dust and brittle from re-use by generations of conscripts.

Lieutenant Zhang gripped his lance with the untamed nerves of youth. The Captain suspected from the anticipation in his eyes that Zhang thirsted for something thrilling such as uncovering smuggled contraband or spies, instead of the usual searches through wagons of cabbage and onions.

The hunched figure's wild, matted white hair obscured his face, but his long, tattered robe could not conceal his shrunken body. Even so, the Captain felt there was something different about him, perhaps an effortless grace, almost a poetic cadence in his movements.

"Halt!" Lieutenant Zhang said. "Old man, you are either lost or on the run. Which is it?"

Captain Yin chuckled along with the others, then sighed, recalling the days when the King's soldiers were disciplined professionals, able to match the Qin or Chu in skill if not in number. They would never have laughed and been so dismissive.

The old man's head tilted up. "Neither," he said.

"Can you not see you are addressing soldiers of the King?" Zhang shouted. "Bow, you fool!" He noticed a rolled bundle slung over the buffalo's back, and pointed his halberd with its glistening curved blade at it. "What is that?"

The old man's weary eyes searched around, as a poet would for the correct phrase.

"It is all that I require. But if you could be so kind as to fill an old man's water sachet, I would be most grateful."

He gingerly slid off the beast.

"Do we look like servants?" Lieutenant Zhang barked. With one swift thrust of his halberd, he ripped off the old man's pack, and knocked him hard to the ground. The other guards broke out in laughter. Lieutenant Zhang's foot lay on the old man's chest. A dog under a master's slipper would have fared better.

The Captain descended from the tower for a closer look. Even beneath layers of mud and dirt, he recognized the patterns and symbols on the old man's robe.

"Zhang, enough!" he ordered.

"But sir, we have orders to search everyone. Bandits and spies come in all guises."

Captain Yin nudged Zhang back. "True, but not in garments worn by officials of old King Jing's court, however ragged they may now be."

He knelt down and lifted the old man's head, then offered a water skin. "I am Captain Yin. Yin Xi."

The old man heaved a dry cough, caught his breath and stood up.

"My buffalo drinks first," he said. "He has earned it."

Captain Yin recalled his father telling him, 'A man who respects all living beings like brothers lives a life without walls.' This was no bandit or spy in disguise. Yin obliged the old man's request before returning to him.

"Sir," Captain Yin said, "you are a long way from home."

The traveler gulped at some water. "Perhaps. But I am closer to where I am going." He returned the water skin to the Captain. "An old man thanks you for your kindness."

Yin nodded towards the gate. "Surely you cannot be thinking of passing through? The prefect has warned of bandits and barbarians beyond this gate, never mind the Qin soldiers who would like nothing more than to slit your throat for a few coins."

The old man shrugged. "No one would find much on these old bones."

Yin studied him as he filled his water sachet. "The Zhou empire shattered like a broken vase, but it prospered for a time under King Jing. Yet you show none of those riches."

The old man's silence and everything about him indicated that riches were of little consequence. Yin had to know more. "What is your name?"

The old man glanced away. "It is no longer of importance to anyone."

"Do not decide for me what is important," Yin replied, to the delight of the other guards.

"Lao Tzu," the traveler whispered.

Yin's face dropped. "Lao Tzu?"

His father had spoken of the man Lao Tzu as though he were a mythical legend. He had supposedly worked in the Royal Archives before King Jing's death, some forty-years ago.

"That would make you almost ninety years old," he said. "That cannot be."

"Indeed," replied the old man. "Ninety-five spring festivals have passed in my lifetime."

Lieutenant Zhang stared at his Captain, barely concealing his anger. "Sir, he takes us for fools. Tying him to a post in this wind and heat will no doubt teach him respect."

Yin held his Lieutenant back, preferring a less primitive interrogation. "Was Confucius not one of your pupils?"

The old man snorted. "Neither Confucius nor I would find comfort in anyone believing that. But yes, he once visited me. He, like many other scholars, traveled from court to court, dispensing theories and counsel. Confucius had already made a name for himself when he first came to see me. For him, the world was still a dream unfolding. He had positioned himself to believe that the chaos of wars, corruption, hunger and greed that surrounds us all would end if leaders exercised their mandate from heaven to rule justly. Those were heady days, full of promise. For some."

"If you are who you claim to be, then answer me this." Yin

squared his body to Lao Tzu. "Which of the twin Princes almost drowned while playing in his father's garden?"

The old man shrugged. "When a river's sorrow swallows our homes, does it matter how cold the water is?"

He tied his hair into a tight topknot and bowed to the Captain before re-mounting his beast. "May Nature reward your generosity," he said. "I thank you."

He stroked his water buffalo, signaling forward movement.

Lao Tzu's quiet defiance annoyed Yin. It was as though he had been toyed with. He was about to let Zhang loose on him when the old man looked back towards him.

"The twin Princes were already young men when I arrived. But it was whispered that our Son of Heaven's wife had the gardens in their inner courtyard drained after she gave birth to them. She forbade anything that would reflect her loss of beauty."

Yin's stomach tightened. "Wait!" he shouted. The urgency of his tone startled his men. "But how can this be? How is it that you have come to be here?"

The old man's eyes betrayed nothing as Yin caught up with him. "It has been a journey no less meandering than a mountain stream which exhausts itself many *li* later as a dry river bed. I have spent two normal lifetimes wandering the earth, reliving lost opportunities, berating myself and repenting my errors."

It was not bitterness that Yin heard from the old man, nor disappointment, but rather a tired sense of acceptance.

"Old Master," he said. "Passing through into Qin territory will mean certain death. I will not allow that. So long as your mind speaks, you still have much to offer."

Lao Tzu looked down at Yin. "I have learned that it is better to leave a vessel unfilled than to attempt to carry it when it is full. When one's work is done, and one's name is distinguished, to withdraw into obscurity is the way of heaven."

Yin stepped in front of the buffalo and bowed. "Old Master. You are Lao Tzu. This is a remarkable coincidence. It would be a great honor for a humble Captain to share a pot of tea with you."

The Lieutenant grimaced.

Lao Tzu motioned Yin to stand at ease. "In the manner of the Way, there are few coincidences," he said. "I prefer to see them as gnarled branches arriving from unexpected paths. But tell me, how is it that a lowly frontier Captain knows enough of the former King Jing's inner court to pose a riddle of the Princes that few could decipher today?"

"My grandfather was once a Royal Guardsmen in King Jing's court," Yin replied. "I was a little boy when he died, but I still remember him clearly, how big he was. He used to bounce me on his stomach. I loved how he carefully polished his halberd, and marveled at the steel tip, and the curved blade that I imagined he used to chop the heads off barbarians. Yet there was also a calm about him. My father said that Grandfather lived his life in harmony after he left the Guard. My father called this harmony 'the Way'."

Lao Tzu flinched. "What do you know of the Way?"

"Little. But I wish to know more, and of the time from which it originated."

"There is..." Lao Tzu stared off into the distance, "There is little appetite for it any more."

"That is not for you to say."

Yin suddenly became aware of the ears of his platoon. The wind at that moment started up again and in an instant everyone was shielding their eyes from the onslaught of the sand. Yin took Lao Tzu and his beast and guided them into a cool shelter.

"This storm could last minutes, hours or even days," he said. "Afterwards, you shall pass with full provisions and an escort as far as the river's bend. But I cannot allow a sage's teachings to be lost forever. I will first record your memories of the Royal Court before you can proceed."

Lao Tzu's eyes bore into Yin. "To record my memories is to know the Way. And to know the Way is to discover one's own rhythms within the natural world. Tell me, is soldiering natural? Is war natural?"

Yin looked at his men, who had also shuffled into the shelter. Except for Zhang, every one of them would have preferred to be with their families, working their farms, tending to their animals. They were no more soldiers than he was a prince.

"Soldiering and war are the failures of peace," Yin replied.

"Indeed, but also the failure of rulers," Lao Tzu said. "Who was your grandfather, that he could speak to you of the court?"

"Yin Lu. Did you know him?"

Lao Tzu seemed to twitch, but it happened so quickly Yin could not be sure.

"Yin Lu, you say? I came to know many in my travels. But know this: to understand the Way is to understand the failures of our Kings. Is this what you desire?"

"Old Master," Yin whispered. "Uttering those words is an offense punishable by death." He glanced at his men. Several including Zhang, who had also just entered the shelter, listened carefully.

Lao Tzu stared at him. "I have been uttering such words for almost seventy springs." He unrolled his sleeping mat and lay down. "You are wise about the storm. Please wake me when the tea is prepared."

Within seconds, he had curled into a ball and was snoring so heavily that he nearly drowned out the fury of the wind, leaving the Captain and his men speechless.

2

Father's Way

The following morning, Captain Yin found Lao Tzu sitting facing the sun with his eyes closed. He was about to turn away so as not to disturb the old master when Lao Tzu spoke.

"For a dry, inhospitable area, I can hear a great many birds here, Captain."

Lao Tzu's eyes were open.

"Yes, I ensure that water and some seeds are at hand for them," the Captain replied. "There is much beauty here if one cares to look."

"Indeed. Life affords us many small pleasures. Tell me, what else do you remember of your grandfather? There was a longing in your voice earlier, a hunger almost."

Yin hesitated. "Much of it is a blur to me now. He was a quiet man, a giant I thought, although everybody seems enormous when one is a child. My father said that Grandfather was an expert swordsman who spent hours training every day. He had been a Guardsman, so he knew the court well and had special duties related to the Princes. Father never went into details, but I believe they were significant. Eventually Grandfather grew tired of the court and just before Father was born, he departed for a quieter life with my grandmother. I know little else about my grandfather and, quite truthfully, there is also little I know of my parents' families. Hence my desire to learn more."

Lao Tzu was silent.

Since Yin joined the Royal Army, he had learned that the Royal Guardsmen had once been its most prestigious arm. They were assigned to protect the Royal City and the King, and to carry out special assignments at the court's request. Only the most skilled and trusted men were included. As such, they were amply rewarded and well fed. Long-serving members were given freedom, official posts, land and wives. Long after the regular army had dwindled to a ceremonial and feeble fighting force, the Guardsmen retained their status. It was rare for one to relinquish such a station, a fact that fueled Yin's curiosity.

"I sensed from what he said that the court was a dangerous place and that King Jing had become..." Yin looked around and dropped his voice to a whisper, "...quite mad. I even heard he once boiled a messenger alive, and served his body to his unsuspecting enemies."

Lao Tzu stirred. "That story is false," he said. "At least partly so. The King could be ruthless, but he was no barbarian. The messenger had dropped dead of fear in front of the King. He was then boiled with pigs' feet and was fed to enslaved traitors awaiting execution who retched their insides out upon learning of what they had consumed. Regardless, the Son of Heaven was in many ways not unlike others without the Way. The Royal Court was all kinds. To call it dangerous would be merely to say that water is wet."

Yin nodded. "And what of the King's twin Princes? I have heard so much to suggest they were fire and water to one another."

Lao took a deep breath. "The court was a rarefied world where silence and submission ruled. Precise rituals, rigid and meticulous minutiae framed every aspect of official business.

Matters of state were typically conducted with a remote detachment. But the twins stood out and could not have been more different. Both lacked the aloofness of most courtiers and Royal family members. Each constantly betrayed his innermost thoughts by word and by deed, and also by the language of his body."

Lao Tzu sat forward, his old bones creaking with the effort.

"I learned details of the court that no scholar dared speak of. And you are right. While the brothers were of similar blood, they were as different as wind and rain. They could not be separated, for they were two halves of the same tree, each completing and balancing the other. Prince Meng, the eldest, was at first reluctant to stay in the court. He preferred contemplation in the many gardens, attending to his birds, or studying with me in the Archives. He left most court matters to his brother and father. At school he had excelled in music, mathematics, rituals and writing, cultivating his mind as finely as wind sculpts pebbles smooth and round. He was no warrior. He had a milky white face with thoughtful eyes, and little taste for the courtesans and luxuries preferred by his younger brother. For a time, Prince Meng may have been the last in the court to understand that when the Way does not prevail in the world, warhorses breed on the border. Through him, the Way might have brought order to stop the endless wars."

He paused again.

"Prince Chao, on the other hand, easily bested Prince Meng in all activities related to soldiering, such as chariot-riding and archery. Yet he also hungered for the spoils of the court and easily maneuvered himself amongst the web of governance and politics. He wore the finest silk robes, each tailored with his signature wide red cuffs."

Yin at first positioned himself across from Lao Tzu, eyes

riveted, ears focused. Then he sat cross-legged on the ground like an eager pupil. He had never before heard such intimate details of the Royal Court in which his grandfather had served.

Just then, a soldier escorted in a man carrying a small bundle. Both bowed towards Yin with clasped hands.

"Ah, excellent timing!" Yin exclaimed. "Master, I sent for our…"

"Scribe." Lao Tzu smiled. "The wares of a learned man are comforting to me, no less than nectar to a bee."

The scribe inelegantly dropped his bundle of blank bamboo strips. He had either missed Lao Tzu's homage to scribes or was indifferent to it. He wore a simple cloth robe tied with a hemp rope. He belonged to the General's astrologer and had traveled more than twenty *li* from the next county. Judging by the scowl on his face, he was likely not pleased to have been summoned.

The scribe unwrapped several brushes, chipped off a chunk of black ink cake and carefully mixed it with water before grinding it with a polished stone. He mumbled something about the cost of his materials and said that should the General learn of what was happening in his prefecture, all hell would break loose. Yin threw him a few spade-shaped coins, which quickly silenced the scribe's grumblings – for now. He would have to think of some explanation for the General, who generally didn't tolerate independent actions among his officers.

"You expect much, Captain," Lao Tzu said. "Tell me, you say you wish to record my wisdom and my memories of the Royal Court. Is that all? Do you also have questions that need answers?"

"What else could possibly stoke my curiosity, Master? Yes, I would be most pleased with a scholarly lesson and a portal through to my grandfather's time."

Yin filled the sage's teacup and handed it to him.

"You move and speak with grace," Lao Tzu remarked.

"You mean for a soldier?"

Lao Tzu nodded imperceptibly.

Yin smiled. "Perhaps I was born in the wrong time and place. A general once said that I drank water as though it were fine wine. He said had I been born the son of a nobleman, I would have made a fortune many times over."

"Captain, think. What matters to you most: fame or your own self? Which should count most, your own self or things bought? Of the getting or the losing, which is worse? He who grudges expense pays dearest in the end. He who has hoarded most will suffer the heaviest loss. He who delights in the slaughter of men will never get that which he covets. Captain, be content with what you have and who you are, and no one can despoil you. Then you shall forever be safe and secure."

"Your counsel might be more comforting and credible had you not been so ready to stagger off to certain death yesterday."

Lao Tzu heaved a sigh. "True, my death might be welcome as my life now lacks fulfillment. It seemed that the Way miscalculated and consigned me to a most inopportune place in time."

"What do you mean?"

"Captain Yin, you search for wisdom while others pursue authority. You search through history while others seek fortune. What I had once espoused is either too stale or not yet ripe. It has not been the time for the Way. And for those such as yourself with a natural curiosity and hunger for enlightenment, you may be similarly disappointed."

"You are so cynical, Old Master. Surely that was not always the case?"

"You are correct. I once saw the world with wide-eyed amazement and eagerness."

Yin motioned for the scribe to start writing as Lao Tzu began his story.

Our family was smaller than most. I was the youngest of five siblings, three brothers and two sisters in the village of Li in Hu County in the State of Chu. My father and number one brother, Foo Gun, were conscripted into a local militia which in turn was absorbed by a larger army in Chu. Thus I had no early memories of my father other than people remarking on his calm heart and sharp mind. My other brother Gao La and my sister Gong worked the fields. My eldest sister Lin Lu was married at age twelve to a widower in a far-away district. I was two years old when my father and Foo Gun left home. I longed to go and join them both: to polish my armor of leather, to stand at attention with my fellow soldiers, to wield a halberd, to hone my own sword into a fine edge to kill bandits and rebels. In the eyes of a child, a life in the fields offered little glory and no hope for honour.

My mother often scolded me for shadow sword fighting. She would say that fighting never fed anybody, and that killing was not praiseworthy. But I paid her little regard when it came to the affairs of men.

One day I found a special fallen branch—straight, thick, perfectly weighted and well suited for my grip. I stripped off the remaining twigs and marveled at my new sword. I lunged at an elm tree, swatted at low-lying twigs and kicked at the thick trunk. My sparring was interrupted when I spied a soldier in a torn tunic with a walking stick, hobbling toward our farm. As he got closer, I saw that his left leg was missing from the knee down. He had thin, graying hair tangled haphazardly.

He stopped before me. "So fearsome and skilled you are," he

said. "But should little warriors not be doing something other than slaying trees?"

I made several more slashing motions towards the tree. "Mother wants me to pick goji berries," I said. "But that will not rescue my father and brother. This tree must die in order to save them."

"Then that old elm tree has but one chance."

I stared at him. Dried blood and dirt caked his uniform so heavily that I couldn't distinguish for whom he had fought. Then he smiled. Despite his rotting and missing teeth, he radiated warmth. I lowered my sword and flexed a bicep. "What chance would a mere tree have against the bravest of warriors?"

He chuckled then hobbled on towards our house.

"Wait!" I raised my sword towards him. "You have not answered me."

He turned around. "Dear child, show me your sword."

I hesitated, then handed him my weapon. He took the branch and checked for its trueness. From his tunic he retrieved a sharp stone. He balanced the length of the stick on two fingers and determined its levelness. Once satisfied, he stripped off the thin bark then chiseled a cleft at the tip.

"Stop!" I protested. "What are you doing?"

"A sword has many uses. Fishing is one of them."

He grinned like a child with a new toy. He started towards the river before I had an opportunity to object further to the transformation of my sword. He beckoned me to join him. Who was this man? I asked myself. And why had a soldier, one who was injured beyond usefulness and unlike what I expected a warrior to be, bothered to speak to me?

I followed him. We stopped often. He told me to close my eyes and listen to the sounds of the forest—leaves falling, birds in song, insects in flight, small animals scampering through the bushes, water trickling in the distance. He told me, still with my eyes shut, to follow the reverberations and smells of the surroundings. At first I thought he was playing a trick on me. I peeked out at him but he was standing silently and peacefully, as if he were part of the forest.

He showed me plants that healed fevers and itchiness, the most delicious of mushrooms, the lairs of foxes. He taught me how to catch grasshoppers, gently remove their wings, then had me stuff them into the folds of my shirt. As we approached the river, we saw several old men fishing, all of whom I recognized. None had caught anything. They stared warily at my new friend.

The one-legged soldier smiled and walked along the river's edge for a way, before stepping into the water up to his remaining knee and running his hand beneath the surface. He closed his eyes and caressed the water as though he were lulling it to sleep. He dropped his walking stick, lost his balance and almost fell in before I caught him. We both laughed.

"Thank you dear child. Now I am no longer missing a leg."

I liked how he called me 'dear child'. It felt like he was calling me 'son'. It felt safe. He motioned me to a spot on the river bank, then tied some hemp rope to one end of my branch and the other end to a piece of sharpened bone. He took one of the grasshoppers and hooked it onto the bone before casting the short line into the water. Within moments he got a bite. The old man looked like he was struggling to balance himself in the water and I tried to take the branch, but before I could do so, the fish swam off. All of this happened a second time, and just as I was losing my patience, he whispered to me, "The restless mind catches disappointment. Be still, child."

I did as instructed, yet still no fish were caught. I was about to ask for my sword back when he suddenly caught a trout. Then he caught several more. With each catch he blessed the fish and the river.

He had me forage for reeds to tie up the fish. Then he had me divide them into four small piles, one pile for each of the fishermen along the river. He asked me to distribute the fish while he took the opportunity to bathe in the warm current. When I returned with the other fishermen following me, much of the dirt had been removed from his heavily-creased but contented face.

"Thank the gods, Lao Kun, you have returned after all these years," one of the fishermen said as he patted the one-legged soldier on the back. "Forgive us for not recognizing you."

The others joined in, celebrating their bounty and the man who had my father's name.

He reached for his tunic.

"Where is your respect?" one of the fishermen said to me. "Help your father."

I stared at my new friend.

"Father?" I said, almost to myself.

Despite his limited mobility, he moved with an easy grace. Father waved his friends off.

"Gentle friends, my son is courageous and keen. Above all he is one with all that is about him, this I can see. How could I feel any more respected? He has honored me so."

With those words it was as though my world had suddenly found symmetry where nothing previously had seemed to fit together. We walked home with our dinner. Father held out my branch of elm and re-examined it.

"The one chance that old elm tree had against you rested not in the weapon you wielded, but in how you chose to see the world. Soldiering can be glorious. But with this weapon, one can also feed the bellies of our family, seek the contentment of our neighbors, and nourish the land. That choice comes not from power, but from vision. Would soldiering bring you contentment?"

Though I was still a child, the answer to his question was self-evident.

I had many questions of my own, all of which he would answer soon enough. Together we returned home, with me racing ahead, yelling out to my mother that Father had returned. She stopped her planting in the field and stood up, shielding her eyes from the late day sun. At first she didn't seem to understand what I had said and who the man limping towards her was. Then she called his name, dropped her basket and walked towards him. When she noticed Father's missing leg, she stopped and fought to contain her tears. He reached her and comforted her by stroking her cheek, but she waved him off.

"Foo Gun, where is Foo Gun?" she asked of my eldest brother.

He shook his head. My mother gasped and staggered but quickly recovered. She turned to me.

"Bring the fish into the house. Tonight we welcome your father home with a feast."

We had many questions for Father. With a heavy sigh, he told us that number one brother Foo Gun had been killed not long after he was conscripted. Father wanted to run home in grief but knew he would be caught and executed and then the rest of us would be killed as well. So he stayed on and fought with his infantry unit. He had lost his leg four years ago while repelling a chariot assault. He was left to die among the many other wounded soldiers until a general learned that Father could read and write and, above all else, was considered trustworthy. The general ordered his best surgeon to save my father in return for scribing duties. Later, when the general retired, he released my father from duty. He had been making his way home for many months.

Injured though he was, Father found ways to help on our farm.

At first he and Mother squabbled over what to plant and how to work. But he convinced her to try new methods and a variety of crops. He possessed a mind that was constantly stirring but he never appeared to be busy. There seemed to be little he did not understand or know, few things he could not do.

One day, our Warlord came by to see how his share of our farm's bounty was increasing. He was impressed to discover how learned Father had made himself and offered Father a job as a clerk. Father accepted but only upon agreement that he would be allowed to speak to others of his farming methods. He came to advise the Warlord on many matters. His views on farming drew the ridicule of many at first, but he persisted for he felt the incremental betterment of the world, one plot at a time, was a duty that no one should shirk. Before long, the Warlord's farms and those around them were yielding the most abundant harvests ever, season after season. I was as tall as my father by age ten, but I never ceased looking up to him.

He smelled of damp bark and earth, no doubt from the pot of licorice roots he always had brewing. He claimed they cleared his stomach and focused his mind. Perhaps it also gave him great patience, for he always encouraged my curiosity and had answers for my never-ceasing questions:

"Father, is it true that Qi warlords boil children for breakfast?"

"Father, how do you always know where to catch the biggest fish?"

"Father, why do some fields go dry after years of good harvests?"

"Why are your farms so bountiful while others are bare?"

Once I said I wanted to be as clever as he. He stopped what he was doing and looked at me with a trace of disappointment in his eye.

"Cleverness takes all the credit, but it is not the clever mind that is responsible when things work out. It is the mind that sees what is in front of it and accepts its course. Cleverness devises craftier means, knowledge tries to understand it, but doing nothing is the most astute approach of them all."

He nicknamed me 'shar pei' after the breed of dog which his warlord owned. He said they could be ill-tempered but were quite independent and intelligent if properly loved. Father knew there could be no life for me except as a peasant farmer if I did not become learned. And so he occasionally took me to the Warlord where I watched the business of landownership and large-scale farming. He taught me to read and to scribe, as well as to do numbers. I hoped to follow in his footsteps and make him proud by becoming a scholar or a magistrate.

But life has few paths of certainty. Our home was located near areas recently overrun by tribes of barbarians. One day when I awoke from an afternoon nap atop a hill overlooking our farm, I saw the barbarians with their dark, crinkled faces and long wiry hair blowing in the wind, charging down the valley on horseback like angry devils. I grabbed a stone and raced down the hill and was about to let out a challenging scream when Shun, my older cousin and my Aunt, who had been picking plums, tackled me down. Shun muffled my mouth with his hand and pulled me behind a bush. I struggled unsuccessfully to free myself from his hold.

"Look!" he said. "We're too late."

Waving axes, swords, sabers and spears, the barbarians howled and screamed as they descended onto our farm and those of our neighbors. It seemed like there were hundreds of them. They struck quickly. We could see Father hobbling in from the field, yelling for my mother. They surrounded him on their horses.

Shun pulled out his slingshot and searched for a rock.

"Put it away you fool, you are too far away," my aunt said.

"Besides there are too many of them. We will be cut down with arrows before we get within half a *li* of your parents. We can only watch and hope these barbarians will be satisfied with thievery alone."

With those words I stopped struggling, and Shun released his grip, though I hung onto my rock.

The barbarians circled Father as though he were captured prey, taunting him with the things they were going to do to Mother. Father picked up a long wooden spade and tried to hold them off. They laughed as he hobbled on his one leg. But he surprised them by swiftly taking the offensive, wielding the spade like a warrior's halberd. He even managed to knock two of them off their mounts before a barbarian cracked a whip, wrapping it around Father's leg. One barbarian who'd been knocked down rushed toward Father and pinned his arms while another with a shaved head drew his dagger. The hairless man bent down over Father and slit his throat. I was about to scream when Shun covered my mouth again. The sweet smell of Shun's plum-stained hands could not mask the bitterness of that moment.

My mother was then dragged into the yard. She cried and begged for mercy, pleading that she was with child. They laughed at her then took turns mounting her before wedging a dagger through her stomach. I almost choked on my own vomit until Shun realized what was happening and released me. Afterwards I collapsed onto the ground, completely stunned.

When the barbarians finally left, we ran to my parents. I stared motionless at their bodies. Then I screamed at Shun for not having released me when we could have saved our family.

"Coward!" I yelled. "You had us hiding like mice!"

I slapped him in the face and flailed at him until he held my hands. When I was worn out and reduced to quiet sobs, he released me.

"Your father didn't return home to have you join him in death," Shun said quietly. "Nor would your mother have wanted to see you die at the hands of those savages. The time to mourn is when you have nothing left to live for. If there had been more of us I wouldn't have hesitated to teach them a lesson. But alone we would have been slaughtered too."

Shun was correct. To grieve was a luxury one never had in times such as those. The unstated edict was that thinking of ill things was to re-live them. I suppose it is no different today. And so I had to swallow that which ailed me. We all had to. My parents were gone. My father, whom I'd known so briefly yet had become my very soul, had been ripped out of my life.

The barbarians had robbed all the nearby farms, burnt whatever lay in their path, taken some of the young women, and also some of the young men to raise as barbarians or slaves. Everyone else they killed, including Gao La and Gong. If the Warlord hadn't conscripted so many of the able-bodied men, our village and the neighboring farms may have been able to protect themselves. If the Warlord had been a man who led without regard for power and dominance, the outcome might have been different; my mother may have been spared, my father might have witnessed my ascension. As a young man for whom moral and intellectual inquiry was encouraged, violence, war and power all seemed pointless and profoundly depraved.

I was twelve and expected to remain with my surviving clan members to work our plot of land, hoping the barbarians might not return. Or I could have remained and waited to be conscripted into the Warlord's army or whatever rag-tag army passed through. But my aunt would not have it. She sent me away along with Shun to her brother, my uncle, in a safer region of Qin. I said my goodbyes, not knowing they would be final.

3

Bitten Peach

Our journey exposed us to scenes of violence, human suffering and tragedies not unlike what we had just left. We hurried through abandoned farms and villages still smoldering from attacks by barbarians or bandits, or from fighting among warlords. We stumbled over the putrid carcasses of soldiers and marauders, as well as of farmers and wanderers like ourselves. But we also found lavish homes protected by high walls and whole armies. These we avoided, knowing that Shun was old enough to be conscripted and that I would be taken on as a laborer. One late afternoon as I gathered kindling near the top of a heavily-wooded hill, I saw two soldiers on patrol creeping towards our campsite. I quickly ducked. I could see that the lead soldier was not much older than Shun, but taller and wiry. The other was older with some heft, but also a confidence in his movements. I became as still as I could as they approached. I scanned about for Shun and whispered his name but he was not to be seen.

"I told you there was someone out here," one of the soldiers said.

"I hope you're right this time. The captain has doubled the reward for every new body we find who can wield a weapon."

"Triple if they're young and strong."

"They'd have to be dumb as you."

"Shhh, over there..." They looked in my direction. I stepped back, snapping twigs as I did so.

"Ahh, a young 'un. Perfect. And where there's one, there's another."

They quickly moved towards me. I dropped my kindling and broke a branch from a low hanging birch. The younger soldier was almost upon me and I slashed away at him. He chuckled.

"Beware, a great warrior is before us." He flashed a small bronze sword and chuckled some more. "What are we to do?"

"Stop," I yelled. "You have foolishly stumbled upon the encampment of wild renegades who will relish in seeing your heads roll!"

My misdirection caused the soldier to hesitate. But then the other soldier scolded him.

"He's talking shit, you moron. Just tie him up and let's be done here. We'll come back for any others after we've eaten. I'm hungry."

The soldier stepped closer and raised his blade at my neck. Without warning something flew out of nowhere and hit the soldier on the head, dropping him instantly. He lay motionless. The other soldier drew a bronze sword as long as my forearm and reached for me. Another rock flew over and hit the back of his hand. He cried out and dropped his blade. As he fell to his knees, another rock just missed his head. He curled himself into a ball and begged for mercy.

Shun jumped out from behind a bush no more than ten arms' length away. His hunting slingshot was fully cocked with a jagged rock sitting snugly in the pouch. He aimed it directly at the soldier's head.

"Move again and you die," he said. Then to me: "Grab the sword."

At first I could only stare at Shun and at the man whimpering in pain.

"I tracked these vermin for half a *li*," Shun declared.

As Shun looked at me with determined ferocity, I retrieved the short sword. "No, get both. Give me the larger."

Shun nodded me away and raised his weapon above the fallen soldier.

No, Shun," I said. "We're not barbarians."

He relented, but not before telling the soldier that our entire clan was in this area and were heavily armed, and should he return, he would be killed before he knew what had happened. The soldier thanked Shun, who then made him crawl backwards over the edge of the hill. We could hear him fall, followed by much moaning and cursing.

Shun fingered the soldier's dropped sword with interest. "We can use this," he said.

He stabbed the air, and then lunged towards the first soldier, still lying motionless, stopping just short of stabbing him. I stared at Shun, surprised to discover this side of him.

"Wild renegades?" Shun asked. "Quite an imagination there, cousin."

I shrugged, but secretly basked in Shun's compliment.

"It was clever and bought a few seconds while I readied my sling."

Shun tied his new weapon to his waist. "Let's move on. Others will soon follow."

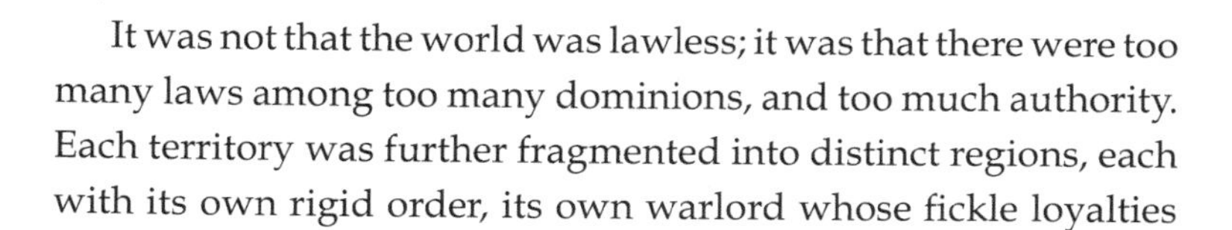

It was not that the world was lawless; it was that there were too many laws among too many dominions, and too much authority. Each territory was further fragmented into distinct regions, each with its own rigid order, its own warlord whose fickle loyalties went to whomever was offering the most opportunity or greatest protection at the time. In essence, there was too much control and too little understanding.

There was one day that remains distinct in my memory. As we rested by a fast-moving river to fill our water jugs, I witnessed a small boy, perhaps no more than five, fall into the rushing waters. He cried out for help as his family looked on in horror, unable to reach him. Shun, who had spent many hours diving for crayfish, untied his sword.

"No, Shun." I tried to hold him back. "You'll be swept away."

"I'll be fine, trust me."

He immediately jumped in, made his way over to the boy and grabbed him. But together they appeared trapped in the relentless turbulence, unable to escape the current. They sank and we lost sight of them. Stunned by this sudden turn of events, I ran along the river's edge, calling out for Shun. I found him emerging further downstream, carrying a coughing but unharmed boy out of the water onto the riverbank.

After Shun accepted the profuse gratitude of the parents, I berated him for being foolhardy but also stood in awe of him.

"But it wasn't foolish. That family certainly didn't think so." He wiped at my cheeks. Only then did I realize I was in tears. "Did I not say to trust me?"

I asked him how he had managed to battle the current and save himself and the boy. He looked at me with his warm, chestnut-colored eyes as though I were a simpleton.

"It was easy," he shrugged. "Why would I battle the impossible? No man is stronger than that river."

I was an imbecile. He had of course known enough to have the river do his bidding. Instead of trying to conquer the river, he had followed its path. Here was my cousin Shun, not yet a grown man and in no way destined to be a scholar, yet he was already immensely knowledgeable about the world. He understood, as did my father, that stillness is often the best option and that following Nature's course is the best guide.

I am here today because Shun took to living hand to mouth and moment to moment as easily as I took to contemplation. He understood which insects were edible, which berries were poisonous and which roots were most flavorful. He ensnared small animals and caught the most elusive fish with ease. He could feel the ground rumble from distant horses and hear hostile whispers many *li* away. In essence, he brought a natural elegance to anything requiring manual dexterity and simple subsistence. Yet somehow my cousin also had the guile of a thief and the sensibility and compassion of an elder.

He tried to teach me many of these skills. While I lacked the ease with which he applied himself, I did learn how to handle a slingshot and set warning triggers. Several times we crossed paths with other travelers or farmers who needed a literate person's eyes in exchange for food or shelter, so I wasn't completely useless. But we both knew I slowed him down. If we wanted to eat, he would have to be responsible for hunting, gathering and scouting.

After many weeks we found my third Uncle's farm in what is now Wu territory. A farmhand took us to a shady spot beneath a tree where Uncle was sleeping. The farmhand, who turned out to be our cousin, shook my snoring Uncle awake.

"My sister's boy, you say?" he said. "Which sister? How do I know you are telling me the truth?"

He was an uncomplicated man with languorous eyes and a wide gap in his teeth that he used to push his tongue through whenever he was thinking. A heavily soiled bandana was wrapped around his forehead, holding down wisps of shambled hair on an otherwise bare head. He jabbed one's chest as he spoke slowly but incessantly about all manner of things, although his accent made it difficult to follow. When he saw Shun's sword, his eyes lit up and he whistled.

"You'd best leave that with me," he said. "Carrying a weapon like that will get you in trouble."

Shun held his sword behind him and stood firm. "Thank you for your concern Uncle, but I'm keeping it."

Their eyes locked briefly. Uncle was about to speak when I offered my sword to him and the rest of our few possessions. He quickly went through them, finding only some clothing, wild yams and some tools for fire-making and cutting. Uncle sighed in disappointment and looked at us.

"Pretty scrawny," he said, inspecting my physique. "You are soft. Your mother likely spoiled you. Why should I take you in?"

"We traveled far to be with you, Uncle," Shun said.

"From Chu, you say?" Uncle looked at us warily. "That is far away. I hear there are many barbarians there. If they come near me, I will snap them." He broke off a thin branch from an elm tree and jabbed us. My eyes were drawn to his tongue sticking out from the gap in his teeth.

"Never mind," he added. "You can stay. I can use four new hands. Warlords have picked through my best laborers. Food and shelter will more than pay for your hard work. This is not an inn." He poked our chests. "You will have to work hard and obey. Do as you are told. I want no lip. When the new landlord Master Xun comes around, remember your place, keep your eyes down and your mouths shut unless he speaks to you. Not that he'd bother with your sort. Otherwise stay away from him, he is a strange one. Do you hear me?"

Before I could answer, he told us that we would be sleeping with the chickens, which we were to guard like brothers. We were to stay away from Uncle's three daughters and treat his four sons like respected princes. He didn't say why Master Xun was strange. But it was not my place to expect an explanation. He walked away, leaving us with his eldest son to show us around.

My Uncle worked part of a farm owned by a noble in the next prefecture. He had nine plots to work, two of which were devoted solely to Master Xun.

It was the middle of the planting season, yet the fields looked to be in a pitiful state, with mounds of dirt and holes scattered about without any apparent order or structure. What should have been a hopeful time of the year among farmers was treated by my uncle with disinterest.

One hot day as I dug rows into the earth with a thick tree branch, the outlines of several men blocked the sun as they stood over me. I was slapped to the ground.

"You bow in the presence of the Master, you worthless swine," Uncle said, swatting me to the ground again.

I got up and bowed to Master Xun.

"Forgive him, Master, he is new... from Chu, need I say more? He has yet to learn proper manners." Uncle glared at me. The Master appeared more interested in my digging.

Uncle scolded me again when he saw that I had not started seeding yet, whereas everybody else had all but finished, covering at least three times more ground than I.

"Forgive me Master, he is my sister's useless boy, weak and soft. I will whip him into shape." Uncle swung his arm up to strike me again.

Master Xun raised his hand and stopped my uncle's next slap in mid-air. Uncle seemed flustered at not being able to fully demonstrate his authority. He had lost face. He puffed his chest out instead and demanded to know why I was so slow.

I could see the Master from the corner of my eyes. Like most noblemen his skin was pale, but his beard was short and tightly shaped into a perfect wedge. Dark, thoughtful eyes surveyed everything within his sight. He wore a loose-cut cloth with a wide silk sash that wrapped around his lower body. It was ingeniously wrapped from the front of the upper body to the back, making full use of horizontal and diagonal lines to complement space and achieve a quietude in motion. Except for a pair of embroidered brocades with wavy patterns suggesting wisdom and intellect, it was sparsely but elegantly decorated.

"Dear Uncle and Master," I said cautiously. "It was my father who taught me how to sow seeds in this manner."

I could feel Uncle's temper rising. He explained to Master that he had taken me in only out of pity and loyalty to his dear sister, and that my father knew nothing about farming. Hearing that said about my father, I could not remember my place nor hold my tongue.

"Dear Uncle, Father's farm was the most impressive in the land. Many farmers came from near and far to learn from him. Our crops always outgrew everybody else's. He knew..."

The Master cut me off. "What your Uncle says about you lacking in manners is true. And you should be more careful: it is one thing to boast of your father and imitate his methods, but quite another to understand them. What is the purpose of tilling the soil this way? Speak."

I glanced at my grinning Uncle, then replied: "Scattering the seeds is a waste, Master. The birds eat more than we do. Father had us first dig into the ground so the seeds would be safe. He taught us that if the crops are grown in rows, they will have more room and mature faster."

I was convinced that the next strike was coming. When it did not, I continued.

"They will not interfere with each other's growth. I am creating a ridge and furrow pattern first, as you can see. Then

I will carefully space each seed before covering it with dirt. But without the right tools, it is slow work."

"Tools?" Uncle laughed nervously. "Master is so kind and generous to give us a livelihood and you speak of needing tools?"

Uncle turned to Master. "Sir, I will beat the cheekiness from this child. You will never have to suffer his disrespect again." Uncle dropped to one knee before the Master, bowed his head and offered an open palm, closed fist salute.

"That won't be necessary," Master Xun said. "Send him to me once his work today is done."

The Master walked on. Everyone stood silently until he was out of hearing, then Uncle slapped my head. "If the Master wasn't expecting you later, I'd beat you now. He better not go easy on you. The last thing I need is a useless farmhand."

Uncle ran to catch up to the Master, no doubt to kowtow further.

I asked one of my cousins why Uncle would say that about the Master.

"It is obvious, you fool," my cousin replied. "The Master's hands are soft, his skin is ghostly. He knows nothing about working the land. Did you not see his fine clothes? He was a silk merchant for many years. Merchants are not to be trusted. They make nothing, and they do nothing, except make money off the labor of others. What use are they? I would rather answer to a cowardly soldier than a pompous swindler."

Cousin spat into the earth then told me to get back to work.

After a day in the field but before the evening meal, I walked to Master Xun's mansion. A single gate was the only passage through the high walls of rammed earth that surrounded the family complex. Once I stepped through, another short wall faced me before I crossed into a quiet, square-shaped courtyard. It was the quietest place I had ever been in. There was a tranquility and calm that was distinctly removed from farms and everywhere else I had ever seen. Skirting the enclosure were numerous rooms, and an upper balcony ran around the courtyard. It was a very fancy house, even more so than the one belonging to the Warlord who once employed my father.

A male servant led me through a sliding door which opened into a corridor that branched both left and right. I waded through a haze of smoke from incense sticks of burning cinnamon and jasmine before I came to another sliding door. I was led through it into a large room brightly lit with torches. I did not have to be told to kneel.

I kept my eyes fixed to the ground, but I could hear people quietly shuffling in with platters of succulent smelling food. A servant named every dish as it was presented: "Bear paw soup, roast capon with chestnuts, fried carp with lotus roots, pork belly with taro, steamed baby mustard greens." No other words were spoken, only slurping and hearty chewing. I had never smelled such pungent aromas. It was as if Nature's bounty had been condensed into steaming wafts of rich, earthy, fruity and salty bouquets. My stomach began to growl, and I feared that it would be heard.

The servant proclaimed some more dishes: "Fried chicken livers with fresh bamboo shoots, wood ear mushrooms in ginger."

Finally some words of rebuke. "This soup is not warm enough."

Profound apologies and begging for forgiveness followed, then more shuffling. I heard a command for more wine from a woman. The growling in my stomach intensified. At last, the eating slowed and I heard a loud burp. Master Xun ordered the dishes removed before speaking.

"Where in Chu is your family from?"

I listened with interest for a reply and was promptly swatted in the head.

"The Master is speaking to you, fool," someone whispered to me.

"Near Li village, Master."

"Your accent is recognizable, but not crude. Where are your parents?"

"My mother and father are dead, Master."

"How?"

I explained what had happened to my family and how I had fled with Shun.

"You are a boy ignorant of the world, yet earlier you spoke knowingly of matters beyond most boys," Master Xun said. "How is this?"

I hesitated. "Yes Master, I am just a boy, but I have seen things no child should have seen. My father told me that in ignorance one could not possibly be wise, but in wisdom one could wrongly choose ignorance. I did not understand what he meant until after he died. There was much that I did not know then. But now I see he wanted me to question my assumptions and be open to learning as much as possible."

"And of tilling the land?"

"He believed that the land is like family, that it needs to be treated as such, that it has to be respected in order to be understood. He saw the land and everything on it, from the earth to the animals, to the trees and ponds and its people, as one."

I glanced up and saw the Master sip some wine.

"And why should this matter?" he asked.

"My father said fields were for either battle or food. Yet he saw what he called a rhythm, a kind of beauty that was to be honored. He said we had to keep everything in a harmonious and sustainable balance. In that way, each element of the land is shaped by its relationship to every living creature on it. Each element needs the other. He saw this as natural and necessary. Much of this I came to better understand only slowly over time."

I paused, awaiting dismissal from the Master. When that did not come, I continued.

"Father learned the use of many different materials and tools while in the army. He learned to fashion them for other uses, such as for the earth. With tools that kneaded the land, our farm's bounty always produced the greatest harvests in the prefecture."

"Give me an example," Master said.

"One device was a board that moved the soil without disturbing it too greatly. This device concentrated the force much more efficiently on the sharp blade of the plough. Such a plough, he learned, was even more efficient if an animal were to pull it."

"Interesting. It seems your father was born to have great ideas."

"Master, he never thought so. He never boasted. He also never spoke ill of anyone. He said he learned much, both through other people's wisdom and follies. He thought wars were the mother of invention, that they forced people into times of creativity as well as madness."

A long silence followed. I heard some movement. I raised my head to sneak a look at him. But he had shifted his position. He was hovering directly above me.

"And you?" he asked. "What do you think?"

I hesitated. "Master, I think there is greatness in all of us - in people's deeds, in their ideas. I did not know my father for very long. But I know he did not aspire to greatness. He wished to merely live his life simply. That he was a great man mattered little to him, thus I saw him so all the more."

"You speak as though you are a learned child."

I told him that each evening as the sun dimmed, Father

and I would explore the forests and streams, or he would use sticks and the ground outside our hut to teach me to read and to scribe. Very quickly I learned many characters. But what Father encouraged most was how to question all things beyond their surface appearance.

I was dismissed by Master Xun and returned to my hut. Uncle and his sons immediately followed me in. Cousin Tuo placed a lamp near my face, inspecting me for evidence of a beating.

"He is unscathed," Cousin Tuo said after looking me over.

"What did the master prick want?" Uncle asked.

"To talk about farming," I replied.

Uncle jabbed a finger at my chest. "What does the new Master care about what you think? Why would he ask you, a boy, about farming?"

"I do not know."

"Did he ask about us?"

I shook my head.

"Did he accuse any of us of thievery?" Tuo asked me. "What did you say?"

I answered truthfully. Uncle spat on the ground.

"Either the Master is playing games with us or you have become his little stoolie," he said.

He grabbed my shirt and pulled me up to his sweating face. I could smell fermented eggs and sweet rice wine on his breath.

"He's no more a squealer than you are a general," Shun said as he entered.

Uncle threw me towards Shun, disturbing the chickens in the process. "You two need to be taught a lesson," he growled.

Shun easily blocked the first few blows directed at me. This infuriated Uncle and he threatened to kick us out. Then Shun seemed to let up, allowing the blows to fall. Even if we had been able to best our Uncle and his sons, it would have been foolish to resist the wrath of our only family elder. We were quickly overwhelmed.

"If you enjoy the Master's company so much you can clean out his shit hole." Uncle spat again. "His merchant nose likes crapping on a bed of pine needles. It's no joy to clean up the shit of a snake. See to it."

After our assailants left, I lay on the ground, too bruised and bloodied to move. Shun tore a rag and dabbed at my cuts, then gently stroked my hair and the back of my neck. "I'll look after Master's shit hole, " Shun whispered. I soon fell asleep.

After that, Master Xun inspected our fields with greater regularity. He never paid me any more attention during his inspections, yet he sent for me several more times to discuss my father's methods and to seek my opinion on matters. He even had me record our discussions. In return, I was fed well and given access to his library and scribing materials.

Master began to draw up more strategic plans for his crop choices and their placement. He had me plan an entirely new irrigation system, all things my father had long-since perfected. Many times I returned from the Master only to find that Shun had already returned from the fields and was cleaning himself up, only to leave again. To where, he did not say. Often Uncle and cousins shared their lewd suspicions and beat me. Shun protected me when he was around, taking many of the blows intended for me. But he was often absent.

Uncle called me all manner of things. "You filthy swine, it's not enough that you carry on like a high-nosed noble making us look bad with your stupid ideas, but to also be the bitten peach of a merchant no less."

I did not know what he meant by a bitten peach and was too frightened to ask. But I would soon find out. Sensing my uncle's displeasure with me, the other laborers pestered me throughout the day with taunts, soiling me with animal manure, overturning my seed bins, and tripping me as I carried buckets of water past them. After yet another day of misery, I returned to our hut and collapsed onto the ground. When Shun returned, I told him everything was intolerable, and yelled at him, demanding to know where he went when he left the farm.

He lowered his head, cradling it in his hands. "Protecting," he whispered. "I am protecting you…us."

"What are you talking about? I get beaten night after night and you talk of protecting me? It was safer on the run. I can't take this anymore. It's time to run away."

To my surprise, he did not disagree.

"We don't have to scrounge for food and hide here, and we are neither prisoners nor slaves. But we are captives of another sort."

He lay down beside me and for a long moment we were both silent.

"All we did before coming here was flee and hide," he added. "Remember the time we stumbled onto what we thought was an abandoned farm?"

"Only to realize it was a brothel," I smiled wearily.

"You talked our way out of that one by pretending you were the magistrate's junior scribe looking for the landowner who owed back taxes," Shun chuckled. "With your sharp mind…"

"Let's not forget that we are here because you have the way of a gentle warrior and the cunning of a fox, a wild fox."

Shun held my hand. "I would prefer gentle fox and wild warrior, but thank you cousin."

We giggled like little boys, then lapsed back into quietude.

He broke the silence again. "While those days are over, I miss the time we had together. Those were dangerous times. We were constantly hungry and tired, yet also masters of our own fate, bending with the wind... Yes that was a freedom I will never forget. But I also know we're different, we're treated differently and you especially don't belong here."

He rolled onto his side and stroked my arm.

"Just promise me something. Don't do anything foolish. I have an idea. Just wait, okay?"

"A plan? What are you thinking?"

"Just trust me. You're good at that, remember?"

I nodded, though it disappointed me greatly that he did not share his thoughts.

Days passed and Shun uttered not another word of his plan. The harassment continued and even worsened. I decided that there was no better idea and that I would somehow leave, though I had no plan. I awoke very early and saw that Shun had left already. One of my cousins came in and told me I had been called to the Master's house. Because Master had done so openly and through my cousin, it meant that another miserable day and another beating would follow at the hands of Uncle and my cousins. I walked to the house and was led to the Master's private chambers where I found him seated. Much to my surprise, Shun was also there, standing off to one side.

"Your cousin Shun informs me you are not content here, and that you have made other plans," the Master said.

I hesitated at first, shooting a wary look at Shun. "Master has been most kind and I am grateful to you."

"You may feel that way. Your cousin here does, though no one else would agree. A merchant, even a former one such as myself, will forever be tainted as an unscrupulous money monger, greedy and not to be trusted. Anyone associated with me is similarly stained."

Shun looked away while the Master paused.

"Your uncle controls all the farmers and laborers. He has

threatened in veiled terms to withdraw their labor if I do not put you in your place. The conundrum is that I need them, while at the same time you have become indispensable to the prosperity of my farms. I profit well from the knowledge you have provided. You have many talents and much knowledge to offer. It will be squandered should you remain. This is not your rightful place."

"My Master is most kind. However, my Uncle thinks I belong…"

"Your Uncle doesn't think, nor does he understand where you belong. The only profession more noble than tilling the land is to be a scholar. Your cousin here proposed something that will benefit us all."

The Master reached for Shun's hand which was balled into a fist, opened it and laid it on his own shoulder.

"I have arranged for you to be taken in as a clerk by a nobleman up in the Sher valley. Like me, he is appreciative of the scholarly mind. In exchange, Shun has agreed to be my… personal advisor, on these modern methods."

"But…" I looked up at Shun who nodded slightly but with his eyes averted from mine. He stepped towards the Master, his arm brushing against his shoulder.

"Master is right, this benefits us all," he said. "But you needn't worry, dear cousin. We will see each other again. I'll find you, wherever and whenever that may be."

Then I understood. Shun, not I, was what Uncle had referred to as the Master's bitten peach. Shun laid out a bundle of clothes, a bedroll and food all ready for my departure. Master Xun had included an ink block, some brushes and several bamboo strips. Even with all these gifts, an unspeakable emptiness prevailed within me. I looked at the bundle but could not move. Shun was the only person I had left in this world. I had assumed he would always be there for me. That was all that mattered at that moment.

"Uncle doesn't bother me so much. I can take it," I declared. But the tears gave me away.

"A cormorant is fantastic in the water as it dives for fish, but in the end, it's still a bird on a rope. As your eldest cousin, I can't allow you to be what you are not. Master here has given you something few are offered. And for that I am grateful." Shun gently stroked the Master's shoulder then gathered together the supplies.

"You will come for me?" I asked Shun.

"Did I not say?" He nodded and turned away, unable to conceal a heavy tear.

I left that morning for a two-day journey to the Sher valley, feeling more alone than I ever had before, and heavy with guilt for the sacrifice Shun had made. But I expected and hoped that I would one day see him again.

4

Alone, Alas

My next Master was an ambitious man who commanded much land along a fertile valley. He traded alliances and loyalties with an ease that blemished all around him. He wasn't unlike many other benefactors I would later meet, some more shrewd, others less enlightened. Not long after I arrived, I heard that a neighboring warlord's troops had swept through the region, destroying much of Master Xun's farm, killing those who resisted and conscripting those who didn't. I could not confirm if Shun was among either group and begged my new Master to release me to travel there and settle my mind. He refused. But I still had many things to live for, so this was not the time to mourn.

After a few years I moved on again, as would be my pattern. My first desire was to return to Master Xun's farm to look for Shun. I imagined finding him and, as we fell into each other's arms, he would admonish me for returning. Alas, that was mere fantasy. I returned to Master Xun's farm and found only one of my younger cousins, a simpleton. She could tell me nothing of what had happened to Shun.

I re-directed my loneliness and focused my mind into a ceaseless questioning of all that was about me. I saw the world's repetitive violence and shame as a failure of leadership. I decried our incessant desire to subjugate the natural order of the world around us. Greed and a naïve belief that the world could be shaped beyond its natural proclivities were blinding us. We had forgotten the harmony with which Nature surrounds our lives; the equilibrium that heaven had given to earth and which coursed through our veins. We had ceased to see that we had all that we needed. And I had come to believe that genuine contentment, real fulfillment, was only possible with a return to these truths. I had marveled at this with my father, who lived in a manner completely in balance with all that was around him. These beliefs, these simple maxims, this possibility—these were the first steps to finding the Way.

I refined such thoughts while finding various employments as a scholar and administrator. At times, I found an audience that would consider and even employ such beliefs. At others, I was summarily dismissed. Thus I learned discretion when sharing my emerging discoveries. Back then, questioning the existing order was even less tolerated than it is now and I was often seen as a disruptive and seditious influence.

Discretion allowed me to find favor with some nobles and minor royalty in the surrounding lands. I served in many roles to many masters as a clerk, advisor, artist, poet, scholar and intellectual. The irony of my service is that in a period in my life when I was most intensely questioning the unnatural order of the world, I was considered particularly adept at creating order. That is to say, many a minor Royal or noble household lacked coherent administration of their records, their history and their wealth. For them, my simple and easily-devised systems of organization and management were well received.

My father was not there to see how his 'little shar pei' strove to honor his name. In my wanderings over these many years, I have often wondered whether my life would have met with his approval. Perhaps in my death, it may become clear.

I came to see the world as utterly parochial, a feeling that continued to gnaw at me. Despite the world's unceasing misery and conflict, I had come to a place of much clarity and precision. It discouraged me that others were drawn into complications when simplicity was all that was required. In all the places I had lived, under all the masters I had served, and in all the places I traveled, I could see that those who were the least troubled and most placid shared certain commonalities. They possessed an unexceptional and uncomplicated manner. They seemingly had little organization, yet also little chaos. There was a natural rhythm to their lives and they lived in harmony with that which heaven blesses our world. Over time, these observations festered. No degree of success as an administrator or as someone else's servant could contain or satisfy my longings to expand upon my contemplations.

After some years, a grateful nobleman left me a small plot of land in the mountains, at a place called Sword Hill. I used it to establish a retreat of my own where I could reflect upon my thoughts without the encumbrance of duty. I hoped that one day it would become a place for myself and others to clear their minds and ruminate on the Way. My first impression of the refuge, however, left me somewhat disappointed. The main structures required much labor to make them habitable and I had neither the tools nor the fortitude necessary. Then an orphaned boy wandered by with a bundle of kindling. His clothes were no less ragged than a worn mop and his face, hands and bare feet were as blackened as the grime on a pig's trotters. His stench made the most odious of outhouses smell floral. He stared with a piqued curiosity.

"Are you the new Master of Sword Hill?" he asked.

I nodded. "But 'Master' is a title I have neither earned nor seek."

"Then what will the Wizened One of Sword Hill do with this place?"

Here was a boy who had already learned the art of sycophancy or had himself become wise beyond his years. I looked at the fallen doors, the leaking roofs, the broken pieces of furniture, the leaves and branches that had drifted in, the scattered animal feces.

"It is a shambles," I said. "It would appear that there is far more to be done than I am able to do. And you are...?"

"People call me many things, but I especially like to be called Li Su. But this place is not a shambles, my Lord. It is a very popular place. Look, a clan of mice in that corner call this home, a family of pigeons above us have rebuilt their nest, and of course the colonies of spiders over there are the envy of the hill. There also used to be a family of red squirrels who could not stop fighting with each other, but they were tasty."

I eyed him cautiously. "So you have been calling this home as well?"

He nodded guiltily.

"Creatures big and small all dwelling together," I chuckled. "But with room for more."

"I hope there is still room for me," he said. "I can hunt, I can start a fire in the rain, I can swing off trees, I can..."

I didn't require much more convincing. He reminded me of when my father gracefully polished me into what I would become. I could not ignore such potential.

As fate would have it, Li Su was a diligent and tireless worker and pupil: Highly resourceful and practical, though prone to rashness, he was unquestionably loyal. Somehow he was always able to obtain materials needed or assistance required and together we removed much of Nature's debris that had crept into the building and was scattered throughout the grounds.

Neither of us was skilled in building and repair, but after two years of painstaking work, and with some help from the former owner, we turned the crumbling manor into an academy with multiple sleeping chambers to accommodate up to twelve scholars. One room was enlarged specifically for quiet study, another for silent contemplation. Another room was re-constructed to carefully store and maintain a growing collection of writings and tablets. The grounds were landscaped to include several small interconnected ponds surrounded on one side by large river stones, and on the other by small trees and shrubs.

Over time, we began to quietly attract scholars who journeyed from all realms to join us. I was never comfortable with their praise and reverence, but it was most satisfying to see the retreat that others referred to as the Sword Hill Academy prosper. Few scholars made the sacrifice to live according to my teachings, that is to liberate themselves from the artificial divisions we had constructed. But those who did achieved a fulfilling contentment. Even Li Su, who never could sustain the focus necessary to be a scholar, still found a place as an indispensable aide. He seemed to love the Academy and the life I had offered him.

One evening, as I gazed at a gentle sunset, Li Su approached.

"Sorry to disturb such a peaceful moment, Master Scholar."

"Ah, but all our moments are peaceful, would you not say, old friend? For I believe I have vanquished the yoke of order. It is most satisfying."

"Indeed, Master Scholar. But even here and now, we cannot entirely remove ourselves from the mundane happenings of society."

"Have we not accomplished this already? Do we not dwell on an island of our own contentment?"

"Master Scholar, we have sustained ourselves well over the years. Yes, we have sown much. But whether it is meat for our bellies, fuel to light our lamps, or cloth for our garments, we have lived off the benefaction of others. This has become a challenge for our coffers. We have ideas that can stir the world yet we sequester ourselves like hermits, all but begging for scraps from nobles, forever disquieted about their own lives."

"What are you getting at Li Su?"

"I have heard that our Academy has been referred to in a positive light among some of the elite of Chu and even Qin. Perhaps we can take advantage of this?"

"Advantage? Whatever are you speaking of?"

"I believe there is material value to be gained from our counsel."

"Hmmm. I have little interest in that."

"How can you have so little ambition?"

I looked carefully at him. "What have you heard?"

He looked away. "The King of Chu is looking for scholars."

"They are always looking for scholars. They are regarded there as fashionable trinkets."

"Many are highly valued and regarded. I have heard they are well-clothed and fed, some even live among the nobles."

"You would sell your acumen and all I have taught you for some hot porridge and a warm fire?"

"You have taught me ideas. I would promote the Way in another manner, for I want to see it in action."

"The Way is not a commodity," I said. "It cannot be exchanged or bartered. I have been in many noble houses where scholars yielded to such influences. But to covet such power is to debase yourself and to risk becoming dissolute. The Way shall ingratiate itself among those who allow it. The Way requires no more clout than the sun needs color. But you know this already, Li Su. You disappoint me."

"Master Scholar, I believe I can do more for the Way by

extending its reach into the state of Chu."

I looked at him with uncertainty for a moment and then shook my head. "This is shallow thinking. I have come to expect more. Much more."

But Li Su would not relent.

"Master Scholar you have always spoken of remaining open to possibilities," he continued.

"Yes, but when have I ever ceded our beliefs for opportunity? It is absurd; there will be no further discussion."

I dismissed him. Feeling angry, I made haste to the nearby village to indulge myself in some preserved egg in congee. I had given up eating meat years ago and the first crunchy bites of pickled turnip atop the velvety salted egg made me forget Li Su's words.

Shortly afterwards, I saw smoke drifting from the direction of my Academy. Before long, flames could be seen shooting upwards. I rushed back, but by the time I arrived it was too late. Flames had engulfed a lifetime's work. I was stunned. It all happened so fast. I was not one to accumulate or to give regard to material wealth, but I felt some pain as years of writings disappeared with the flames. But they were insignificant compared to the lives that were lost in the fire, many of them people I had known for years. I had lost much in my life already, but nothing in my teachings or experience prepared me to face the loss of friends, companions and scholars who so revered me. I had always shunned tears, but now I wept—for them, for my father and mother all those years ago, for Shun who was very much the elder brother. I had taught others to not fear an absence of order and to embrace the spontaneity of life. Yet Nature had dealt me another blow so unkind that it exposed how cruel its impartiality could be to anyone, from the scholarly to the simple-minded, from the rich man to the beggar. We are all equal in death. Many died that day while I had a childish tantrum and filled my belly with rice porridge.

Li Su survived the fire and supervised the clearing of the debris, salvaging what little that was left. Curiously, all his possessions survived. But I could barely face him or anyone. I had become a false master, filled with vacant ideas. I alone deserved to have perished in place of the others.

Thus when a Royal messenger arrived with word that Yi Ban, Minister of Rites within the Royal territory of Zhou was to visit the following day, I was ill-prepared. I assumed that he was coming to arrest me at my weakest hour for spreading provocative ideas. What I taught had never endeared me to most of those with a privileged station and perhaps this was a visitation of ironic justice. I waited for him in my garden amidst the wreckage and rubble of the Academy. If I was to be arrested, I wanted to see his Royal nose itching at the smell of cold ash and cinder as he performed his duty.

Until I met the Minister, I had never before set eyes on Royalty of such rank. Yi Ban was responsible for social and diplomatic matters, court etiquette and rites, as well as religious and educational affairs. Even so, he walked in alone, without any soldiers or attendants. I bowed and he greeted me with reverence and a sympathetic smile. Both his manner and his attire startled me. I had not left the mountains for some time so I had not seen anything quite as elaborate or ostentatious as his Royal yellow robe with wide blue hems on the sleeves and base, and a wide blue silk sash hung from his lapel. The robe was richly embroidered with silk threads patterned into blue orchids and red cranes, an ironic choice really given his tall, thin frame and long neck. A black leather belt with jade adornments suspended from silk ribbons completed his attire. I wondered how many families could be fed for the price of such an ensemble.

I did not know it at the time, but he was on his way back with the King from the annual paying of respects at the Royal tombs for the Qing Ming Festival. Yi Ban had left the Royal entourage to personally come to speak with me. He inspected the charred remains before we sat to share a pot of sweet and sour fermented apple cider.

"Forgive me, my Lord Minister, for being so direct," I said, "but why would someone of such importance as you grace someone as unworthy as me with your presence?"

The Minister sipped his cider. "But it is you who graces me with your presence. The works and teachings of Lao Tzu are recognized for having much practical value."

"You jest, my Lord."

"Not at all, dear scholar. Your treatise from many years ago on the re-organization of several minor Royal houses is a model still copied. You created systems of classification, you organized structures that safeguarded treasures, and you gave rise to whole new areas of study. While you also espoused ideas contrary to the current state of governance and society, they circulated among the literati and some of the nobility. Yes, they were not widely embraced, but they merited discussion and are often cited. At the very least you have sparked much-needed debate."

I bowed to the Minister. "I am pleased to hear that my efforts have eased the work of others."

"But I did not come to praise you, Lao Tzu. I need you. Zhou needs you."

"My Lord?"

"The Royal House… how can I say this? It would benefit from your creativity. The Royal Archives require your organizational expertise; the court itself could use fresh ideas, new and trusted faces."

His candor was startling and, again, his presentation was

surprising. Most of the court ministers and many of the nobles throughout the Zhou dynasty were bound to the King by blood relations, though ambition might dilute it as surely as water does wine. At first, I had judged Yi Ban to be no different. Now, he asked that I travel with him to re-establish the Royal Archives in the capital, Chengzhou.

I looked at him as I gestured at the ruins surrounding us. "My Lord, you can see where my work has taken me. My dreams have perished, ideas have gone up in flames, and lives were lost. I am humbled by your words, but I do not see how I am deserving of such an honor. Why would I even be considered for such a responsibility so soon after this disaster?"

"How does one burn an idea? For a scholar, you have much to learn still and you underestimate yourself."

The truth was that I was ill-prepared for such a purpose. I was already an old man and I had fully expected to die in the mountains.

I sought to discourage his interest with some of my thoughts on leadership. "Most rulers practice a form of rule that is heavy handed. They demand love, compliance and obedience among their subjects. Yet the best rulers are scarcely known, the next best are loved and praised, the next are feared, and the next despised. These latter ones are rulers who have no faith in their own people, and their people become unfaithful to them. When the best rulers achieve their purpose, their subjects claim the achievement as their own." I paused to allow my words to bite. "Where do you suppose King Jing falls?"

Much to my surprise, Yi Ban laughed, almost spilling his cup of cider. It was refreshing to see such an unrestrained response from a man in such a position.

"Bold words, Lao Tzu. But you have answered your own question. You are more likely to be trustworthy for having no personal ambition. The King can be unyielding, and bronze-fisted. But even he will eventually come to understand that his maturing sons need to be among men of the modern world."

I could not see a place for myself amidst shifting palace alliances and intrigue, and told him so.

"I would not argue that the Palace has challenges," Yi Ban acknowledged. "But remember that above all else you are a scholar. A thousand years of history is scattered within the shambles of the Archives. I know these to be irreplaceable riches and relics there. Unless they are salvaged into presentable form and their value demonstrated, I fear they will be forever lost. Already there is discussion of turning the space into part of the armory and selling off its contents. As a learned man, as a man who has made a life of providing method and order where unruliness existed, how can you allow this opportunity to pass? My dear scholar, you are precisely the man for this task. If that alone were not enough to persuade you, let me make my appeal more personal: I need your fresh eyes, your un-jaded ears and your voice within my Ministry."

I confess I was tempted, but still not convinced. I had heard more than a sliver of perfidy about the Royal Court. As I looked at the ruins about me, I could not forget my role in the death of friends and colleagues who had just perished. I could imagine their alarm at my leaving for Chengzhou. Yi Ban sensed some reservation and suggested I take until the next morning to decide.

I wanted to seek out Li Su's thoughts. I found him tying up several bundles. I told him of Yi Ban's offer, and he seemed relieved to hear it. Then I noticed that one of the bundles he was tying was a blanket.

"Li Su, what's going on? Where are you going?"

"Master Scholar, I had tried to tell you before the fire, but you were most angry. I am leaving. I am going to Chu. Now I am more resolved than before to go. The Academy is finished. Now you can make your way to Chengzhou."

"This is unbelievable! Is this what I taught you, to run when a challenge presents itself?"

"No, Master Scholar, but you never said anything about stagnation and wasting away. I have given you an opportunity. Take it. Take the Way wherever you wish. But remain here, and you will die with it alone."

"What do you mean, you have given me an opportunity?"

Li Su looked at the scorched ruins. "One must follow the path laid before him. You have always said that. But I believe we must also create our own destiny. The world is out there, Master Scholar."

Li Su tried to return to his packing but I grabbed him by the arm.

"What are you saying? Did you have something to do with the fire?"

He looked at my hand then flung it off. "I regret that lives were lost. But I recognized some time ago that acquiring wisdom and knowledge are pointless if they are not used. It is time for you to go as well. Stay if you wish. But do you really want to rebuild atop the ashes of those who perished? Do you have the will, the strength? Now you can leave without any guilt."

He returned to his packing, all but oblivious to my protests before quickly departing along with another scholar. For twenty years I had given him a life, nurtured him and mentored him, tried to teach him the meaning of the Way. Where had I failed? Had I expected the impossible?

By the next morning, I had made a decision. I had few options left, and so I resolved to view Yi Ban's offer as a legitimate and honorable path. Here was a man who had sought me out, who had praised me and shown me respect when it wasn't required. He knew that my thoughts on governance were clear. I had long preached that when opposing things such as ill-willed governments, it is best to begin to reduce the ruler's influence through expanding it; that is to say, by subtle means from within. I had always expounded the view that change whereby the weak overcome the strong should be handled delicately. Fish should not leave their depths, and swords should not leave their scabbards.

As the youngest son of a humble farmer, I was a long way from the village of my birth. For me to be appointed to the Royal Court was as unimaginable as a prince riding a donkey into battle. This offer of renewed purpose was unlikely in the extreme and perhaps ill-begotten through Li Su's suspect actions. But it was also serendipitously timed and not easily ignored. Long-lost youthful impulses re-asserted themselves and directed me to accept.

At my insistence, Yi Ban traveled ahead of me to the capital with his retinue. It required a few days and much heartache for me to conclude the past twenty years of my life. One of my scholars offered to join me while others left in disgust, seeing me as hypocritical and self-serving, just as I had seen Li Su. I understood how they felt, though I did not see myself as a traitor. I saw myself rather as fulfilling a destiny.

Before I left, one of my scholars came to warn me that the previous archivist I would replace was said to have been a spy. He had poisoned the guards before fleeing to Chu with a chest of jewels and treasure. The Son of Heaven already trusted few others besides his sons and now he would see even less value in yet another intellectual. This should have been warning enough. Yet strange as it may sound, there is a certain freedom when one is ill-regarded and little is expected of you.

And so it was done, twenty years of work. Two days later I released all who remained and began my long walk to Chengzhou, accompanied only by a donkey.

5

The Road to Chengzhou

A GENTLE SUN had barely managed to dry the morning dew when I set out towards the capital. As I left the valley, I encountered two peasants knee-deep in mud, struggling with a wooden plough in a small plot of young millet. Neighboring plots had similar crops, as well as soybeans and water oats. One of the peasants was shirtless and likely the grandfather of the young boy beside him. The elder had sagging, crinkled skin with recent scarring, probably from a master's belt. The younger one could not have been more than twelve years old, around my age when I fled with Shun. I thought of Shun often, wondering if he had survived the perpetual violence, the many wars, and whether he had been able to have a peaceful life.

The elder plodded stiffly through the mud, each movement laborious. He stopped for a water break. His eyes barely left the ground and he hardly acknowledged my greeting when I approached. I offered him a preserved duck egg that I had bartered from a farmer in exchange for some sesame flat cake purchased in a village. He studied me with suspicious eyes before accepting my offering. In return, he passed me his water vessel.

I explained briefly who I was. He replied in a tone that implied I was an imbecile.

"If you're hoping that Tian, our Heavenly God, will protect an elderly scholar travelling these dangerous roads alone, then think again."

"But I am not alone," I replied. "I am never alone, and neither are you."

I pointed out that I was sharing the moment with him, and that wherever I walked, I had all that Nature had created around me.

He cracked a toothless grin. "I once believed in the justice of the gods, their generosity. That was long ago."

"True. But I suggest you look beyond them. Look inwards."

He gave me a puzzled look, then told me that his family had for many generations farmed a large and productive plot sixty *li* to the west. But his eldest son had disgraced the family by becoming intimate with a girl who was promised to a lord and the clan was thrown off their land. His shamed son ran off and joined a lord's army battling the Qin and the rest of the family also scattered, hiding their humiliation as best as they could. The plot he currently worked belonged to a nobleman landlord adjacent to him. He explained that all arable land was divided into nine compartments, each a hundred paces long and only one pace wide. Eight families labored on their own, leaving the ninth plot for all to work in the King's name, or for a noble currently in his favor. The outer-lying farms, such as his, fell under the domain of the lesser-ranked landlords, whereas those closest to the city walls enjoyed better protection from the military and rich landlords.

He shared his story without malice or anger. In his mind, this was simply his fate. For others, though not for many from what I could see, their Gods of Nature had been in a good mood for some time. It had been many years since their anger swelled the many rivers and flooded the vast territories. Nor had their God of Sun recently punished the world by hardening the land and withholding water from even the smallest of life. I wondered how long this blessing would continue, as wars forever raged. Indeed the rich mud and pungent manure told me that food should have been in abundance here.

I shared meals on the road with the many peasants who were forever on the move. Not all shared equally in Nature's harvest. The lucky ones had straw shoes, but many wore only the mud on their soles. Those with wearable tunics, or who possessed animals, appeared content despite their station.

After a week on the road, I had witnessed many a hungry family, mostly farmers, each actively searching for a better life. One such family likely saved my own journey from disaster. Not long after I entered Chu territory, my donkey was stolen as I slept. Perhaps I was too easy a target for thieves. I naïvely assumed there was an unwritten code of honor among travelers. After that, I followed the narrow road to Chengzhou much like a beggar. Most of the farmers I encountered along the way refused to feed me, decrying their own lack of stock and recent robberies. None of them looked especially robust or healthy, and as I wore the robes of a scholar, I looked better off than they.

Feeling weak from hunger, I admonished myself for not having taken Yi Ban's offer to leave with him for Chengzhou. The sentimental side in me had drawn out my goodbyes with those of my former students who had not already left and were still speaking with me. I had never really had an orderly parting of ways and transition into a new life. I felt so old, so foolish even thinking of it.

At last I encountered a more convivial family of twenty-six members, composed of three generations, coming from Chu territory. The head of the family was an old soldier named Tang Dengjie. I heartily accepted his invitation to share their camp. This was a fairly lucky group of peasants. Though they were homeless and dispossessed, they were free, and their situation was in many ways preferable to servants and slaves. They travelled with ample stores of food and were well-clothed, as exemplified by their well-kept hemp pants and cotton shirts. They had the same wrinkled, weathered skin as all peasants who had endured life's challenges. But they were lucky because they shone with a joyous spirit and were filled with an uplifting mood.

They had snared rabbits earlier in the day with sling shots, reminding me of Shun. I helped them pick mushrooms and fern roots for a stew and despite not having eaten meat in years, I had what was my finest meal in many days as we sat around a roaring campfire. Tang had an energetic, youthful smile, unusual since the lines around his bright eyes and forehead suggested an age closer to mine.

His wife matched his geniality. She made an astonishingly invigorating pot of licorice root tea that reminded me of my father's.

"It's a dangerous world for an old unarmed man to be traveling alone," she said as she poured the steaming tea.

"Indeed, the world is filled with evil, I tell you," Tang said.

"Such a cynic," Tang's wife admonished her husband. "I said dangerous, not evil. You forget there are good people, heroes among us."

"Good people, yes. But heroes?" Tang scoffed.

"The White Renegade, you old fool. Don't forget him."

"Who?" I asked.

"The White Renegade. Have you not heard of him?"

I shook my head.

She stood up and expanded her chest and slowly panned the forest with her eyes. "He's powerful as a wolf, cunning like a fox and swift like the wind," she said.

"If he exists at all, he's a thief and a murderer, and so are his band of outlaws," Tang said.

"Oh, and did I forget wise and handsome?" she chuckled.

"Killing and banditry are not laughing matters," Tang reproached his wife.

"He kills only those lacking in virtue, and if you call it thievery when he takes only to survive and feed his fellow man, then I will share his saddle any time," she said as everyone broke out in laughter.

We shared tales well into the night most evenings. One night, Tang, with his remaining arm waving in the air and his finger pointing upwards for emphasis, shared his family's story.

He had lost his arm fighting for a baron many years ago. When he returned to farming, the baron compensated him for his service by reducing the tithe to be paid by his entire clan to farm. A neighboring warlord who killed those loyal to the baron overran the area but Tang and his family were spared because his father had once fought for the warlord's father. However, their taxes were raised again and most of their harvest and livestock confiscated. The warlord had Tang and his wife beaten, and forced them to sell one of their granddaughters to him. With another war brewing, Tang knew his remaining grandsons would be forced to serve. He decided they must leave the land his family had farmed for as long as anybody could remember.

"Our journey will take us to my cousin in Qi. He lives west of Linzi," he told me. "It will be safe there and you are welcome to travel with us. My grandchildren and their children could use a scholar, even an old and feeble one at that."

He and the rest of the clan laughed.

I told him I had business in Chengzhou, with the Palace. He fell silent and stared into the fire. He didn't appear impressed, but rather concerned. With his remaining hand, he gripped mine like a brother and said if things did not work out, I would always be welcomed in Qi.

We parted after four days of shared travel. By then, I had learned the names of each family member and shared much merriment. I felt a sensation of familial belonging that reminded me of the few years I had spent with my own family more or less intact, and also of the years at the Academy. The Tang family lived at ease, each member in harmony with the other, a formation that seemed as effortless and instinctive as wind fanning trees. Without knowing the Way, they lived it. Such honest people use no rhetoric, perhaps knowing it often cloaks deception. Many enlightened people are not cultured, and culture is not enlightenment, but people such as the Tang clan are content. And their lack of riches did not diminish their acquisition of contentment. They lived with an unforced and instinctive sense of charity: the more one gives, the more one receives. And these people were most adept at giving. At a fork in the road, they turned north and I continued east into the Royal territory that ensconced Chengzhou, but not before they insisted I take enough food to last me the rest of my journey.

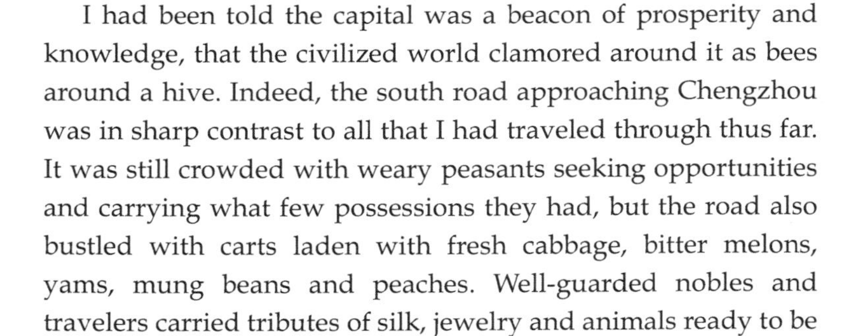

I had been told the capital was a beacon of prosperity and knowledge, that the civilized world clamored around it as bees around a hive. Indeed, the south road approaching Chengzhou was in sharp contrast to all that I had traveled through thus far. It was still crowded with weary peasants seeking opportunities and carrying what few possessions they had, but the road also bustled with carts laden with fresh cabbage, bitter melons, yams, mung beans and peaches. Well-guarded nobles and travelers carried tributes of silk, jewelry and animals ready to be slaughtered for the King.

From a distance, the high walls of the city looked imposing, standing perhaps twice my height. I knew that three gates guarded each of the four walls of Chengzhou city. Each wall ran a full nine *li* on each side. A younger man than I would require at least two hours just to walk the full length of one wall. Yet as I passed through the main south gate under the watchful but weary eyes of heavily-armed soldiers, I could see the wall was made only of beaten earth and that sections of it were crumbling.

I joined a column of wagons and other travelers awaiting clearance to proceed. Some were pulled aside and randomly searched. I overheard many rumors swirling about.

"Teams of assassins disguised as entire clans have been sent by neighboring states. They are intent on killing King Jing and other nobles."

"That would be foolish. They'd never get through. Moles from within the Palace are more likely to succeed."

"Does anybody even care any more?"

"He is still the ceremonial leader of the Zhou dynasty."

"Yes, but that and two whores will get you two whores."

Mere figurehead or not, the King's throne and what it represented still mattered to many. Breakaway territories had spies everywhere, seeking potential allies as well as identifying possible enemies. The Son of Heaven could not control the subterfuge, but he did attempt to douse the whispers of discontent with public beheadings and the burning of farms. I presented Yi Ban's stamped pass to the guards, which allowed me to bypass much of the column.

As I stepped through the gate in the wall, I walked onto the only stone road in the whole Empire. As wide as the outstretched arms of two men, it ran four *li* from the middle gate to the main entrance of the Yellow Palace. When the sun shone, quartz on the surface glistened and sparkled like a river of enormous jewels, beckoning towards a paradise of riches and purity. It was said that a Son of Heaven of the past had become so consumed with avoiding dirt and filth he had ordered this road paved to ensure that his wholesomeness would never be threatened by the filth of the street. I could not help but smile to myself at the foolish notion that a newly-laundered robe and a fresh bath could place a person closer to heaven than the most moral of mud-covered farmers.

My eyes wandered over the throngs, more people than I had ever seen in one place in all my days. Teams of beggars competed for space and attention with street vendors, newly-arrived homeless peasants alongside shoppers, merchants and servants. Regardless of their station, all had to be watchful for pickpockets and to dodge the horse-drawn carriages of nobles, as well as the pushcarts hauling manure. The air hung heavy with the choking smoke rising off the small fires of the many craftsmen, toiling away on sunken dirt floors under thatched awnings.

In the distance, past the throngs and narrow mud roads, loomed the towering Grand Celestial Hall, the very heart of the Yellow Palace, the Royal Residence and the core of the Zhou empire.

A large gathering of peasants and villagers surrounded a small, raised platform not far from the gate, filling the air with excitement and regular applause. Just below the stage, a trickster juggled four peaches through the air. Several other performers formed a human tower, standing on each other's shoulders, stretching towards the sky. A fortune teller foretold of unexpected wealth ready for the picking. A blind charlatan stopped me and implored me for a coin, saying that, "in return much grief shall be spared." I glanced at him not only because he was rather hideous but because, except for the vacant look in his eyes, he closely resembled my Uncle on Master Xun's farm decades ago. I was distracted away from him as the attention of the burgeoning crowd focused on the platform nearby.

I had witnessed enough executions and had no desire to see another and I was about to move on when I overheard some of the peasants nearby.

"For a farm girl, she is an extraordinary beauty."

"Yes, but look at those tiny hands; at thirteen she should not be so delicate. Her family will be lucky to get twenty *dao*."

"Perhaps. But that's good for a jug of rice wine and a water buffalo."

"Forget the water buffalo: the stubborn beasts are only good for hauling manure. Take three jugs of rice wine."

Laughter broke out.

So it was a slave auction, not an execution. The charlatan startled me by touching my arm. "The gods have decided," he proclaimed. "She has been chosen."

Bewildered, I looked at him but he merely pointed into the din of the crowd. My eyes scanned the gathering and came upon a young woman, really not much more than a girl dressed in rags, surrounded by people examining her. I asked the charlatan what was going on.

"That is old Li Wei and his wife," the charlatan replied.

The charlatan didn't seem to notice that he'd just blown his pretense at being blind. But his deception mattered little, as there can be few moments as painful as when a mother and father sell off their flesh and blood.

"One would have to possess the heart of a barbarian to not feel remorse for them," the charlatan continued. "It's not enough that a plague of hungry locusts savaged their crops and a fire destroyed what little they had left of their home. If not for that girl's alertness, they would have all perished. Nevertheless, they are now snake-bitten and cursed. Her sale is all that separates them from starvation and keeps the debt collector from delivering the final blow to the family. To those who only see with their eyes, she appears to be worth little now—a few goats, perhaps some chickens."

I looked at the charlatan and suddenly felt that there was more to him than his hideousness and similarities to Uncle's gapped tooth and bald head. "This is nonsense," I replied. "What madness continues to befall people that women can still be sold for a few animals?"

"My Lord, you have been removed from the real world too long. These are the ways of the world. Do not deny that you have seen this many times over. Instead, see beyond the unrecognizable. For I have, and I know there is purpose for her. The gods have seen to it. Please sir, a single coin?"

"For what? Even had I a *dao* to give, your pronouncements are meaningless."

"Then heed this, Master Scholar, 'an ill wind scatters seeds of hope, but even the calmest breeze harbors pestilence'."

I was about to reply when the auctioneer's voice boomed out, seizing my attention. He enticed a merchant to shout out an offer of ten *dao* for the girl. A farmer countered with two sacks of millet, three chickens and a large jar of barley sugar.

A butcher offered six freshly slaughtered chickens and three goat heads.

The crowd oooo-ed and ahhhh-ed.

The auctioneer pleaded with the bidders.

"Honorable masters, though she is small, her father, a loyal subject, swears she is very obedient and will learn fast."

The auctioneer pointed at the parents, still fighting back tears.

"Surely you can offer more for such fine pedigree!" he urged. He tried to pry apart the girl's lips to reveal her teeth but she resisted. She was about to push his hand away when our eyes locked for a moment, and she relaxed and let him do it, while still standing tall and proud.

"Wang Wei, be careful!" one of the peasants shouted. "She might not be strong but she could still bite your pecker off—if she could find it."

The crowd broke out in laughter and jeers. A Major of the Royal Guard, a towering man, stepped onto the platform. He was carrying the longest and most intimidating halberd I had ever seen. Its bamboo shaft was capped with three glistening blades, one like a spear, a short blade spiked off one side of the shaft, and a final blade shaped like a crescent. He had a deep scar running from forehead to cheek and a thick, woolly beard tied into a single braid. His dark, humorless eyes surveyed those watching as if he were ready to pounce at the slightest provocation. He raised a Royal standard, and banged the butt end of his halberd down on the platform, effectively quieting the crowd. Then he nodded towards a phalanx of armor-clad bodyguards approaching from behind the crowd, along with the King's carriage.

"The King! Look away," the crowd whispered. We dropped our heads to avoid inadvertently looking at the Son of Heaven, an indiscretion punishable with twenty lashes and in some cases death. From the corner of my eye, I could see he was well-hidden behind a curtain.

The Major was about to drag away the young girl when she looked up at him, revealing her diamond-shaped face, dark and inquisitive eyes as shiny as the finest lacquer. This startled the Major and he hesitated for a swollen moment before he returned the glance. Then he gingerly took her hand and, fulfilling his duty, led her to the King's procession.

The auctioneer feigned a protest, but an official clanked a small bundle of spade-shaped *dao* coins onto the platform, some spilling over. The auctioneer could not hide his glee.

The Royal carriage and the Guardsmen moved on. Many in the crowd went over to congratulate the young woman's parents whose honor at having their daughter taken to the King's private realm would improve their social standing. The parents failed to reciprocate the enthusiasm, though the crowd dispersed into pockets of excitement.

"The Son of Heaven already owns the most beautiful women in the world. Why take a raggedy farm girl?"

"She may be a farm girl, but she can wash my feet any time."

"Dream on, you old goat. If she or any other women in the Palace so much as touches anybody else's feet, the King would see that two heads will roll—hers and the idiot who couldn't keep his stalk where it belonged."

It suddenly occurred to me that the charlatan, as bad as he was at pretending he was blind, seemed to know who I was. He had referred to me as Master Scholar. I turned to query him, but he had disappeared.

Lao Tzu's voice faded as he stopped to take a sip of water. A full day had passed since he had begun telling his story.

Captain Yin shifted in his seat. He was enthralled with all he had heard, but could not help but question what he felt was a digression.

"Old Master, please excuse my impertinence, but what does the farm girl have to do with the Way, or with my grandfather?"

Lao Tzu poured himself some freshly-boiled water.

"Everything and nothing." He gently blew on his water. "The Way surrounded her as it does me. As it does all of us. The harmony of Nature flows freely. It is the very rhythm of life. This order allows us to act without action and to do without doing, such as when Shun saved that drowning boy."

Lao Tzu sensed Captain Yin's confusion, and so he elaborated.

"My good Captain, the Way is not a block of wood to be carved, nor is it a set of edicts from our rulers to be studied and practiced. Yet through it, all things are done. It is by how you live that you see and understand it. I had asked you if soldiering and war were acts of nature or human folly. Was this girl's life, or even that of the King's, fated and fixed? Were they part of the stream running with the wind, or were they logs thrown in to dam its flow?"

Yin pondered his questions while Lao Tzu sipped his water.

"But Old Master, if it is order and structure that you question, consider where we would be without it. Laws, leadership... these are foundations of Zhou, of all life."

Lao Tzu sighed. "There are laws and order to everything, especially in Nature, it is true. But these possess a very different cadence from the ones advanced by people such as Confucius. He believed that order and stability are the foundations of society. He, along with many other scholars, counseled our Son of Heaven, the dukes and the lords with such ideas. Through this, many such scholars came to wield enormous power."

"And you?" Yin nodded. "Did you not have a similar standing within the court?"

Lao Tzu put his cup down.

"If you understood the Way, you would refrain from asking such a question. I have observed that those who gain what is under heaven by tampering with it do not succeed. Those that grab at something, lose it. For among the creatures of the world some lead and some follow, some blow hot when others blow cold. Some are vigorous just when others are worn out."

Yin straightened and nodded for Lao Tzu to continue. He would measure at another time what he had heard.

6

The Forbidden Royal Palace

I STAYED AT an inn near the Palace for a few days, awaiting Yi Ban's instructions. When he and an aide finally appeared, his warm sympathetic smile greeted me once again. He enquired about my journey and stay in Chengzhou, but his casual disposition was short-lived. He immediately began preparing me for an audience with the King.

"The Palace is a solemn place," Yi Ban declared. "Matters of state, in fact any matters involving the Royal Family, are conducted with the strictest etiquette. The King is never to be addressed as such, nor as a person. He is Heaven's representative, hence he is to be addressed as the Son Of Heaven. My aide will brief you further on some of the finer details of protocol and ritual so that you will be presented in the best possible light."

Yi Ban edged toward me. "Lao Tzu, you may be wiser and more enlightened than many scholars within the Palace. But here, your past and your credentials may not hold much currency. You will be viewed with uncertainty and misgivings until you have proven the doubters to be misguided, and even then there may still be those who seek to profit from your virtue. You must learn to view others in like manner."

I smiled. "To what end can an archivist gain or profit from his standing?"

"Do not be so dismissive of yourself or your situation. With heaven's grace you will soon be in the corridors of power. It is a position and an opportunity that leaves few unchanged, and regrettably taints many. Your outsider's counsel and fresh eyes will be invaluable... if you can maintain them."

The Forbidden Yellow Palace was located in the exact centre of the city. Its perimeter was perfectly squared with a thick wall that paralleled the city's walls. Guarding the only public entrance and exit was the arched Heavenly Gate. The heavy oak gates were painted gold and adorned with phoenixes symbolizing good fortune. It was framed by battlements that faced south and stood four stories high, with yellow tiles on multiple, steeply-constructed roofs.

Entering the Palace required advance permission, or good standing among the military, with at least one reference from either nobles or government officials, or else Royal assent. Once again, Yi Ban's seal served me well and I was ushered in, but not before undergoing a lengthy search by grave-faced Royal Guardsmen. Once through, I was greeted by stone lions the size of small horses. Above me on the battlement, a platoon of soldiers and ready archers followed my every movement.

I was instructed to follow a silent Royal Guardsman. He led me onto the stone road that led directly through a wide, dirt courtyard. Legend said nothing was able to grow in this area, not even the hardiest weed, because of the salt from tears and pools of blood spilled from all the executions carried out over the centuries.

Within the grounds before the Royal buildings, there were numerous walled compounds of many different designs. Some had higher walls, some additional stories or more elaborate décor. It all depended upon on when they were built, for what purpose, and most importantly, for whom. These compounds included the living quarters for some high-ranking ministers, together with several buildings such as barracks and armory for the Royal Guardsmen, servants' quarters, housing for livestock, official guest quarters, the kitchens and the Archives. Sadly, the Archives structure appeared unkempt.

Privileged slaves and servants lived in thatch-roofed, mud brick, single room huts which stood within the grounds of walled villas belonging to their masters, each one surrounded by their own complexes and by high walls pierced by wide passageways. It was as though the Palace consisted of many inner cities within itself, each with its own hierarchies and allegiances. I heard of many young noble women who had never ventured beyond their own walls, let alone outside the Palace; and of slaves born within the Palace and who spent their entire lives there. Death threatened any who strove to escape from their masters, and such punishment was rarely required. Many outsiders would gladly have traded places for the relative safety and full bellies such servitude provided.

Precisely three thousand paces from the city wall and through the Heavenly Gate in a perfect north-south axis, loomed the Grand Celestial Hall. The Zhou had long boasted that it was the largest building in the world. Giant carved dragons hung over the entrance, dragons of course being our rulers' favorite symbols of authority, fertility, goodness and above all else—strength.

The Hall was erected on a raised terrace of beaten earth, adding to its dizzying height of five stories. Whereas all other curved roof structures within the Palace had yellow tiling, the Hall's massive roof tiles were painted blue to symbolize the sky. This enormous weight rested on a complex system of beams and brackets constructed from the stoutest of Tibetan cypress trees, decorated with bronze joint plates with coiled serpent and dragon motifs.

It was boasted that inside, the Son of Heaven could preside over audiences of up to five hundred people.

Flanking the Hall were four identical buildings, two on each side. The two on the western side were private chambers for the King and Queen, and for the Princes. The two on the other side were for the concubines, servants, visiting family, dignitaries and celebrated guests of the Royals. Each was connected by elevated covered walkways to shield the Royals from mortal eyes. Behind this flank of buildings were the Royal Gardens, courts for gamesmanship, and the King's private stable and armory.

Seven hundred years ago, the Zhou must have thought the world was ending as thousands of barbaric nomads on horseback swept over the plains, slaying the King and plundering the old capital of Daoyang. The remaining Zhou Royals fled from their western power base, relying on the lords of Qin and Jin to provide for their safety. Eventually, they established Chengzhou as their new capital. I am sure they thought their new walls would stand for a thousand years. However poor construction and the constant wars had left the walls weak to their core. Yet weakened walls and decaying morality are like rot and disease—they occupy the same branch of a dying tree.

Though our rulers still favored yellow for the Palace walls and had everything painted accordingly, it had obviously been some time since they had seen a fresh coat of paint. Dry, cracked lines and peeling sections were found on most walls, except for those in the inner court, and many appeared like the ordinary dried mud walls seen everywhere else. But even as I searched for faults about the Palace, I could not help but feel wonder and awe at the enormity and scale of the Palace's grandeur, in particular the beauty of the ceiling, which was painted like the night sky with the constellations

This symbolized the King's mandate from heaven to rule. Rulers are put in place by heaven and may continue to rule so long as they do so with justice and wisdom. When they cease to rule in the best interests of their subjects, the mandate of heaven requires that they be overthrown. For those such as myself, whose lives were largely unaffected by the ceremonial and functional roles of the King, how they lived their lives and how they presided had little bearing. But now, as I approached the apex of ceremonial power, I had to re-examine this. I could not disagree that moral and just leadership should be divine in origin and reflective of heaven's natural creations on earth. This made the failure of leadership so much more tragic. But what if leadership could be otherwise, what possibilities could there be?

Over the centuries, the Palace had burnt down several times due to lightning strikes, invasions or general carelessness. Despite this, repeated reconstructions followed principles that sought to revere heaven, and there was thus little deviation in architectural design, and the liberal use of torches and lanterns still brightened the Hall like a summer day inside.

A phalanx of torches and Royal Guardsmen lined the imposing walk to the King's dais, casting fleeting shadows along the way. Lanterns were placed above enormous bronze vessels on fine lacquer bases depicting Zhou rulers and their past victories - none of them recent. Round bronze mirrors hung from posts, warding off evil spirits.

As if to compensate for his dwindling power, King Jing became perhaps the most accessible of the Zhou rulers in memory. He had never known hunger or want, and had never shared a meal with anyone outside of his lineage or official circles, which was not unusual for the Son of Heaven. Yet he fashioned himself as loved and revered by his subjects. Executions, while still common, had become less frequent under his reign, and taxes had not been raised in some time. Once a week, the King and other members of his family presided over an audience with their subjects, hearing matters of state, as well as arbitrating disputes. The King had invested heavily in the tutelage of his sons, his heirs, and generally encouraged their counsel, particularly when holding court. That common folk were regularly allowed into the Palace, albeit after a thorough search and under heavy guard, was a remarkable symbol of openness. Many regions had become oblivious to centralized Royal rule. The idea of there being a universally-acclaimed enlightened and beloved King was as much an illusion as the idea of their lofty stature.

I was among a small group of pre-selected subjects to be presented on that day. Once inside, we were surrounded by scores of Royal Guardsmen in ceremonial uniforms. Within this cocoon, we knelt before King Jing, as did the Ministers such as Yi Ban, the Ministers of Law, State, Civil Administration, Social Welfare, Justice and Works, and the all-powerful Minister of War and their aides.

I stole glances in the ruler's direction. Facing south, he sat in the centre of the Royal dais, which stood several feet above the ground. His twin sons, the Princes, who were eighteen years old at that time, sat on either side of him: Prince Meng to his right, Prince Chao to his left. The Queen sat one step below the males, though she might as well have been a thousand *li* away to judge from the remoteness in her eyes.

Prince Meng was the elder of the siblings by a span of minutes. Custom dictated that the elder would succeed to the throne, though there were occasions when this tradition had previously been broken for political or personal expedience if the King so chose.

My introduction was one of many items of minor business presented that day and I was able to observe all matters of the day preceding mine. This included a prisoner who was dragged in by two guards. His hair had been erratically cut short, marking him as a prisoner, and his wrists were bound behind his back with hemp rope, while fresh bruises covered his bloodied face. One of the guards bowed and bellowed, "Your Majesty, this filth has been charged with stealing from the Royal kitchen."

The King nodded at his Princes.

It was said that Prince Chao was like his father from birth: stubborn, proud and forever vigilant. There were those who believed he slept with his eyes open. Though he was younger than his brother, one might have thought he was vying to take the throne himself, as he showed no lack of confidence in court.

"Heavenly Father, you always say a crime against us is a crime against heaven," Prince Chao said. I stole a quick glance in his direction. His raised chin suggested authority. The lustrous sheen of his hair, and the manner in which it was tightly bound in a top knot covered with a hat, suggested boldness and confidence.

"Ah Chao, you have the memory of a lonely concubine," the King chuckled in reply.

Prince Meng, on the other hand, had the calm, thoughtful qualities that his father and brother rarely displayed. He looked at the servant. Instead of a hat like his brother wore, his head was covered with a square piece of cloth.

"Heavenly Father," he said, "is this not a man whose family has served our family for generations? The village of his clan was recently burnt to the ground by roving soldiers who had deserted the Chu. Perhaps we should consider this before we condemn him. I believe that to be just."

"Heavenly Father, the Gods and our other servants will take note of any weakness we show." Prince Chao emphasized the word 'weakness' and, judging from his tone, I could imagine him shooting his brother a scalding look.

"They will also reflect on any compassion and mercy we display," Prince Meng responded.

The King rubbed his chin and grinned at his two sons. "Excellent. I see the fruits of my wisdom. There can be no greater comfort than knowing my success as a father and as King. This dynasty will pass into capable hands. Each of my princes profits as though one were a fisherman, the other his indispensable cormorant."

"But what if the fisherman's hand should prove to lack the necessary firmness and strength?" Prince Chao said in a clear reference to his brother.

The King's laughter filled the court. "Prince Chao, your elder brother may not have your skill with a bow or your daring on horseback, but he is not without acumen, and he is by rights my heir."

I listened closely. Prince Meng could have built on his father's affirmation of his right to rule, but instead he ignored his brother.

The King nodded towards Prince Chao. "You are quite right. Forgiveness is a weakness I cannot afford. This thief's right hand will be fed to the dogs. His left hand will be branded with my seal. The world will see how I reward disloyalty. He can learn to herd sheep. They will have less to steal from."

The prisoner whimpered. Prince Chao made no effort to conceal his smugness. Then the King looked to Prince Meng whose eyes had remained on the servant. "And his family will receive a sack each of sorghum and millet each spring for ten years."

The Queen adjusted her gold hair pin and giggled like a little girl with a secret. An awkward silence followed, then I heard the King's heavy sigh and what sounded like a mumbled rebuke at his Queen.

An official shouted out to those in attendance, "His Highness King Jing is all powerful and merciful! May heaven continue to bless us with his wisdom!"

Those present repeated these phrases in perfect unison while remaining kneeling on the ground. The prisoner was dragged out. The official then shouted out, "Minister Yi Ban, the Honorable Minister of Rites!" And Yi Ban stepped forward and knelt before the King.

"If it pleases the Son Of Heaven, may I present to you, your new Royal Archivist, Lao Tzu, esteemed scholar and former master of the highly-regarded Sword Hill Academy."

I stepped up, knelt, then bowed three times and remained prone. I could feel the King's eyes studying me as though I were a snake that might strike once his back was turned, or simply slither away.

"Another great scholar. Another great representative of the literati. Hmmph. The last archivist was a thief and a spy. Do you know what fate shall befall him once he is captured? Speak, scholar."

I remained bowed and spoke clearly. "If it pleases the Son Of Heaven, I trust my predecessor's very own soul has already passed judgment on his failings and that the wisdom of the heavens will exact their providence. As for this court, the repugnance which it must feel will no doubt be matched by an earthly retribution of its choosing.'

A silence followed. Yi Ban quickly repeated my credentials to the King, who sighed.

"Neither a battle-scarred warrior, nor a noble of impeccable peerage, yet you are ready to fill us with your wisdom, righteousness and arrogance." He slapped his knees and laughed again as though he was at a cock fight. "Rise, Lao Tzu.

Look at your Son of Heaven so that I may see your eyes. How enlightened and kind will you consider me if I banish you and ban all your teachings?"

The Son of Heaven wore a long braided beard tied with gold foil. For a man who had likely never toiled for a moment in physical labor in his life, his face and hands were surprisingly creased and dry. Large dark eyes attempted to burn me like flaming arrows, but I had long since learned to live with fear and found them no more frightening than summer fireflies. His hair was bound in a tight bun held together with a jade hairpin fashioned into a dragon.

"If it pleases the Son Of Heaven, he may banish wisdom and discard knowledge from the people. For they may benefit a hundredfold still as ignorance is ultimately blissful. Banish forced duty and insincere kindness, for compassion will form of its own accord. Banish that which motivates profit, for thieves and robbers will disappear. If without these three things your people find life too plain and unadorned, then let them have simplicity to contemplate, and the un-carved block—the uncorrupted mind—and allow them selflessness and a repudiation of frivolous desires."

The King rose, glaring at me as he stepped off the dais, his hand resting on the hilt of his jewel-crusted dagger. The fireflies had developed darts. I should have better minded Yi Ban's protocol instructions. Conceivably I was arrogant, or else I had unwisely forgotten fear. Or perhaps my father was correct in advising that my naiveté would be my undoing. Though my life dangled in the balance, I betrayed no panic, for I felt none. Whatever my destiny, I had come to realize I could preside only over that which I could govern. He must have sensed this contrast to the usual court acolytes, and it had given him pause.

His voice thundered throughout the hall: "You will be

watched every moment of every day until I am satisfied that you are neither a spy nor a thief. Be gone!"

He stepped back onto his dais and sat down.

And so it was done. The Son of Heaven had imposed on me the same conditions as for any other new staff within the Palace. I had for now, passed heaven's scrutiny.

7

The Royal Archives

Until my arrival at the Archives, I had never witnessed disorder on such a scale. The state's accounts were in complete disarray, and there was little method to the classification and storage of records, relics and treasures. Intricately threaded robes worn by previous kings and queens were bundled like common tunics and trousers. Seven hundred year-old vases were haphazardly stacked. Accounting tablets and paintings were heaped in piles without regard for historical period or category. What wasn't layered in dust showed clear signs of water damage and mould. I have seen chicken coops more thoughtfully organized. This disarray supported the rumors that the previous Royal Archivist was unfit for the task, and that he had employed his mind and pocket elsewhere. Perhaps he was indeed spying for the state of Chu. The large collection of ancient records, bamboo tablets and paintings of the many gods worshipped long ago by the Shang and now by the Zhou, could not have been more chaotic if the hand of the Wind God, Feng Bo, had ripped through them. Then there were the centuries-worth of tributes and gifts from kings, nobles and sycophants thought too worthless even to merit a shelf in a far-off room within the Palace.

The original Royal Archives had been housed within what was now the armory, but evidently knowledge and scholarly pursuit were no match for the storage of the King's ceremonial chariots and carriages. The new Archives compound was much smaller and was part of the old servants' quarters located in the remote southeastern corner behind the blacksmith. Altogether it was no larger than the mansion of a minor noble, but each room was bursting with history. And it had a saving grace—the adjacent courtyard garden.

It was small but promising and had once grown vegetables. It still contained fruit trees along with numerous interesting shrubs and plants that attracted an array of birds and insects. I wanted to replicate the quietude and calm of my former life and so my first order of business—pleasure, really—was to weed the garden. The trees and shrubs also received a much-needed trim. As with my former Academy, I had limestone boulders brought in and I had two small interconnecting ponds dug and filled with fresh spring water, then stocked with goldfish and danios. While it wasn't the Academy, I quickly replicated a harmonious balance of wood, water, stone and flora, giving me a reflective escape from the tension and demands of the Archives.

In those first days, I reviewed my staff. Most had been friends or family members of minor officials. They handled fragile materials with the same delicacy as digging a trench. The few genuine scholars and clerks on hand were poorly-trained scribes. They lacked knowledge of the proper handling and storing of priceless and irreplaceable treasures. Moreover, their lackadaisical approach abetted thievery. I disappointed myself with how quickly I came to harbor such cynicism about my subordinates. Perhaps recent memories of Li Su's falseness had jaded me. I so wanted to avoid a repetition and I wondered whether it was a portent of an inevitable descent into the malevolence of power of which Yi Ban had warned me.

To resolve this, I dismissed those who tended to speak poorly of others or beat the commoners who provided the menial labour. One of them, Kao Shin, would become my most trusted assistant. I learned long ago that an untrained mind is more valuable than an intelligent but corrupted one. My remaining staff received daily lessons in scribing, cataloguing, storage and preservation, and also in the Way. I wanted those around me to understand not only the scope of my philosophies, but also the tempo to which it related.

Reorganizing the Archives required fortitude. While I professed the wisdom of submitting to the unpredictable cadences of the natural world, I could not similarly allow the disorder of the Archives to persist and I did not foresee any objections to the prescribed re-organization it clearly required. The entire collection, as immense as it was, needed to be itemized and catalogued. The previous system saw items stored according to each king's reign, but limited space had rendered the strict implementation of this impossible many years ago. I required each article to be numbered anew according to their age, then grouped by element or category—bamboo tablets with other bamboo tablets, bronze vessels with bronze vessels, tax records with tax records... I estimated this task would out-live me.

I proposed expanding the storage space available and including rooms for quiet study and contemplation. I foresaw the collection as a bastion not only for the preservation of history but for pursuing understanding of that history. At the same time, I wished to greatly enlarge the current cellars and add cedar shelves throughout. This would allow me to secure the more delicate ceramic items in a predictable temperature, away from the ravages of sunlight and the still-unrepaired leaky roof, and with less threat of fire and pilfering. I presented the expansion plans to Yi Ban as being necessary for proper storage and growth of the materials. At first he hesitated, believing that the Royal family would only see the Archives as a repository for their own vanity. But after moderate persuasion, he came to see the wider purpose of the Archives as a hub for higher learning. He approved the expansion, but added that such an undertaking would also need the King's approval.

I had hoped to have as many of these changes as possible in place before a visit from the King. It was at Yi Ban's suggestion that the King inspected my work to date before ruling on the expansion proposal.

On the appointed afternoon, the Son of Heaven arrived and my minister Yi Ban was nowhere to be found. The King made a sweeping entrance with his sons and officials and several bodyguards. Still there was no sign of Yi Ban, who had told me he very much wanted to be present, no doubt to check my tongue and personally present the project. Along with several of my junior archivists and clerks, I dropped to my knees.

"The Son of Heaven honors us with his presence," I said. "Forgive me, but the Minister of Rites…"

"Is not required," the King interjected.

He ignored us and walked around with the Princes, poking among the shelves and unrolling several bamboo strips sewn together with silk threads.

"My Minister of Rites advises that I should examine the progress you have made to date, but I did not need his advice to bring me here. I am well aware that this may be a new strain on our treasury. I prefer to see this for myself without his badgering presence. Neither the future Son of Heaven nor I have ever been here, and from what I see, there is little of interest or value."

After only a perfunctory glance at the tablets, the King tossed them down. When he said, 'your future Son of Heaven,' he made no clear indication as to which of his sons he was referring to.

"I was led to expect more," he continued. "I was misled.

Clearly I must direct my Prime Minister to restrain this project and take closer scrutiny over our state's accounts and the treasures here."

"Indeed, Heavenly Father," Prince Chao agreed. He picked up and opened a faded bamboo tablet. "Look at what an ugly being is depicted here."

I glanced at the tablet. The King commanded me to rise and explain it.

"The Son of Heaven is gazing upon an image of Yu Huang, the Jade King, the Heavenly Ancestor."

"Why does he appear so angry?" Prince Meng asked.

The Prince had a perfectly smooth, peach face absolutely bereft of lines or facial hair. Large, soulful eyes looked around with curiosity. His fine silk robes could not hide slight shoulders that sloped like a pigeon's. His hands, which took the tablet from Prince Chao, were so delicate that I could not say which was more fragile, the Prince's hands or the crumbling artifact. I answered the elder Prince's question.

"As the Son Of Heaven is well aware, the legend of Yu Huang tells us that he created men from the mud of the Yellow River. He left his creations in order to scold a slave who had not yet prepared his meal. With his attention diverted, the clouds unleashed their fury and rained on Yu Huang's work. Those figures over whom he had shown greatest care had already dried before the rain. They were those in his likeness and became the nobility. Those made with greater haste but still preserved became the farmers, servants and slaves. Those made with the greatest haste which melted in the rain became people with deformities."

I glanced at the King to gauge his reaction, which was now attentive, as were the Princes, so I carried on.

"Yu Huang was angry because of his carelessness, your Highness. He did not anticipate the rain."

From the corner of my eye, I could see the King studying the painting. "How do you know he left in order to scold a servant?"

"The Son Of Heaven surely recognizes that it is a legend only."

"Legend or not, you are wrong. Yu Huang was not careless. He fulfilled his duty, his servant was likely inept and required admonishment. It is one of many burdens of power. Rulers must remind subjects of their place." The King turned to the Princes. "We make difficult decisions, even if it hurts those we serve."

"Only the Son of Heaven among us can appreciate the burden of governing," I said. "Yet I believe the lesson is not the carelessness with which he may have dealt with his servant, but in misunderstanding the pulse of the Way. Had he danced with the wind, scented the air and touched the clouds, he would have easily seen the rain coming."

The King stared directly at me. I immediately regretted my impulsiveness. I had heard that others who had spoken out of turn as I had just done could find themselves chained to the Palace gates, but I could not allow an opportunity to correct blindness to the Way, nor misunderstandings of it. I expected the King's next command would be to at least admonish me for my insolence. Showing impeccable timing, Prince Meng broke the silence.

"Father, in your wisdom you have said it is a Prince's right to question, to think critically in order to learn. If so, I would like to see more of these and study them."

The Prince looked at me as though seeking my permission.

"The Son Of Heaven's Prince is correct," I responded. "And there is much to see. Your Highness' collection is vast, the treasures irreplaceable and the Archives overflowing with such works of value."

"Study them to what purpose?" Prince Chao interjected.

"Why bother? How much room do we need to store worthless old relics and tablets of numbers? This area could be used to enlarge our armory, the yard for archery practice, or even to play *cuju*. The men would love the additional space to kick a ball about."

He had the same dark eyes as Prince Meng, but they were eager and energetic, as one ready to stretch his bow to its fullest. His face was more weathered and angular than his older twin's, his nose slightly crooked, perhaps from a break. His hands were perfectly manicured but sinewy like an archer's. His robe was more elaborate than his brother's, with deep red cuffs, and he wore it with purpose and confidence. The King stared at his two sons.

"If the Son Of Heaven will allow me to speak..." I said, my head bowed, not wanting to antagonize him further.

He grunted his consent.

"This collection is immense. You possess original copies of the classics. There are four hundred years of records, from taxes collected, valuable artifacts, and treasures received. Nowhere else does such richness exist. Nowhere else does the potential to sift out a complete picture of human history possible. The correspondences and tributes alone would suffice to produce the complete annals of the Zhou dynasty. With all the evidence collected here, there can be no disputing the place the Zhou have in this world. If the Son Of Heaven would allow me to reveal but a single treasure, perhaps I can better explain."

The King nodded, and I directed their attention to a table where a number of small bronze animals sat. I picked one up. "If it pleases the Son Of Heaven, this horse is one of twenty-six different animals, each representing a King from the House of Zhou. Each piece has carved on its base a different King's name, his reign and details of his glory. My research has unearthed the fact that these were a gift from a far-away kingdom. They were presented to the Son Of Heaven as playthings upon the occasion of his fifth birthday. I understand that the Son Of Heaven cut himself playing with them. Consequently the previous King deemed them unsuitable and had them placed in storage. The craftsmanship is not especially unique. But they symbolize the richness of all that we house. The one I hold before you is engraved with the Son Of Heaven's name—King Jing, but nothing more. Its final details await your instructions."

I placed the bronzed horse onto its base and held it up to the King as I bowed. He inspected it, then cast his eyes onto the rest of the collection. I could hear him take a breath.

I continued. "By comparison, my Son Of Heaven's position in history alongside these illustrious Kings is precariously recorded and poorly stored. Our Son Of Heaven's role cannot be properly honored and respected if these treasures are not secured properly to retain this legacy. Your deserved place within the structure of history demands more rigorous preservation. I propose to clean and polish each of these bronze animals and display them and other treasures of the House of Zhou. Visiting dignitaries and noblemen will marvel at such objects of history. Scholars will flock to study such greatness and take such knowledge back to from whence they came. The name of Zhou will become even more respected. It will be spoken of as the only living remnant of the past through the present and into days to come. You will be known as the protector of the House's annals, and the treasures enshrined here. Though it will take some time and a necessary expense to bring order here, as your servant and Royal Archivist it is my aim and duty to make it so."

I briefly explained my plans for expanding the building and enlarging the cellars. King Jing and Prince Meng were showing more than a casual interest, but then Prince Chao interjected:

"At what cost to the state treasury? Heavenly Father, one archivist has already robbed us. Now another proposes to burden the state with extra spending and building projects. Who is to say what else has already been stolen? It unsettles me how such valuables are being managed and guarded. I propose we double the guards here to have all those with access searched daily, as well as their homes."

Again, Prince Meng demonstrated his maturity, ignoring Prince Chao's provocation.

"Father, you have expressed concern over whether history will recognize and remember your greatness. Perhaps the answer lies in the degree of care and management of this dusty collection of forgotten treasures."

The King stroked his long beard and looked at me. "Show me what more you have."

I led them through the collection, passing by the mundane to focus their attention on shelves of tablets of official homages, poems and acknowledgments from foreigners and nobles, and silk paintings depicting the divinity and courage of King Jing, as well as that of other previous Kings holding court or in peaceful outdoor scenes.

"Why have I not seen these before?" he asked.

"Many Sons of Heaven in the past have preferred more practical tributes such as rolls of silk, slaves, bronze vessels, gold, jade and weapons. They may have had little interest for items that were less immediate and more… thoughtful."

The King nodded, his eyes alight. "There is much value here. These Archives should not merely be a warehouse. They will be a gallery of my greatness, and that of my forebears. Scholars and nobles will flock here and be astounded by the richness of my reign and of the Zhou dynasty." His eyes bore into me. "You will see this is so. But first, what is this 'Way'?"

His question sought a simple answer, as if knowing the color of the sky could foretell all there was above. I explained that it was both simple and complex, obvious yet obscure.

"I am the Son of Heaven of Zhou. There is little I am not capable of knowing or understanding. Need I repeat my question?"

"I beg the Son of Heaven's forgiveness. One of the basic principles of the Way is that it cannot be adequately described in words, and to do so would be insulting to its unlimited power. Still, its nature can be understood, and those who value it understand it best. If it pleases the Son of Heaven, there was something formless yet complete that existed before heaven and earth without sound, without substance, dependent on nothing, unchanging. Its true name we do not know; the Way is merely the name I have come to give it. But in the tablet we just saw of Yu Huang, I interpret his failure to be an inability to enjoy the simple and the quiet, the natural and the plain. That is how he failed to forecast the rainstorm that altered the shape and placement of man. That he had been distracted by going to scold a new slave shows adherence to an artificial division among brothers. Yu Huang's allegiance to such a fabrication set the boundaries for the caste of human divisions. He ultimately failed to live within his inner self and in accordance with the laws of Nature.

"All this in a painting?" the King asked.

"If it pleases the Son of Heaven to see this otherwise, let his own eyes be his guide."

"Heavenly Father, the scholar's interpretation appears sound," Prince Meng said. "I would be pleased to hear more."

But the King's curiosity was not long sustained. He chuckled and wondered why so many scholars spoke in riddles. The King then declared that they had other pressing matters and would like to hear more, but at another time. Then he walked away, exiting the Archives with the others following.

I knelt and thanked him. As they departed, I could hear Prince Chao's slight chortle.

Not long after the Heavenly Family left, Yi Ban walked briskly into the Archives, short of breath. "Forgive me Lao Tzu, the King often toys with people, in this case with a sudden change in my schedule. He sent me to a conference with the Minister of War on the most trivial of matters. Thus you were left without the support of my presence. I am most distressed."

"Your concern is welcomed, Minister, but may not be necessary. The Royal inspection went well. It would appear we have the King's support, and perhaps that of the elder Prince as well."

"Excellent, excellent! That is a tremendous relief."

I shared more detail about the inspection. Then Yi Ban asked my thoughts on the Princes and the King.

"It was as I sensed when I was initially presented at court—that there is a tension between them," I said. "It is unclear whether it is the mere rivalry of siblings or a contest of power. It would also appear the King either purposely baits their rivalry or is oblivious to its adverse potential. As for the King, he is an uncomplicated man, likely appeased with strategic reminders of his greatness, however inflated they may be."

"Undoubtedly," said Yi Ban. "How the Princes' rivalry bodes for the court remains to be seen. The King has at times encouraged this division, but for those such as myself who are more interested in good governance, a clear and unequivocal succession is needed. Until then, we must all be attentive as to who stands with whom."

"Is this necessary, Yi Ban? These are matters beyond my knowledge."

"You must learn to re-make them so."

"But I have already accomplished much without playing the

game of the sycophants."

"I am not asking you to be anyone's toady," Yi Ban sighed. "I respect your candor and value its freshness. But you are my appointee. Should you act improperly or unwisely, it is I who will suffer. Learn the craft of court and you will accomplish much, to the benefit of us both. You must be aware of your place, Lao Tzu, and what it requires of you. Your performance today suggests an ability to bend with the political world here. And have no doubt, this is a different world."

After Yi Ban departed, I returned to the tablet of Yu Huang, the Jade King, the one that Prince Chao thought to be ugly. I realized that what he saw to be ugly was merely a reflection of how he chose to see the world.

8

Mei

Some months later, I sensed that the Royal Guardsmen had ceased to shadow my every movement. At this point, I began my wanderings. I sought to escape the strain of work within the Palace. I would borrow the garments of one of my scribes and quietly leave the Palace, shuffling through the Gate of Divine Purity into the heart of the city. It was on one such occasion that I encountered someone who would play a role in the history of Zhou.

When I had first arrived in Chengzhou, I was too overwhelmed by its enormity to gauge all that it was. Its perfectly squared city walls surrounded nine east-west streets and nine north-south streets. Each was wide enough to accommodate nine carts in parallel, whereas the main streets of most villages can barely accommodate a single wagon hauled by a bony donkey.

Between the main streets were dirt roads, but always straight and intersecting at right angles to form a perfect grid. The districts closest to the inner city of the Palace were walled and reserved for lower nobility and officials living in homes made of mud and wood. The wealthier and more powerful had lavishly-furnished homes of brick with tiled roofs, courtyards and walkways lined with jugs of wine. The air was scented with flowers from the gardens and from spices in pots of food steaming on stoves.

While I lived near the Palace, my own abode was of no such opulence. I was assigned a two-room dwelling that was attached to a smithy. The previous archivist's home was apparently rather lavish, but Prince Chao had seized it after that archivist fled.

Within this perfect delineation stood the centre of the world, the Son of Heaven's Yellow Palace. Just outside its west wall stood the most important shrine in the kingdom, the Temple of Heavenly Worship. Traditionally this was where Royal ancestors were buried and worshipped, though subsequent rulers such as Jing's father built their own tombs on grounds further away. Nevertheless, it continued to be a place for making offerings to the gods. Anything of importance, whether it was ascending the throne, a Royal marriage, the bestowal of great honors or blessings for going to or returning from war, occurred within this temple.

There was a time when the King's mandate as heaven's representative on earth was absolutely revered. He possessed supreme power among mortals, and embodied the will of the gods. But now, as if to show their preeminence among the clans and above religion itself, the Zhou Royals boldly broke with tradition and built their own places of worship outside of the Palace.

The temple remained an impressive sight, with seven halls and thirty *chi* in height —a dizzying height equivalent to more than five grown men atop one another. Tradition stated that mausolea for dukes could have no more than five halls that were twenty-seven *chi* in height, those for a senior official three halls and fifteen *chi*, and for a junior official a single hall nine *chi* high. But I had seen many self-proclaimed kings in breakaway territories who had built even larger and more elaborate temples, as if to imply the Zhou's moral authority was irrelevant. In different times, this boldness would have incurred the wrath of a powerful King and central government.

To the east of the Palace wall was the Sheji altar for worshipping the God of Land and the God of Grain. In front of the Palace was the Central Square, often used as a market catering primarily to the servants of nobles and government officials. On this particular day, a number of vendors who had traveled some distance were hawking farm equipment, tools and weapons, silk robes, textiles and ornaments.

A man dressed in farmer's clothing but looking too well-kept to actually be one, stood by wagons ladened with strange-looking metal tools. "Stronger than brittle wood ploughs, your farmers will triple your yield with these new metal ploughs!" he shouted. "And they are guaranteed to last forever."

Nearby a soldier modeled body armor made of metal similar to that of the farm tools shaped into square plates, riveted then tied together. A stout merchant beside him put a finger to his lips as if whispering a secret. "Bronze is yesteryear's metal. No one can feel safe without these new inventions."

He swung a tree branch against the armor, hard enough to split the wood. "These suits were built by the finest craftsmen in Qin and acquired at tremendous cost. Imagine the respect competing warlords will show when they see your militia in them. I can offer them at a special price, but today only. I have many interested parties only a short ride away."

The largest gathering centered on a fierce-looking warrior showing off a horizontal bow with an intricate bronze trigger that could fire short arrows accurately in quick succession. The arrows flew true into a distant outline of a man drawn on the side of a building, drawing gasps of delight from the onlookers. I failed to share in their excitement and moved on.

Several merchants hawking vessels inlaid with gold and silver received little attention whereas the jade vendors drew much interest in their display of intricately carved discs, hairpins, candle holders and ornaments.

"What a waste of time and money," I overheard one merchant say to another. "We travel hundreds of *li* but we'll be lucky to break even. These noblemen and bureaucrats are a bunch of old ladies, sitting on stories of glories long forgotten by everybody else."

I understood their disappointment. They likely had families to feed. But to profit from the machinations of war, and to help maintain the opulence of those already hoarding money was offensive. It created and maintained divisions among men, the very antithesis of the Way.

Thus I generally avoided the congestion of the main streets with their fine shops, exclusive merchants and artisans catering to the elite. Instead I threaded my way through narrow side lanes, even though they passed cramped hovels, brothels and gambling parlors with teams of pickpockets often evident. City planners once had the foresight to construct proper water distribution channels but these had long since turned into cesspools.

But outside the city gates, I found places where plainness and simplicity flowed, where the common people, however ignorant of the formal teachings of the Way, led uncluttered lives with unhindered purposes. I strolled the markets of the ordinary people, walking among the villagers and enjoying the freedom of anonymity, though it came with some risk. Roaming about outside imperiled one's standing as well as safety. Bandits roamed freely, and spies were said to be everywhere, watching for opportunities to advance their interests even at the cost of besmirching the good names of honest people.

My favorite destination was a quiet inn on a hill just outside the city, overlooking a village by the Luo River. They served millet porridge with preserved duck eggs. It reminded me of the days, seemingly a lifetime removed, when I lived in the mountains at my Academy. For a moment, I could not reconcile my new status within the Palace with the memory of my past. But the calm of the meandering river, the unpretentious conversation of fellow customers at the inn and the uncomplicated ruckus of people passing by made the hours disappear easily and soon my ambivalence dissipated.

On this particular occasion, the peace was broken by several soldiers who entered the village below, questioned, searched and hit some of the young females. They then moved on to ransack several houses and overturned baskets and wagons. I spied someone covered in a cloak creeping up the hill from the village towards the inn. The soldiers hadn't noticed this figure, but they began making their way up the path toward the inn and the person crouched behind the surrounding wall of loose stones. I looked closer and our eyes met. It was a young female.

At the first sign of trouble, the locals in the inn had fled, leaving me alone there.

"Old man!" one of the approaching soldiers called out to me. "Why are you still sitting here? Could it be you are hiding something?"

I stood and gave a cursory bow as they surrounded me.

"Good soldiers of our Son of Heaven, I am Lao Tzu. I work in the Royal Archives. I sit so here because the world is best viewed from such a position of ease. Perhaps you would care to join me?"

One of the soldiers overturned my table, sending my bowl of porridge crashing to the ground.

"You lie old man," he said. "Remove your tunic before we make you crawl like a maggot."

The soldier untied a whip from his waist. From the corner of my eye, I could see the young woman still cowering behind the wall. She shifted, causing a stone to topple. One of the guards overheard and turned in that direction.

"Stop, my good soldiers!" I cried out to distract them. "It is cold for an old man and my tunic serves best on these bones. Perhaps if I knew what it is you seek, I may be of service?"

The officer ripped my tunic and pushed me about. The soldier moving towards where the woman was hiding turned his attention back to me.

"We have reports of thievery from the Royal kitchen. Perhaps you are a part of it. You wear the tunic of a Royal servant and look well-fed, yet you are a quite a way from the palace."

His gnarled face and tangled beard were in contrast with the orderliness of the Royal Guardsmen serving directly within the Palace. He tightened his grip on my tunic and sneered.

"For one who is so close to death, you show neither fear nor anger. Only a spy could be so cool."

"If I am a spy then my fate is sealed, whether I beg for mercy or resist. Perhaps there is wisdom in the words of our King whom I have heard say, 'Truth above all else shall prevail, in my time or in heaven.'"

"Falsely invoking the name of the King is an act of desperation."

"Do you sense desperation?" I asked. "Do you believe our Son of Heaven lacks such wisdom?"

He blinked at me. I continued.

"Yet I sense compassion in you. For compassion is the finest weapon and the best defense. If you establish harmony, you would surround yourself with compassion like a fortress. Then a good soldier need not rely on generating fear, just as a good fighter need not display aggression. Honorable officer of the Royal Guardsmen, I would submit to you that a good leader does not engage in unnecessary battles and a good leader does not exercise authority where none is required. This is how you may best win the cooperation of others. This is how to build the same harmony as exists in Nature."

The officer's face slackened. He relaxed his grip, letting me go.

"What you say is full of riddles. If it is trickery, I will find you out, Lao Tzu, and you will be treated no better than a wild dog taking its last breath."

He ordered his soldiers to move on towards some nearby farms.

I picked myself up and re-tied my torn scribe's tunic. When we were truly alone, I beckoned to the young woman.

"You may come out now," I said, but she barely stirred at first, probably because the voices and movements of the soldiers were still audible in the distance. Then she stood up, stepped over the wall and walked into the inn. Her hair was braided like a man's, and her shirt and trousers made her appear as would a farmer. But there was no mistaking that diamond-shaped face, the milky skin, and the dark, small, inquisitive lacquered eyes. She had been the King's purchase at the slave auction on my very first day in Chengzhou.

She saw me glance at the small bundle of food wrapped and slung over her shoulder.

"Neither you nor I look as though we need to risk our lives by stealing food."

"You are correct." she said. "But to do nothing would mean my parents and sisters would starve. It is a risk I am ready to take."

In response to my questions, she told me they worked a plot for a lord not far away. But after years of successful millet crops, a plague of locusts and a fire forced her parents to make heartbreaking but necessary choices.

"You must miss them," I said.

She turned away as if to hide her emotion. I shared with her some of my father's technique of alternating and mixing crops, giving the land time to heal and replenish itself. I had since seen these methods used effectively in several other regions. She seemed interested and we spoke at length about farming matters.

Then she asked, "Why did you risk yourself?"

"Followers of the Way do not distinguish between themselves and the world. The needs of other people are our own. I try to do good to those who are good, but also good to those who do not do good. Goodness then becomes my all. I trust those who are trustworthy and also trust those who are not trustworthy."

"I trust no one," she replied. "Except perhaps the Black Serpent."

"The Black Serpent?"

She nodded. "I do not know how the Black Serpent learned of my need to bring food to my family. But a tablet with his insignia was left in my chamber with a note advising me to wait until the time he designated. When that moment came, I found a sack of food with instructions on how to evade the Palace Guards. It has happened several times. He has not failed us once."

"Interesting. An ally exists for you within the Palace."

"Others would say a spy."

"Perhaps even a potential follower of the Way, someday," I said.

"Who are these followers?"

"Followers of the Way live in harmony with the world, and our mind is the world's mind. So I nurture the worlds of others, as a mother does her children's. And as a daughter would her parents in return. As you are doing."

A hint of a smile broke through her tight face. She dropped her sack to the ground. "They were right, you do speak in riddles. What is this Way?'

I returned her smile. "You have borne witness to it. But tell me, what is your name? Or should I ask someone in the Royal Court?"

"I thought there was familiarity about your face as well."

I reached for some sweet rice cake on the ground that hadn't been completely ruined. I broke off a piece for her and then for myself. She untied her sack and put most of what I had given her into it. We nibbled away in silence, though her eyes darted about at every sound, no doubt still wary of the soldiers. We could hear peasants returning, cursing the soldiers as well as the King's name.

"Our indiscretions bind us," I said. "Though I suspect yours will cost you far more than mine."

She nodded. "Such is the lot of women and servants."

"And the risk of feeding one's family. Perhaps you had best continue on with your purpose."

She looked at the waning sun, re-tied the sack and hefted it over her shoulder. Before leaving, she turned a last time to face me.

"Mei," she said. "My name is Mei, my Lord. May I know yours?"

"Lao Tzu. I can be found in the Archives. But I am no lord. I am simply…"

"A man who surrounds himself with compassion like a fortress …."

"Is forever strong," I interjected.

Mei smiled. "Perhaps someday I may learn more of this Way?"

Then she scampered over the wall with the ease of a deer running in a meadow. I nodded at the diamond-faced thief as she disappeared into the bushes.

9

Prince Meng

"This young woman... Mei," Captain Yin said. "She returns to your story."

Lao Tzu nodded and sipped his tea. "The good Captain is surprised that a woman could have a place with the Way?"

"Perhaps." The Captain shrugged. "The role for women is limited. Such has been and always shall be the case."

"Not so, Captain." Lao Tzu put his cup down. "The universe is not drawn in divisions of men and women. At the deepest level of our being – in our very essence – we are neither. Here in this world, in this life, we inhabit either the energy of a male or a female body. But beyond that, we are equal and are essential to one another.

"So it is her story as much as it is that of the Princes and you?"

Lao Tzu sighed again. "We are all here because of the balance of energy between male and female. You of all people will come to see that this young woman's place in the story is no mere aside. Be patient. Let us move on first with the Princes, then all shall become clearer."

The Captain nodded.

It pleased me that I had been able to convince the King to see the value in the dynasty's forgotten treasures and records. But his command to create a permanent record of his greatness was unfeasible. Indeed, it was naive. It did, however, accord me the much-needed credibility that Yi Ban had spoken of. I knew the King's idea of greatness was not in keeping with the Way. If he were truly great, he would fulfill his purpose and have no interest in self-aggrandizement regarding what he had done. He would fulfill his duties as a good ruler and not boast. He would fulfill his obligations to lead but take little pride. And he would fulfill his role, but only as a role that could not be avoided.

Yi Ban suddenly had many demands on, and expectations of, my perch in the bureaucracy. None, however, were more tedious than sitting through certain state functions. Though politics was part of my role, I had little personal interest in it beyond that which promoted the interests of the Archives. Yi Ban insisted that I at least familiarize myself with court protocol and matters of state in order to be presentable at all formal occasions. It was on one such occasion, during a state dinner with the newly-arrived emissary from Chu, Duke Huilan, that there occurred an early harbinger of the future.

Many states such as Chu openly disregarded the Royal Family and had reduced their tributes to the Royals. The King made no secret of how incensed he was. The lack of deference from these territories had become a burning humiliation. Exacerbating this was the expectation among some of the states that the King should provide military support in order that the Royal territory remain secure from barbarian invasions and lawless renegade attacks. To demonstrate his wrath, the King had expelled the previous emissary of Chu, but not before he had the emissary's messenger's tongue cut out and boiled with pigs' feet, making a soup he drank to show how ruthless he could be.

But Chu was increasingly powerful and more strategically located than any of the other breakaway states. Knowing that the weakened Zhou family had little bargaining room, Chu now exhibited much swagger and showed little apprehension in dealing with the King and the few allies that he could mobilize. This was all common knowledge, and none of it would have concerned me had my station not brought me into such close proximity to these leaders. Indeed, this was made clear when Duke Huilan arrived at the west gate of Chengzhou.

I was told that most emissaries arrived only with an aide or two and some servants. But Duke Huilan also came with a battalion of heavily-armed infantrymen and a platoon of battle-hardened cavalry. Needless to say, he was refused entry.

"It is a provocation," Prince Chao announced to the court.

"And an insult to the Son Of Heaven," Yi Ban added.

"The Duke's entourage is meant to intimidate. But surely he must know that armed troops cannot enter our gates," Prince Meng said.

"We can easily overwhelm them, if it pleases my Son Of Heaven," General Wu stated.

"That may be precisely the tactic he hopes for," Prince Chao replied. "I say leave them there to rot."

"Heavenly Father, I suspect the Duke is responding to the way we treated the previous emissary's messenger," Prince Meng said.

"It was justified," the King replied indignantly. "The emissary should have known better than to make such demands, especially through a worthless servant."

"What does the Duke think he's doing?" Prince Chao asked. "It is a token force he brings, loaded more with a message than any real threat."

"Heavenly Father, he expects us to cower and quiver," Prince

Meng said. "Instead let us disarm him with hospitality and drink. We should welcome him and his servants into Chengzhou. The rest of his escort will be feasted as visiting cousins, but shall remain outside our gates. In so doing, we would blunt his message and remind him that he is before the Royal Court, under the roof of the Son of Heaven."

The King pondered Prince Meng's counsel, then nodded his approval.

And so a banquet in the Duke's honor was hastily arranged for two nights hence, with the Grand Hall turned into a massive banquet room. The Duke entered wearing a flowing saffron robe with purple trim simply adorned with a jade amulet in the shape of a crane. The King's clothiers had easily bested that as he arrived in a fiery red silk robe emblazoned with gold-threaded dragons with huge black eyes. A deep blue sash on both the wide collars and billowing sleeves completed an outfit that likely would have cost dozens of farms several years' worth of production.

The menu included many different preparations involving the six cereals—rice, millet, corn, sorghum, wheat and wild rice stems; the six animals—horse, cow, sheep, pig, dog, and chicken, and the six liquids—soup and five wines, including spring and pear. As with other formal banquets I endured, food was secondary to the reciprocity of etiquette, of whoever offered the choicest bits of food to whomever first, and to the polite refusals back and forth until the food was cold and nothing really was consumed except for the wine. That evening, however, the King and the Duke carried on like old friends and enjoyed the evening's offerings. I knew this civility was merely in keeping with protocol and waited to see how the underlying tensions would be addressed.

While they ate, rhythmic clanging began to fill the Hall as the orchestra of stone chimes, ox skin drums and racks of bronze and wooden bells struck up to entertain the audience. Five young women seemed to float into the Hall from behind a curtain, each adorned in the finest ruby silk gowns with gold-threaded embroidered dragons and tigers. Jade jewelry dangled from their ears and covered their thin, birdlike fingers. The dancers' movements were slow but precise at first, then gradually grew faster as the music swelled in volume. They deftly flicked their wrists, and turned their bamboo fans with each beat of the drums, playfully hiding different parts of their faces. Their hips swirled in time to the racks of bells. The ballad was called 'Yellow Moon Rising,' and was meant to convey youthful vigor yearning to be free. Despite the dancers' uniformly fixed smiles and heavily-painted white faces, I identified one dancer among them—Mei. If she recognized me, she gave no indication.

The final movement came to a climactic close with the dancers holding their fans above their heads, eyes gazing upwards, exposing their bare wrists and forearms. The men gasped, and the King and Duke nodded to indicate their approval and pleasure. Had I been one to be charmed by women, Mei in particular would have earned my attention. The Duke took an extra long glance at her, which left the King grinning. Mei also clearly transfixed Prince Chao.

Prince Meng politely applauded, prompting others to follow. The Duke leaned into the King.

"The Son of Heaven has outdone himself by surrounding the court with the most beautiful women in the world. They are jewels, especially the one on the left." He pointed towards Mei.

The King leered at the young women.

"The Duke is most astute. I personally selected them from all parts of Zhou."

Like young noblemen regaling one another with stories of their conquests of women, the Duke and the King exchanged knowing glances. The King signaled for more wine.

"Perhaps our Son of Heaven has found the elixir to our complicated world," the Duke said. "We expend too much energy on disagreements. We should focus more on the pleasures of our stations—fine drink, lovely women, sweet music, and the good health of our Son Of Heaven and his heir."

He held up his goblet and nodded to both the King and Prince Meng, then drank the wine. The King followed suit, toasting the Duke.

Perhaps Prince Chao was offended by the Duke's gesture towards his father and brother while ignoring him. He stiffened and his face reddened. He was about to say something when the Queen started to giggle uncontrollably. Then she started to tear up. An aide handed her a drink which she flung away with a pout. The King gave her a reproachful look then motioned for the dancers and musicians to be dismissed. Mei gave no sign of recognition in my direction as she exited. The Queen soon left the table while humming a nursery rhyme.

With the entertainment and food dispensed with, it was time to proceed with business. Duke Huilan began.

"The Son of Heaven honors me, yet I am not worthy of his gracious hospitality. From the moment my party arrived in Chengzhou, I have been humbled by his generosity. I understand my predecessor may not have been satisfied with his reception, which was most regrettable. It is my hope that I can better represent the great kingdom of Chu."

The King nodded, and the Duke continued.

"As this court knows, Chu stands for peace. But our Son of Heaven must be aware that the messenger was acting on orders from his master, the previous envoy. He was merely conveying the views of my esteemed King. That a Royal messenger was received in such a manner is not in keeping with the good relations we have enjoyed. Kang, the King of Chu, has instructed me to give the Son of Heaven an opportunity to rectify what some might interpret as a slight."

The King shifted in his seat, while Prince Chao instinctively reached for the hilt of his dagger. The Duke carried on.

"As a gesture of goodwill, I come bearing tribute. Our King sends a gift for both the brave Princes as well as for the Son of Heaven."

The Duke's assistant brought forth a cushion upon which sat three bronze belt hooks inlaid with exquisitely carved jewels. Such objects had recently become fashionable among Royalty and nobles.

The King examined each of the hooks with curiosity, then dropped them back onto the cushion. As he spoke his voice was heavy both with the sweet jade colored wine and indignation.

"Tell Kang that a hundred of these would not cause me to express any regret for my actions. It is he who lacks respect."

Prince Chao jumped in. "Furthermore, there is no King of Chu. Need you be reminded that you are addressing the Son of Heaven? This court is the divine ruler of all lands under heaven. Chu's arrogance is inexcusable."

The Duke looked at the rejected belt hooks and hesitated. He had likely hoped for a more favorable reaction.

"If the Son Of Heaven may allow me to explain this gift," he said. "Neither craftsmen of Chu nor of Jin, nor anywhere in Zhou made these hooks. They were captured from nomads who recently overwhelmed the defensive towers to the north that were built by your ancestors many generations ago. Someone should have told your engineers that a wall, a great wall and not just a weak system of towers, is needed to keep out the barbarians. The Royal Tombs of your parents south of Dai would have been plundered if my King's followers had not intervened."

Many years ago, in what had become northern Chu, the King's father, in preparation for his death, had built an elaborate tomb to resemble his Palace on a smaller scale. An enormous mound of earth was layered then dug out. Thick-timbered beams and clay bricks held up the many chambers with their richly plastered and decorated walls. When he finally died, in accordance with his instructions, his son, King Jing, mourned him for six months, then buried his father along with his many possessions, including his still living concubines, eunuchs and horses.

Upon hearing of the near plundering of his father's tomb, King Jing lurched up from his seat. "Why was I not informed of this?"

"Informing the Son of Heaven of the incident is one of my tasks as the envoy from Chu. I might also add that our King should not be seen as anything other than a loyal cousin. It is your other subjects neighboring you, the Qin, Jin and those tattooed barbarians, the Wu, and any number of other warlords, whom you should guard against. The Royal House requires friends who will stand up for it. We performed our duty in safeguarding the Royal Tombs and in protecting the hinterlands from incursion from barbarians as well as from disloyal neighbors. However, these actions might best be met with some gratitude in the form of recompense from the Son of Heaven."

The King could not hide his contempt.

"Chu is not the guardian and protector of Zhou!" he shouted. "You forget you are addressing the Son of Heaven, the King of Zhou. Such statements are reckless."

"My Son of Heaven," the Duke replied, "I am but an emissary conveying a message. The King of Chu desires nothing more than peace. Your crops have been bountiful, trade is thriving, and the treasury must surely be bursting. Our King knows this. And he also believes that if it were not for his friendship and protection, you might not have the splendor of this Palace and of Chengzhou."

The King slammed his hand down on the table, causing several ministers to jump.

"Chu is playing with fire, Duke. I could easily have you and your escorts interned for your insolence. Perhaps that is a response Kang would begin to understand?"

"It would hardly merit the Son of Heaven's effort. Our King has asked me to inform you that he has fifty thousand soldiers within two days of the Han Gu Pass. Killing me would give Chu a pretext for war. I doubt that you are prepared for this. I ask the Son of Heaven to reconsider."

The King flinched and was silent. The Duke continued.

"Perhaps we can all save face. Perhaps I was too obtuse in suggesting our King required something that sounded like a form of 'compensation.' Shall we rather call it a contribution, or even an investment? This, in addition to safe passage for all craft belonging to Chu and her friends to ply the Yellow River and all it's tributaries?"

The King's eyes widened. He lost all diplomatic restraint, and bolted up from his chair.

"And where would Chu be if I sealed the borders and blocked all trade along the Yellow River from Lu to the western mountains? You have few friends. I am the Son of Heaven of all Zhou. I could slowly choke the lifeblood out of your people. How high and mighty would your precious King be then? How will you trade your precious little trinkets then? And as for you, your nearest companions are days away. Do you think you have enough time left?"

The Duke didn't flinch. "My Son of Heaven, my King's generals expect to hear from me within five days. Should that not happen, they will act. My life is hardly worth the bloodshed that might follow."

The King stepped towards the Duke and pointed at him. "Perhaps you are the one who is ill-prepared."

"My Son of Heaven, this is a complex matter. It may be best for you and your court to take advantage of the next few days to discuss this. I shall be pleased to remain at your disposal to construct a message of peace to send to our generals."

Yi Ban approached the King and whispered in his ear. The King returned to his seat.

"Rise, Duke Huilan, emissary from Chu," the King commanded. He signaled to his Royal Guardsmen to surround the Duke. The Duke's face finally started to lose some color.

"You are dismissed. My Royal Guardsmen shall escort you to back to your chamber. You may await my answer there. I will send a Royal messenger to you."

The Duke kowtowed before leaving the Hall. The King dismissed all the guests but for the inner court and his advisors.

Prince Chao took the initiative.

"That filthy dog of a Duke can call it what he wants, but it is blood money, blackmail, extortion... Heavenly Father, it is time we end this humiliation and stand up to Chu."

The Minister of War and several generals nodded and chimed in with warlike bravado. Only Yi Ban disagreed.

"Your Highness, fifty thousand troops are not to be trifled with. They could be upon us before we could mount an effective defense. Chengzhou would be plundered, and the court would have to evacuate. There would be little glory in this, your Highness."

"Heavenly Father," Prince Meng added, "it could hasten the end of your reign. There would be..."

The younger Prince interrupted him. "You speak with little faith for one who aspires to the throne. You ignore the fact that we are not without loyal followers. Let us ally also with Qin, Jin, Zheng, Chen and even Wu. They distrust and hate Chu even more than we. We could create a trade and military alliance that would surround Chu. If they move against any of us, together we will snap their necks like the wild dogs they are. To show weakness as some would argue…" He glared at Yi Ban and Prince Meng, "…would condemn us forever to be their stepping stools. Our people expect more of a future from their leaders."

The King stroked his beard and nodded in agreement. Then he looked at Prince Meng.

"Heavenly Father, our people think that for building a house, the best place is upon the ground; for friendship, they value gentleness and truth; and in government they desire good order and effectiveness. In each case, they prefer what does not lead to imbalance and strife." The elder Prince stole a look in my direction. He was paraphrasing words I myself had once said, long ago and in another place.

Prince Chao laughed.

"Zhou is in need of courage and bravery. Instead, my dear eldest Prince recites meaningless philosophy. And not just meaningless, useless too."

"And you counsel war," Prince Meng interjected. "We have heard this talk of alliances many times before, of rearming for glory. Yet no one will openly join with us; no one dares stand up to Chu's cavalry. We may be Zhou's portal to heaven but we must not overestimate its current position. It cannot hold together a fragmented alliance. Being belligerent towards Chu plays into their hands. They would like nothing more than a pretext to undermine our authority."

"How dare you besmirch this House?" Prince Chao shot back.

"We barely have a House around which to rally an army," Prince Meng retorted. "Our farms and villages hide their remaining men of fighting age. And is it any wonder? Who would be left to harvest the crops?"

"If you are such a man of the people then perhaps you might bring the harvest in yourself, dear eldest brother." Prince Chao said, smiling coldly.

"Enough!" The King commanded, raising a hand. He looked at each of his sons. "I am well advised. Each of you speaks a harsh truth. I will not need days to decide upon a course of action."

The next morning, as I approached the Archives, a servant scampered to me with news that Prince Meng was already in the study hall and was perusing tablets. This was his first visit to the Archives since accompanying his father and brother. I walked quickly to the study hall where I bowed and welcomed him.

The Prince returned the scrolls he had been perusing to their shelf, then stared into the garden and spoke.

"Yi Ban says that your Academy was renowned for a new way of thinking, and that you have few intellectual equals anywhere. Yet you make little effort to show this, unlike most of those in the court."

"Your Highness, I am hardly worthy of such praise. Minister Yi Ban is too kind. He exaggerates greatly. I can only hope to live up to the praise he has so generously bestowed."

The Prince's voice became soft, almost reverential.

"He also said you could be trusted and that your loyalty whether to slave or master was unquestionable. Yet he also said that your head often floats amongst the clouds, or dances with the butterflies."

I grinned. I had often been accused of being a dreamer, but never by Royalty.

"Your Highness is also most kind. May I offer you some tea?"

He declined, but accepted a tour of the garden. We strolled at a leisurely pace, unlike during the previous visit. He asked the names of various plants and bushes and marveled at the birds quenching their thirst in the pond.

"I would have liked my mother to allow such a pond in our grounds. I understand we once had one," he said.

Such a personal comment startled me. I felt he was in need of a sympathetic ear.

"Your garden is most impressive," the Prince continued. "I recognize the burdock. That is a gingko tree, and of course the peonies."

"Your Highness possesses much knowledge in this area. And that one is rhubarb. Like many of the things in this garden, it is a wonderful contradiction. Its stalk is a useful laxative, but its leaves are poisonous."

The Prince fondled the rhubarb leaves for a moment and then moved on. He finally agreed to some tea, over which he had many more questions.

"Lao Tzu, tell me of Sword Hill Academy. What kind of people become scholars, what homes and lives did they leave, and why did you abandon it?"

His use of the word 'abandon' stung. For an instant it forced me to re-examine my purpose here. I dismissed the thought and re-focused on the Prince, who seemed to have an unflagging interest in every little detail of ordinary life and in what went on outside the Palace walls and beyond Chengzhou. Everything I said, he reflected upon before responding. He marveled at how lives could be so unrestrained.

The Prince gazed upward. "As rulers, it has always been our belief that what people desire most is safety and security," he said. "In government, it is good order, yet governing is complex.

'If princes and kings could follow the Way, all things would by themselve abide, heaven and earth would unite and sweet dew would fall. People would by themselves find harmony without being commanded.' Sound familiar, Master Lao Tzu?"

There was no hiding my satisfaction.

"Yes Your Highness, these are words I spoke I cannot remember how long ago."

"However long ago, it was recorded by a wandering scholar. But tell me, Lao Tzu, was it not trifling of you to say that the needs of the common man are simple yet their lives purposeful?"

"Not all are striving to lead, to govern, or to master all that is about us," I replied. "The highest good is like water. The goodness of water is that it benefits all. It does not discriminate and is content in places that all men disdain. It is that which makes water so close to the Way."

Again, the Prince quietly reflected on what I had said. He then asked many questions about the Way. His eyes searched mine as though he were a curious scholar, not a ruler-in-waiting in the style of his father.

After several hours, one of his servants came in and knelt before the Prince.

"Your Highness, the King has requested your counsel. Your presence in the Royal Court is desired."

The Prince sighed. As he turned to walk away he nodded as if to say goodbye, a common but most un-royal gesture. As he left the Archives, he stepped over the threshold and pulled at the hem of his long gold-threaded robe. He could have been preparing to shed one costume for another, one spun with coarse hemp threads.

From then on, Prince Meng visited me in the garden regularly. Each visit lasted longer than the preceding one, as his curiosity about the world expanded. I also became aware that his visits either preceded or followed discussions with his father on matters of state. One day I was playing with two orphaned gold finches in a cage when he came into the garden. His forehead was creased with worry but his eyes said he was pleased to be back.

"They are beautiful... so delicate, so frail," he cooed, and blew gently into the cage.

"Your Highness, they are in need of a new home, I can think of no one who would be a more devoted guardian than yourself. May I present them to you?

He smiled, then gazed into the cage.

"You are not only generous with your wisdom, but also of the heart. But I cannot accept them. My father forbids birds within the inner Palace."

"Then they shall live under your care here in the garden."

His eyes lit up much like a warrior-child's when given his first sword. We spoke about birds and some new plants I had acquired through southern merchants, but I could see his mind was drifting.

"Lao Tzu, have you ever found yourself wanting to be elsewhere?"

"Your Highness, where else would I wish to be but in your service?"

"Please Lao Tzu. Protocol may require that you flatter me, but my character does not."

"It was neither flattery nor duty your Highness."

He smiled again, but a troubled look overtook him.

"Why is it that in a world as rich and advanced as ours, conflict is never far away? Surely this is not just."

"Are your Highness' concerns to do with matters of the court?"

He nodded. "There are those in our court who foolishly believe there is merit in returning to a strong central government at any price, binding all the lands together even if driven by the point of a spear. After the banquet with Duke Huilan, the King waited until the final hour before responding to him. Even then, he chose to insult the Duke by sending a lowly messenger from the Ministry of Public Works to deliver his answer."

"I see," I said. "The King delivered a small but deliberate diplomatic cold shoulder, similar to what the King himself received from the previous Chu emissary."

"Our King had little choice, not with fifty thousand hostile troops only days away and friendly forces unprepared to intervene. So he relented, granting to Chu free trade along certain rivers. It might hold off Chu's ambitions, but not for long. My father has also directed the Minister of State to initiate secret talks with our neighbors Qin and Jing, offering unimpeded access along the Yellow River as an incentive for an alliance. From the Minister of War, he demanded a rearmament and modernization strategy as soon as possible. To General Xie, he assigned a dangerous mission to the far north to learn what he could from the northern barbarians, masters of the horse and of new weapons including one which shoots arrows from a short, horizontal bow."

I nodded. "I have seen such a new killing device, just beyond these walls. This appeasement and rearming strategy… it is an interesting alchemy. Yet it is as old as yesterday's broken promises."

"My father looked at my brother and said, 'Peace and prosperity make great rulers.' Then he turned to me and said, 'But glory rains on those victorious in battle. Our moment is not at hand, but we shall be ready for it when it comes.'"

"Your Highness is of another opinion?"

The Prince stiffened. "The King showed resolve and has appeased Chu for now. But it is pride and face-saving that drive us. After so many hundreds of years, it is not easy to turn back the loss of such power to the throne and heal the many divisions within our realm. But I long for a different course and I am sick of contending with my brother at each and every step that I take. He hounds me endlessly, as though I alone am responsible for all that pains his world."

Prince Meng's calm but weary voice hardened as he spoke of his brother. "He wastes no opportunity to beat his chest in front of the King and play me for a simpleton unprepared for rule. I am the first-born. He should not be so foolish as to forget that. And as for my father, I would have hoped for more."

"Your Highness, our Son of Heaven and the Mother of Our Nation are also your father and mother. As with all families, they cherish their kin, they bestow their love and..."

"No. They bestow duties and obligations. They require that we suffer through endless and repeated formal customs and rituals. They surround us with servants and underlings charged with wiping our bottoms, grooming our hair and polishing our nails. When I feel pain, where is my comfort? When I grieve, who offers me a shoulder? If this is family, it is no wonder our house is but a façade."

I was stunned at such candor, but also pleased that he trusted me. During moments such as these I had to remind myself that ever since his royal birth, Prince Meng had been destined to struggle with his brother for his father's attention, and for the throne, even if he did not share his brother's relish for the fight. Every moment of every day of his life, he had been told to prepare to be King. Ill will towards his sibling had been encouraged, had been designed to promote mettle and had become a natural force within the court. It was clear that the love and comfort that I had received as a child were as foreign to the Prince as servants had been to me.

"Your Highness, no lure is greater than what others have, and no disaster greater than to be discontented with what one already has. Truly, he who has once known the contentment that comes simply through being content will never again be otherwise."

"I do not know what it is to be simply content," the Prince said in a whisper barely heard.

It pained me to see him so forlorn. I imagined that paternal instincts were similar to what I felt and I wished to console him.

"Your Highness, are you not content in this garden? Do you not feel contentment caring for your birds, being lost in a book, or in a painting? There are many moments when worries and concerns are banished and you are wrapped in a child-like joy."

The Prince paused. "Perhaps. But these moments should be never-ending. And they could be so if my brother were of a different nature, less ambitious. I believe my ascension will be the most peaceful and successful path for the reunification of Zhou. If Prince Chao were to ascend to the throne, his recklessness would mean endless bloodshed."

I urged the Prince to purge these ill thoughts and feeling from his mind, but I knew there were no words sufficient to heal this sibling feud.

He bowed to me and walked away. He could not have bestowed more gratitude than that.

10

Prince Chao

Unseasonably warm air fueled the excitement in the capital and the nearby surrounding villages as the mid-autumn moon festival approached. A good harvest and a recent lull in the many armed conflicts between the divided regions allowed the people, both privileged and poor, to enjoy a rare period of calm. The women within the Palace frolicked with one another as they picked mulberry leaves, while the men engaged in archery and hunting excursions. Prince Chao won most of the archery competitions, some of them fairly, and whenever an animal was trapped, he would never need more than a single arrow to finish the kill.

Prince Meng was a reluctant warrior. He much preferred activities of the mind and was more likely to be found in my garden or immersed in a tablet within the Archives than out hunting.

But on one particular occasion, it was not Prince Meng but Prince Chao whom I found sitting in the garden with a recently acquired tablet.

"So this is where my dear elder brother's head can be found," he said. The Prince was heavily suffused with his favorite jasmine scent, which I found rather repugnant.

I bowed. "Your Highness, I am honored. How may I serve you?"

The Prince held up the bundle of tablets. "Have you read this?"

"Yes, your Highness, that is a draft of General Sun's book on military tactics. He has peculiar views of war. In fact he sees elements of art and strategy as paramount to simple raw power."

"A General?"

"Yes, your Highness. He served under King Helu of Wu. He is also known as a philosopher and a strategist."

"But of course, General Sun Wu. With almost nothing to work with, he turned Wu's pitiful army into a force that even Chu is wary of. Who else could say, 'If you know your enemies and know yourself, you can win numerous battles without a single loss.' For him the first lesson of war is to master deception. Correct me if I am wrong, scholar, but I do believe he thought strategies and tactics mattered far more than superior manners and civility in times of conflict. In fact, nothing matters more than winning. Do you know your enemies, scholar?"

"Your Highness, it is my manner to try and endear myself to all."

The Prince laughed. "Perhaps you should not try so hard. Do you think my dear brother would enjoy this book?"

Oddly enough, I had seen Prince Meng reading General Sun's text on numerous occasions. Without waiting for my response to his question, Prince Chao placed the tablets down as he noticed Prince Meng's caged goldfinches. He broke off a twig from a plum tree and poked at them through the bars.

"Your Highness, those goldfinches are Prince Meng's personal favorites," I said.

A wicked smile crossed his face. He proceeded to snap off a larger twig and was about to thrust it in the cage when he stopped himself. Disappointment replaced his smile and he sighed.

"My dear brother would like nothing more than to foul my

name in front of the King, however petty the cause."

It seemed conflict avoidance was in Prince Chao's character after all. "I suppose I should thank you, scholar," he said, and laughed.

"Your Highness?"

"My dream-headed brother is rarely in court these days, and when he is, his counsel is gutless and weak, hardly what one might hope for in a Son of Heaven. I believe you have had some influence over him."

"Your Highness, I am but a servant of the court. Perhaps Prince Meng believes a leader does best when the people barely know he exists. Perhaps when his work is done, he feels his goals will have been achieved and the people will say, 'We did it ourselves.'"

"Well then, my dear brother has accomplished much. Not that it matters. The people barely know him. His mark is that he often misguides the King with silly notions of natural order and benevolent rule. He even has the King believing that his legacy will only be assured if work here within your tomb of books is supported. At least it has secured you a position, for now. As for what the people say, I'm sure they sleep better at night knowing that the Archives are well-managed."

He picked up several pebbles and threw them into the pond, disturbing the fish.

"I understand a scholar in Chu has requested an audience with you, a man named Confucius. He seeks the Master Archivist, the philosopher to the Heavenly Royals, the Most Esteemed Scholar, and the great and venerable Lao Tzu. Is Yi Ban aware of this?"

My long pause no doubt gave away my surprise.

"My dear scholar, could it be that a mere simpleton prince knows more of the world of the literati than the Master Archivist himself?"

I had become accustomed to the Prince's cutting barbs, but never in my own garden.

"Your Highness, there is nothing I keep from Minister Yi Ban or from the court. I was not made aware of this request. Nevertheless, Confucius shall be granted the utmost respect if he visits."

"Indeed he will. As for your Yi Ban, he likely knew nothing as that is his usual state. He is an incompetent and a dreamer like my brother. If not for his Royal blood, he would have been removed from court years ago. But you… even an archivist has his ambitions, am I not correct?"

"Your Highness, were I to desire to change the world, I could not succeed. The world is shaped by the Way; the self cannot shape it. Trying to change it, you damage it; trying to possess it, you lose it. Some such as our Son of Heaven will lead and others will follow. Some will be warm, others cold. Some will be strong, others weak. Some will get where they are going while others will fall by the wayside. I assure you my only ambition…"

He waved me off. "Spare me scholar. I know how you speak of rulers and nobles as oppressors of the people. If true justice were to prevail, this would be my court; and such talk which incites ill-regard for the masters, would be akin to treason." He stared into me.

"Your Highness, my work at the Academy in the past has been called noble and truthful. If the court is not pleased with my work here, I would willingly leave. But it is not in the nature of the Way to incite disregard for anyone. To be alone and in want is what men most fear. Yet I have seen other princes and dukes avail themselves of extravagance while surrounded by such men. Truly, such things are increased by seeking to diminish them and diminished by seeking to increase them. These are maxims that I have used in my teachings. Show me a man of violence that came to a good end, and I will take him for my teacher."

"Have I just been cleverly insulted?"

"Your Highness, I would never..."

"You think I am a man of violence, that kind of a teacher, don't you?" The Prince asked as he studied my face, grinning. "You are either extremely clever, and thereby dangerous, or a hopeless romantic. Which is it, scholar?"

"Your Highness, if desiring peace is extremely clever, then I am dangerous. If unity is a hopelessly romantic idea, then let me be known as a hopeless romantic. You thirst for a different path, one I am sure you believe to be the most advantageous for Zhou. However, I believe my goals are not so removed from yours. Surely we could drink together."

The Prince hesitated before he replied. His usual sharp tongue and impulsive temper were restrained.

"You truly are a romantic," he said. "As if a Prince would care to drink with a commoner!" He laughed. "I find all you dreamers hopelessly self-righteous, and even more dangerous than these men of violence that you warn of. You are perilous in that you fail to understand that trust is a rare commodity here and should not be dispensed so easily. Once it is bestowed, your final defenses have been breached. Perhaps my brother has charmed you. But do not be deceived, scholar. He plays the role before you of the reluctant heir. I see through his ruse. He actually seeks to command the stage, but his grip on the succession is not clad in bronze."

I sensed the Prince sought a strong reaction from me. I purposely betrayed none, though I was curious.

"My dear scholar, you can no longer be considered a novice at court. Surely you have wondered about the Mother of our Empire? Thought her to be somewhat peculiar, perhaps?"

"Your Highness, it is not for me to judge the Queen or to open my ears to idle gossip. I am..."

"You are romantic and naïve." The Prince shook his head in amazement. "Can it truly be that improving your position is not a goal of yours? Or is your intellect so vastly above the pettiness of us simple Royals that you do not need to bother? Perhaps I can enlighten you."

I bowed slightly.

"Believe it or not, there was a time when I was able to convince my dear brother to engage in fun and games. One such pastime we called 'royal invaders'. As children, Meng and I would imagine ourselves hiding deep in barbarian territory, or in actual fact from some of our more slow-footed, dim-witted Palace servants. With all of its rooms and corners, the Palace offered a range of splendid hiding places. The servants were commanded to find and then 'capture' us within a set time. I never knew whether they deliberately let us win most of the time or whether they were just dim-witted, but that is beside the point.

"We were eight years of age and it was exactly this time of year, during the mid-autumn festival. It had rained hard for many days and most of the festivities were cancelled. Many guests had traveled far for the celebrations, including my father's family from western Jin. They were staying in one of the Royal guest chambers. With time on our hands and hordes of servants to commandeer as barbarians, Meng and I scurried from hiding place to hiding place. This time, it seemed as if the servants were particularly committed to capturing us. We could hear them shouting out to each other: 'The Hall of Longevity is free of those vermin Royal intruders!', 'The Royal Garden is empty, but I can smell them nearby!', 'They are running out of rooms, we have only the south balcony and school left to search!'

"We were indeed slowly being cornered. Meng's face soured and he wanted to surrender, but I refused and took his hand. Our only escape was to cheat and to hide in one of the areas forbidden to most of the servants—the guest chambers. We slid along the corridors, through a circular doorway, and found ourselves in a small antechamber used as additional living space for guests. I could smell oil and varnish on the rosewood furniture and lattice. We stifled our glee as the servants continued past us in the hallway. Then through the thin walls, we heard giggling and a familiar voice from the adjacent room. These days, Prince Meng doesn't show much resolve but back then he took the initiative. He crawled up to the door and gently pushed it open.

"'What do you see?' I whispered? His body stiffened. I pulled up beside him and looked in, saw our father and his youngest sister, Aunt Feiyan, both naked. She was on her knees licking his stalk. He said, 'Uhhmm, our Queen could no more excite me than a tiger could fly.' Meng jumped away and in so doing, he alerted my father whose head shot up. His eyes burned into mine for an instant. Aunt Feiyan shrieked and reached for something to cover herself. Father pushed her off then sprang out of bed. Before I could make it out of the antechamber, he grabbed me and threw me down. He raised his hand and was about to slap my face when suddenly he smiled. He placed me on his bare thigh. I had never before seen his naked body. He had nipples with wavy hair. His long narrow torso and round belly glistened with sweat, and I nearly gagged at the intense odors he gave off. I tried my hardest to avert my eyes from his stalk, but I saw that it had shrunken into a wrinkled, wet mass.

"He told me that my mother was ill, that if she was to find out what I had seen, she would get even sicker and perhaps die. He said I needed to learn to be strong, to make difficult decisions if I was ever to be considered for the throne. Good kings always keep important secrets, he emphasized. He asked me if I wanted to protect my mother. I nodded. He made me promise never to speak of this to anyone. I nodded again. He said that if the rain stopped we would go hunting the following day, just he and I.

"I marched out of there as though I had just been given a royal directive. Meng had not waited around. I joined the other servants and searched and searched for him, but he was nowhere to be found."

The Prince held me in his gaze, and for a moment I stood speechless. "Your Highness, I am at a loss for words. Why, why…"

"Why would I utter such filth and vilify my own family, and to you?"

I bowed humbly. "Yes, your Highness."

"Because you may be the only one within these Palace walls who does not already know. You see, I kept my promise to my father, however awful it felt. Yet the Queen still learned of it. She could only have done so through the courage and valor of my dear elder brother. I can picture him crying like a boy in need of his wet nurse, running to her. It's not difficult to imagine him saying, "'Mother, mother, father and Auntie Feiyan were in the same bed! Prince Chao made me go! I didn't want to!'"

Prince Chao's face conveyed absolute revulsion, but then he calmed his features and continued.

"It stopped raining the next day, though Father and I never did go hunting. Instead he charged into my bedchamber, clutched me with one hand and slapped me with the other. He accused me of having betrayed him. I said I hadn't, which made him angrier. He said I had been his favorite, but now I would never be King, that I'd failed him, the family and the dynasty. His slapping got harder and harder. I could have said I was not alone yesterday. I could have said that Prince Meng had been there too and had run off. Instead, I silently withstood Father's fury until I passed out.

"I believe my mother confronted Father. He may have denied

it, or he may have beat her too. You see, she can't tell me. She took poison afterwards. Or maybe it was given to her. But it was not enough to kill her. As you have undoubtedly noticed, she is little more than a well-dressed vegetable. She laughs endlessly when a serious manner is appropriate. She cries when joviality is called for and talks like a child during formal announcements. Father will only allow her to be seen if she has been docile long enough for him to believe any embarrassment she causes will be minor."

The Prince picked up several more pebbles. His face no longer betrayed any malice or anger. He had adopted a tone bereft of any anguish, as if he were recalling some mundane event. Then his voice resumed with a taut edginess.

"So on that mid-autumn moon festival when I was eight years old, I had my nose broken, I saw my mother go mad, I was abandoned by my gutless brother, and I learned to see my father for what he is: a man. Simply that. Not the Son of Heaven, not the divine ruler of the world, just a man. He later found far more effective means of punishing me. He ensures that no peace is possible between my brother and myself. I believe he enjoys this intense war he has fostered between us, a war whose poison-tipped arrows are made of a loud, piercing silence. There is no Royal Proclamation about it, but it is omnipresent, in the air we breathe, in the water we drink, and it is woven into our fine silk robes. He dangles the crown before me, knowing I would be a more suitable protector of the dynasty's destiny. Like you, he chooses to ignore Prince Meng as he really is—a mouse to all appearances, but not a frightened little mouse. He is a smart, opportunistic one. When he believes his moment is at hand, he will pilfer that which he does not deserve."

"Your Highness, if matters are as you say, then you and Prince Meng were innocents, you were children. You were in a situation not of your own choosing. Neither of you can be faulted. Your continued quarrels will only lead to chaos, regardless of who reigns. I'm sure Prince Meng would agree."

"Ah but my dear scholar, good fortune follows upon chaos. Who can say how things will end? Perhaps there is no end, for honesty is ever deceived and kindness is ever seduced. Men have always been like this."

He surprised me again with an additional quote from my very own teachings, albeit without the full context. The Prince resumed tossing pebbles into the pond.

"There are many scholars doing the rounds among the nobles and the breakaway territories," he said. "Some, like Confucius, are as popular as the fiercest warriors. My father thinks they are vultures and has little use for them. Yet I believe there may be some ideas that should not be so quickly dismissed. I understand Confucius is a friend of good order and government. I would not be averse to engaging with such a mind. You will see to that for me. Perhaps there will be a place for you after all."

"Your Highness, consider it done. If you will allow me to say, your leadership skills among men are already highly regarded. You even quote from my own writings and know of traveling literati such as Confucius as though..."

"As though I'm not a cabbage-headed, hot-tempered Prince?" He laughed. "Never underestimate a hungry wolf, dear scholar. The world is changing. If there is to be a place for one such as yourself, it will be at my behest. Those who work with their heads will rule, while those who work with their hands will serve. You will work with your head, but you shall also serve. I know what power you wield. It is not just the wisdom of noblemen and kings that shapes the world. I have heard what you scholars say. I have witnessed its influence in other kingdoms. Whole governments, farms, villages, cities, armies... they all see with one vision and live with a singular purpose."

"You speak of peace."

He stopped his pebble throwing and stared at me as though I were a child.

"I speak of power. Power, you foolish scholar. You either have it, or you are among the various classes of fools."

Did he view himself as a ruler, or still among the classes of fools? Was he saying that his Royal house lacked singular purpose unlike the growing powers within the now-fragmented empire? As he turned away, I felt a twinge of self-doubt reminiscent of my judgment of Li Su and the fire at the Academy. I had since left the Academy to release the Way to a larger pool, but I now questioned whether that pool was not only muddied with want and power, but also poisoned with a moral blackness.

Prince Chao's tale left me bewildered. Why had he confided in me? Was this a play to create suspicion between myself and his brother? Or were his emotions genuine? Did he wish to reveal dimensions of himself and others that I might otherwise never consider? I could not help but feel for a moment that my own course might have been compromised, that its flow could no longer simply meander and evade the imbalances around me. Even more, I began to question the natural bearings I had relied upon the Way to provide. Within that natural order, lucidity and simplicity reigned, the world is unambiguous. But human beings blur and obscure that which should be apparent. Humans are not simply either good or evil, just as the sky is not just dark or bright. Much lies unseen between.

11

Nature's Sorrow

As Lao Tzu slept through the starless night, Captain Yin stood alone beside the scribe, reflecting on the old man's reminiscences. Initially he had hungered only for knowledge of his grandfather and of the Way, but Lao Tzu's stories of the Royal Court were proving to be so intriguing that he craved more.

As the light of dawn was about to break the dark sky's grip, a disgusted-looking Lieutenant Zhang marched up to him with several guards in tow.

"So it is true—the old man remains," Zhang hissed. "What if he is a spy? He could slit your throat as you sleep. Have you thought of that?"

Captain Yin took another look at Lao Tzu who between heavy snores was sleep-talking about cleaning out bird cages. "If he is a spy plotting to slit my throat, then he is a well-rested one," he said.

"The General won't stand for soldiers playing nursemaid to homeless beggars," Zhang retorted.

"A moment ago he was a spy, now he is a homeless beggar. Next he will be a goddess in disguise."

Several of the men laughed and Zhang's face turned red. "Captain, I must..."

"That is correct, Lieutenant, I am the Captain and you are

dismissed."

The Lieutenant performed an exaggerated salute and stormed off.

"It seems your young lieutenant doesn't share your interest in history, nor in the Way," Lao Tzu said from inside his bedroll.

The Captain looked down at Lao Tzu, sighed and shook his head.

"It is not his fault. Nowadays many soldiers are recruited as professionals but trained as spies. I would not be surprised if he sends a sharply-worded message to the General. Did you sleep well, Old Master?"

Lao Tzu nodded. "Finest sleep I have had in many moons, and far better than you did to judge by the bags beneath your eyes. Guarding against throat-slitting spies, perhaps?"

The Captain smiled. "Hardly. A good sleep isn't something that ever comes easily to me."

Lao Tzu sat up. The Captain motioned to his corporal to pour some tea. The corporal complied, though he could not have moved any slower.

"Captain Yin," Lao Tzu began after they had drunk. "I would be interested to know why an enlightened man such as yourself chooses to remain a soldier?"

The Captain exhaled noisily and then smiled.

"To be honest, I don't know why. My father was a farmer before he was conscripted just like me. He became a fine archer. His father was, as I said, a Royal Guardsman. So perhaps my fate was sealed from the beginning, although you will likely tell me that one's fate can go in many directions. Perhaps I might have been more content if I had become a scholar."

He paused for a moment, then changed the subject.

"I have no actual memories of my grandfather. Do you suppose his years in the court gave him the opportunity to have contact with intellectuals and scholars, and with the Princes? You have not spoken of him so far."

Lao Tzu was already staring off into the distance. After a pause he spoke.

"But I *have* spoken of him, only perhaps in too discrete a fashion. Your grandfather was an honorable man in many ways. He endeared himself to many. He was very much an important part of the Royal Court and knew many of the intellectuals who did the rounds of the nobility and royalty, in the manner of traveling acrobats or magicians."

"Such as Confucius?" the Captain asked.

Lao Tzu nodded. "Confucius had worked for the Duke of Lu. After leaving his post there, he wandered through Qi and Chu promulgating his beliefs and was generally received warmly. The Zhou court may have been among the least receptive to his ideas at first, as it feared spies, but he was allowed to stay at the court. Shortly after I had my conversation with Prince Chao, Confucius sent word to me that he hoped to view the Archives and discuss my views on rituals and traditions. By then I had heard of his ideas on reforming administrations and shaping society, as if people can be bent like young bamboo stalks."

"You sound skeptical." Captain Yin said, interrupting the old man.

"Captain, I am too old to be skeptical, but no longer young enough to remain idealistic. You wished for a portal to understanding. I once thought I could provide the same for others. I once believed my ideas would be more than that, that the Way was the inevitable and correct path for all. But I have witnessed how even the truest ideas can be corrupted. All I desire now is to complete a final journey."

"Confucius. He corrupted your ideas?"

Lao Tzu heaved a sigh and was silent for a time. Captain Yin wondered if the old man would continue at all. But he did, and the Captain signaled to his scribe.

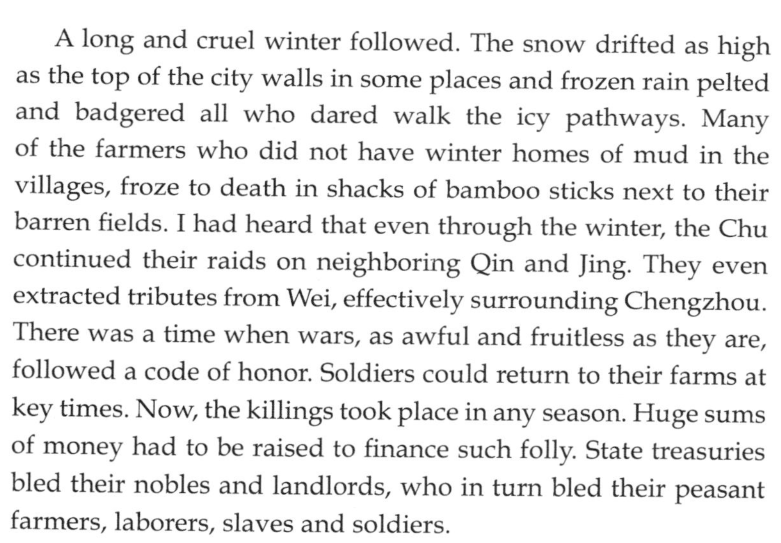

A long and cruel winter followed. The snow drifted as high as the top of the city walls in some places and frozen rain pelted and badgered all who dared walk the icy pathways. Many of the farmers who did not have winter homes of mud in the villages, froze to death in shacks of bamboo sticks next to their barren fields. I had heard that even through the winter, the Chu continued their raids on neighboring Qin and Jing. They even extracted tributes from Wei, effectively surrounding Chengzhou. There was a time when wars, as awful and fruitless as they are, followed a code of honor. Soldiers could return to their farms at key times. Now, the killings took place in any season. Huge sums of money had to be raised to finance such folly. State treasuries bled their nobles and landlords, who in turn bled their peasant farmers, laborers, slaves and soldiers.

Nature's harshness finally ended with the fall of warm droplets of rain so gentle that each bead might have been a sparrow's kiss. When the frozen earth began its slow thaw, the traders and merchants from distant parts arrived. Some had evaded Chu troops or else paid hefty taxes to them. In Chengzhou, they flaunted intensely blue, semi-precious stones. Many nobles could not purchase the new gems fast enough.

The thriving spring trade signaled not only a thaw in the weather, but also the adherence by the King and by Chu to an uneasy peace. For now, Chu were not likely to spread their tentacles further through Jin and into Chengzhou. But it was as if their gods had decided the world had to be cleansed. Black clouds burst open and oceans cascaded down from the heavens.

This went on for weeks. The remaining snow and ice melted faster than a garden snake fleeing a mongoose.

The rain continued without end. Even old timers such as myself had never seen anything like it. When the sun did break free, it turned the earth into an enormous steam cauldron, leaving us to walk the world in layers of drenched clothing. But these brief respites from the rain created their own grief. The sun's fire stoked the pests and gave scavengers, both human and animal, brief opportunities to forage for food. Farm plots yearning to be planted became seas of mud. Pregnant rivers surged like water demons claiming all in their path. Bloated carcasses of humans and animals floated everywhere. Chengzhou became a city of sludge. Most homes, rich and poor, suffered from the flooding.

In most of the regions surrounding Chengzhou, what little food could be preserved, bought or bartered could not be cooked because of the lack of fuel. After all the rain, drinking water reeked of rotting corpses and human and animal waste. Whole families could be found huddled under trees or other shelters, begging for food. Others lay together in water-logged shacks, arms across swollen bellies, too exhausted and hungry to fend off the insects covering their dirt and tear-streaked faces.

The Royal Palace itself was not immune from the unending deluge. Workers in the Celestial Hall struggled to keep its enormous floor clear of pools of water. The Royal Kitchen and armory were flooded for days at a time. Many of the lanterns lining the walkways and terraces were blown away or destroyed. My Archives would have suffered significant losses had it not been for the recent additions and renovations that included new drainage channels on the roof and in the cellar. These all withstood the elements.

But nothing could move through the mud without the greatest of effort. Wheels remained bogged in the quagmire. Soldiers did not stray from their barracks, leaving the general population to fend for themselves. My personal assistant Kao Shin, who was a quick learner in the Archives, also turned out to be a master scrounger. He and I were unable to find much food or fuel, but my station as master of the Archives afforded us privileges of food.

After several weeks of this calamity, King Jing finally reacted and called a meeting of the court. He ordered the Minister of State to instruct the army to make piles of corpses in preparation for disposal in mass graves. A strict curfew was implemented, as was a travel ban. Venturing beyond one's immediate area was forbidden without Royal or military approval. This measure served to safeguard those in the wealthier districts, but it meant many peasants died in their homes as they were unable to seek food or assistance. This drew a rebuke from Prince Meng.

"Heavenly Father, such measures serve only our nobles and the families with means. I have reports that demonstrate that many poor are condemned to die where they are. They cannot search for food and clean water; they cannot search for missing family members, they cannot..."

"They cannot loot the homes of our nobles and our Royal Granaries," Prince Chao interrupted. "Nor can they gather themselves into armed, roving, drunken, lawless bands. Surely we can offer more Royal backbone to our kind. Heavenly Father, the gods must be punishing us with good cause. Whatever has been done to incur their wrath has yet to be determined. Perhaps more silent prayer will reveal this. But for now, our best course is to safeguard what we have and protect our Palace and those around it."

Prince Meng argued back. "Heavenly Father, as we speak, hundreds of bodies are being buried. Many families have not had an opportunity to identify their missing members. Surely the living and the dead deserve some dignity?"

The King nodded. "Indeed, the heavens must be displeased." He glanced at both of his sons, making no other effort to stifle their disagreement.

"Perhaps my dear eldest Prince would like to assist our soldiers in dignifying these rotting corpses?" Prince Chao continued with an exaggerated flair. "We have not had rain for three days now, it might make for a pleasant stroll. I understand the odors of our dear fallen subjects are particularly… robust. Heavenly Father, it is quite conceivable that my brother speaks wisely. I suggest that we review such restrictions and I propose that Prince Meng inspect our brave soldiers to ensure that the martial law you have ordered is actually necessary and is being properly enforced. Furthermore, that he also personally examine the burial and disposal of our departed subjects."

Prince Meng was silent while his brother and his sycophant aides smirked. In my private moments with him, I had come to understand much from Prince Meng's smooth face; from wide-eyed, child-like curiosity during our discussions of the Way, to indignation regarding political and court matters, to profound disappointment with his brother. Until this day, he had never revealed such imbalance and apprehension. It was as though he were trying to choose which of his arms to cut off. Then he spoke.

"It is not for either myself or Prince Chao to make Royal Decrees. But if my Heavenly Father commands me thus, I shall of course obey."

The King agreed, and issued the command. Prince Chao offered to alert the military, barely able to refrain from chuckling as he did so.

"Master Lao Tzu," Prince Meng said to me afterwards, "yet again I have allowed my brother to draw me into matters of which I am not an expert. It is one thing to suggest to my father to rescind a bad edict, but quite another for me to inspect soldiers and disaster plans. I was speaking only of reports I had received. Perhaps I was hasty."

"And who gave you such reports?" I asked.

"The Royal Archivist and his loyal staff," he said with a smile.

"Then the Royal Archivist, old man that he is, shall accompany you."

The next day, dark clouds hung low as I sat beside the Prince in a horse-drawn carriage. Royal Guardsmen accompanied us on all sides, forming a tight column. We drew back the curtains as we exited the Heavenly Gate to the Palace and continued along the stone pathway. Except for the central stone road, all the streets were a mess of muddy lakes and largely empty except for soldiers milling about. I could hear the occasional cry in the near distance. The simple act of breathing took much effort as the air hung damp and heavy.

"Water gives us life yet is also the bane of many an existence," Prince Meng said as he gazed out at the scene. "It is difficult to imagine anything drying under such conditions."

"Your Highness may recall that we've spoken of how the best of men are like water. Water benefits all things, yet it in itself does not contend with others. It merely flows in places that others disdain, often with tragic consequences. At other times it nourishes all life. This is where it is in harmony with the Way."

We continued in silence on our way to the city's South Gate. All we could see were the high walls of courtyards and the rooftops of homes belonging to noblemen and high-ranking civil servants such as myself, which crowded in the areas closest to the Palace. As we moved further away, the walls became progressively lower, the buildings smaller and more poorly-built.

We approached the first military checkpoint. Large numbers of soldiers clustered about, doing little more than biding time. As soon as they saw a Royal carriage and the Guardsmen, they snapped to attention. An officer ran to the head of the column and bowed to the commanding officer of the Guardsmen.

"Captain sir, Corporal Shui at your service. Forgive me, we were not informed of your inspection. Allow me to…"

"Where is your commanding officer?" the Captain asked. "Prince Meng is here to review the area and a slovenly detail greets him? Heads will roll, beginning now."

"Captain, never mind," said Prince Meng poking his head out the window. He looked at the corporal. "What can you report? Why are so many of you stationed here?"

Evidently Prince Chao had made no advance arrangements for the inspection.

"Your Highness, we have been assigned to maintain security along the Royal road. I am pleased to report it is secure and free of looters. I will call for the commanding officer overseeing this district at once."

"That won't be necessary. How much looting has occurred?" the Prince asked.

The corporal hesitated, then replied that no looting had occurred in the districts surrounding the Palace.

"Then how many lives have been lost?" the Prince asked.

The corporal paused again before replying that there had been no fatalities in the areas surrounding the Palace. The Prince and I exchanged glances. The Prince asked where most of the damage and looting had occurred. The corporal indicated to the west, off the main roads in the slums, and along the river banks.

I told the Prince I was familiar with the area, but that it would be impossible to reach because of the mud. He ignored me and directed the carriage driver and the Royal Guardsmen to head in that direction.

"Your Highness," the corporal attempted to interrupt. "Your escorts may protect you, but there is much disease and filth. Rats the size of cats are preying on lost children. It is not a sight for Royal eyes."

"A corporal dares to tell a Prince what is fit for him to see?"

The corporal dropped to his knees and quickly kowtowed several times as he apologized for his stupidity and begged for the Prince's forgiveness. The Prince ignored him and ordered the carriage to move on.

The main road remained clear but quiet. We peered through our curtains at the narrow side streets where people scattered at the sight of the procession. The Prince ordered the Captain to move off the stone road and into the muddied side streets. The Royal carriage lurched to a sudden stop as its wheels sank into the mud. The Royal Guardsmen broke formation and began pushing and pulling to bring the carriage out of the morass. Several of them slipped into the thick mud as they struggled. Then to my surprise, the Prince halted their exertions.

"We will never break free with our weight anchoring the carriage," he said turning to me.

He stepped out of the carriage and in an instant, his red gazelle leather boots sank into the quagmire. The sludge-smeared men stood still in shock, then dropped onto their knees and hands. The Prince waved me out of the carriage, ordered the drivers off, then commanded the men to rise. He directed them to place anything flat and solid beneath the wheels. When he looked around and found nothing in the immediate vicinity, he ordered the men to remove their tunics and place them under the carriage wheels. They took their positions, this time with the Prince counting to three and pushing alongside them. Within seconds the carriage was free. The men and a small crowd of locals cheered and applauded the Prince.

One look at the river of mud ahead told us it was futile to carry on. But the Prince continued to surprise me. Without a word, he stumbled through the quagmire on foot, oblivious to the splatters of mud on his blazing yellow robe. Though he had to struggle with each and every step, he moved forward with a relentless determination. Weary residents slowly inched out of their hovels to watch and I could hear word spreading that the Prince was in their midst. Most had likely never seen him up close, and certainly never in their neighborhood and acting so human.

The Prince's eyes scrutinized his subjects, many of whom were so weak they could barely stand, let alone bow. Their ragged clothes hung loose on their bony frames, and dirt streaked their gaunt faces. The smell of rot and decay and of feces was everywhere. The Prince, angry but resolute, focused on a boy no more than six years old, leaning against a crumbled mud wall. The child had swollen, cracked lips punctuated by deep lesions. He was oblivious to the mosquitoes feasting on his flaking skin.

"Where is your mother?" the Prince asked.

The boy's sunken eyes looked up at the Prince, but they could only blink. The Prince repeated his question. Still the child gave off a vacant stare. The Prince looked behind the wall. The straw roof had caved into what was a tiny room not much larger than the Prince's carriage. Inside lay a woman, the boy's mother, whose body looked as though every drop of moisture had been sucked out of it. She smelled of rotting fish and fresh feces. The Prince turned around and staggered away, fighting back his vomit. Several men instinctively rushed towards him, then stopped. Ordinary hands on a Royal would have meant serious punishment. His personal attendant was called for, but the Prince waved him and the soldiers off.

"Cholera," he said to no one in particular as he struggled for air. He ordered fresh water for the boy. The men looked at one another.

"What are you waiting for?" he shouted. I had never heard the Prince raise his voice before.

A soldier offered forth his own leather drinking vessel. The Prince held the boy and gave him water which he swallowed in large gulps, spilling much of it onto the Prince's robe. The Prince took out his silk handkerchief and wet it before wiping clean the boys face and arms.

The Prince visited several more homes and provided the same succor. Soon the detail had dispensed all the water and whatever food the Royal kitchen had loaded onto the carriage. By then, a crowd had formed, but the people did not to beg, nor did they seek favor. They were there to quietly bear witness to heaven on earth bearing pity at last.

The next day, Prince Meng and I made another foray into the slum areas, this time with wagonloads of food, water and clothing and a full battalion of soldiers re-assigned from the areas surrounding the Palace. The Prince directed them to assist the people in whatever way they could. As supplies ran low, another convoy of troops and supplies approached. Work teams placed planks over the muddy expanses to enable the wagons to ride more easily over them and penetrate deeper into the slums. One of the vehicles was a Royal carriage which came to a standstill by myself and Prince Meng.

"My dear eldest Prince, the heaven-sent savior of the poor and wretched, I do hope you brought a change of Royal clothing," shouted Prince Chao from inside as he surveyed his brother's muddied robe. "Or were you thinking of borrowing some of the local attire in order to be even closer to the people?"

I could see Prince Meng wanted to choose his words carefully, but even so he lacked diplomacy. "Has hunting season started, Prince Chao? Or has a new brothel opened up in the area?"

Prince Chao gave off an exaggerated laugh. "Both humane and humorous, what a wonderful combination. You inspire me, dear eldest Prince."

"What are you doing here? This is my responsibility, you saw to that."

Prince Chao began fanning himself. "Yes, but did you really think that you alone had the sway to re-assign a full battalion of troops, not to mention a month's supply of food and water from the Royal warehouses? No, dear brother, it was I. You may thank me if you wish, but the love of my subjects, many of whom no doubt await me, is all that I desire."

With him was the Royal Guardsman, Major Huang. I recognized this towering man with his deformed face and dark, humorless eyes from the day Mei was sold to the King. The Prince ordered Huang to direct the convoy onwards, but he couldn't resist one last jibe at his brother.

"Stirring heroics yesterday and today, my dear eldest Prince," he shouted from the carriage. "You didn't turn back any barbarian hordes or defeat any rebellious warlords, but it is inspiring, utterly inspiring. So much so that I persuaded our Heavenly Father to double the love for our people and have us both save these wretches. Now if you'll excuse me, tears of gratitude and undying loyalty await me."

Even while undertaking noble and compassionate deeds, the twins could not refrain from sniping at one another.

On the third day of the court's relief efforts, I traveled with Yi Ban into the most affected areas of Chengzhou. Prince Meng remained behind to oversee logistical efforts from the Palace, while Prince Chao continued to distribute aid, although he was content to do so while basing himself within the confines of a nearby nobleman's mansion. He left the relief efforts to be overseen by Major Huang, who surveyed the work with his right hand gripping his halberd.

"He is a rather intimidating sight, would you not agree, dear scholar?" said Yi Ban.

I agreed. "He has the stance of a sentry, and the scars of a warrior, but I also see much complexity in the way he surveys all around him."

Yi Ban chuckled. "It is not complexity I dare say, but his duty, which he takes especially seriously. He is a soldier, after all. Thinking is not needed. Evidently you do enough of that for all of us. Nonetheless you are correct. He is rather unique."

I pointed to Huang's long weapon. "It is not often we see an officer wielding a halberd."

"Ah, that is Thunderclap, his weapon of choice," Yi Ban replied. "In an era where chariots are losing some of their luster to calvary, the long spear is falling into disuse among officers. The Major may be the only senior ranking officer in all of Zhou to wield it on a daily basis. His is also likely the heaviest weapon ever fashioned, yet notice how he moves it as though it were weightless. No man could get close to him without getting speared, chopped or sliced."

"Indeed," I nodded, "the Major's long reach with his halberd would make him a formidable opponent."

Yi Ban continued, "I am told he cherishes that weapon more than wine and women, and that he personally polishes the blades meticulously. It was forged for Huang's grandfather who also served as an infantryman before the Royal Guardsmen recruited him. Then it was in the possession of Huang's father when he was a lieutenant Guardsman, before he was killed while dealing with the leaders of the Tai farmer uprising some twenty years ago. That bundle of red horsehair tassel you see around the spear includes samples from each kill. Now the Major brandishes it."

"A veritable Royal Family of Guardsmen," I said.

"Truly, and Major Huang has done especially well. There are few top appointments that a commoner can achieve in the military. The Major has advanced on merit. No doubt you have noticed that hideous scar running from his forehead down to his cheek."

"Impossible to miss."

Yi Ban nodded. "It happened while he was a young corporal. He was among a platoon of Guardsmen escorting the young Princess, now our Queen, returning from Feishan. Bandits ambushed the outnumbered Guardsmen. Most were hacked to pieces. Huang stood by the terrified young Princess and her servants, wielding Thunderclap like a demon. He was seriously wounded but he kept his adversaries at a distance. His gallantry inspired the remaining escorts who along with Huang, rallied and chased off the remaining bandits. The Princess and her entourage returned to Chengzhou, where Huang was immediately promoted to sergeant. He has risen steadily ever since. As Major, he commands all the Guardsmen and he is not to be overlooked. Not that you could."

"That tale sounds like it's grown over the years," I said.

"Believe it scholar, for I was a younger man once and one of the few who survived that attack and chased off the bandits."

"Like I said, the story has grown over time," I repeated and we both chuckled.

As Yi Ban finished his account, a Guardsmen patrol appeared, leading a bedraggled group of prisoners with heavy boards around their necks. The prisoners stumbled through the mud and were brought to a stop before Major Huang. Onlookers and soldiers gathered around. Yi Ban and I could not help but look on as well.

A corporal saluted the Major.

"Sir, we have rooted out the looters and black marketeers as you commanded. Their leader appears to be one of ours, as you suspected—Sergeant Pu-ji."

Major Huang took a deep breath and glared at the prisoners. He lifted Thunderclap's blade beneath the board of Sergeant Pu-ji, forcing him to stand erect, however shakily.

"It is not enough that you would embarrass my command and dishonor your brothers with your actions. But you also did it under false pretenses after I granted you leave to attend to your family," he said and flicked his blade, sending the Sergeant sprawling. "You disgust me," the Major spat at the Sergeant. "Get up."

The Sergeant staggered back onto his feet and caught his breath.

"I am not worthy of forgiveness, but I beg you sir, have mercy on me," he said. "I have served you well for many years. I was with you at basic training, and long ago at Anyi when we were all but certain of death. I have been a good soldier. I do not know what madness overcame me. Please...please, old friend!" He clasped his hands together beneath the board and started to whimper.

"We go back many moons together, this is true." Major Huang ordered the board removed. The Sergeant collapsed to his knees, and prostrated himself towards his commanding officer.

"Thank you old friend, thank you," he cried.

Major Huang took a big step back. He raised Thunderclap with both hands, spun his body around and in one long swift arc chopped off his Sergeant's right hand. The Sergeant's scream reverberated around us. He rolled onto his back, feet pounding the mud, and the screaming continued.

The Major towered over Sergeant Pu-ji and wrapped the scythe-shaped blade around the Sergeant's neck.

"Another sound, and I will take off your other hand."

The Sergeant went quiet though his eyes revealed deep shock and his nostrils exploded with phlegm.

"Take him out of my sight. Take them all away."

After the prisoners were removed and the crowd dispersed, Yi Ban and I approached Major Huang.

"Major," Yi Ban said, "allow me to formally introduce..."

"I know who he is, another... scholar," the Major interjected without looking at me.

"So you have met?"

"There is no one who enters the Palace that I do not know," the Major said as he wiped the Sergeant's blood off his blade.

"Messy business I see," Yi Ban said, looking at the blood.

The Major nodded out of deference to the Minister's rank.

"Major Huang, what will become of your 'old friend'?" I asked.

"He ceased being a friend the moment he lied to me, stole from the people he was sworn to protect, and ultimately dishonored the Royal Guardsmen. That was some time ago. I have only now found evidence. All that he owns, and all that his family possesses will be confiscated and sold. They themselves will also be sold or imprisoned."

"But of course, such is the King's justice... punish not one but all," I said.

The Major tightened his grip on Thunderclap. I could clearly see the contours of his scar, smell his sweat and sense his focused energy.

"Do you not think the Sergeant's family's wealth was ill-begotten?" he demanded. "Are you questioning our Son of Heaven?"

"It is not the Son of Heaven I question, it is our world which breeds human failings, which are in turn met with limited humanity and much brutality," I replied.

"And you would have me ignore those who commit such brutality? This is foolish talk. My Lord," he added, turning to Yi Ban, "may I carry on with my duties?"

Yi Ban nodded.

Just as the Major was about to turn away I said, "Major Huang, let us suppose that twenty years ago the Son of Heaven had not decided to raise the taxes of farmers in the western region of Lu? Let us further suppose he had realized he could live quite comfortably without taking their livestock, their produce and their boys and men for wars that never cease. And suppose he had not sent in troops such as your father to restore an order that already existed among people who were now merely fighting for the simple life they knew. If that were so, you would not be here now, but your father and many others might be alive. Surely there is much to be gained by an enlightened disregard of commands, do you not agree, Major Huang?"

The Major stood rigidly. "But… but order must prevail. It is not possible to look the other way."

"You perspire, Major Huang. And not only because of the rigors of the task you have just performed. You wear a thick woolen tunic beneath your armor as though the spring chill is still upon us, though it has clearly passed. We cannot ignore the changing seasons any more than we can the brotherhood that is within us all."

"We are no more brothers to such vermin than are animals and humans."

"Ah but we are. Amidst the Royal collection in the Royal Archives is a rare painting. Swiftly sketched with deft strokes and washed with color, a woman stands in prayer attended by a phoenix and a dragon. It is a masterful piece of art, regrettably ignored. Therein lies evidence of brotherhood even across different manners of beings."

"That is a false and ludicrous notion, conjured by someone with too much imagination and not enough worldly sense," the Major snorted.

"Perhaps. But no more so than when a man rests with his beast of burden or his stallion. The possibilities are limited only by an over-reliance on archaic notions and a lack of imagination."

The Major's eyes flickered, then he marched away.

Yi Ban nodded towards the departing Major. "Lao Tzu, did I not advise you to be cautious? He commands the Royal Guardsmen and answers only to the Royal Family. I have long suspected that he knows and sees more than he lets on. He is not one to alienate."

"I don't believe I have done so. Quite the opposite."

"We can only hope. Alas, I must now depart. Some junior ministers demand my attention."

12

Confucius

Nature's wrath bared its anger through the flooding, the starvation, the diseases and the ensuing violence, killing tens of thousands throughout the kingdom and the break-away states. Some no doubt whispered that such tragedies were harbingers of a shift in the mandate of heaven, legitimizing the indifference many already felt towards the Royal House. For myself, I knew that even these calamities in the timeless world of the Zhou Kingdom would barely merit a line in the dynasty's annals. More significant to this story is that not long after the floods subsided, Confucius entered Chengzhou's city gates.

He arrived on horseback with a servant and two pupils in tow. My immediate reaction was of mild astonishment—a horse is worth many servants yet he was purportedly of quite humble origins. Nevertheless there were no airs about him when we first met. He showed me all the deference one expected from a junior, dropping to his knees and kowtowing.

"Please rise, it is I who should be bowing to you, Master Confucius," I said.

"You flatter me, Master Lao Tzu," he replied. "Many moons have passed since I first longed to be in your presence."

There was nothing particularly striking about Confucius. He stood taller than most men, though not especially so. His appearance was more youthful than I expected, though at the time, he would have been in his late twenties. He carried himself exceptionally well. There was confidence in his tone as well as an economy in his movements. When he walked, it was as though he glided. When he gestured or nodded, it was with a graceful ease. Cavernous eyes searched slowly but perceptively, taking in everything around him. Such refinement and his full face indicated that his days of hunger and want were long over. I have no doubt he came to similar conclusions about me.

He presented me with a small, simple lacquered box. The box's value alone could feed a family for weeks. I opened it and gazed upon its contents, which were several square pieces of thin, stiff blue fabric bound with a thread. I picked them up and examined them with fascination. The first piece was a wonderful likeness of a scholar in contemplation atop a mountain. Other pieces were inked with wonderfully formed words. Together they made for an odd type of book.

My curiosity was piqued.

"Fascinating, and... beautiful at the same time. I have never before laid eyes on such a peculiarity. Forgive my ignorance, Master Confucius, but what is it?"

He smiled with a self-satisfied expression on his face. "They are raw silk fibers. Layered, then dyed. As you can see, it is quite light and pliable. While in Linzi, I taught a nobleman's sons for a period of time. He collected strange and interesting objects and traded this for a jade goblet with a merchant who died shortly afterwards in a fire. Apparently it takes many hours and much material to make, far too much for it ever to be of any practical value. But ink spreads nicely on the material and the nobleman had several of my sayings inscribed onto it as a parting gift."

I read the first saying: 'Do not do to others what you would not want yourself.'

An odd gift with an odd saying, or so I thought at the time. Was it an indirect way of him telling me to treat him with respect? Or was it an honest expression of the power of reciprocity in guiding our actions? Though his gift was unique, it had little real use. Perhaps that was its intent. Perhaps he was honoring me with a simple object crafted with time and patience, a reflection of the Way. I remember thinking how strange it was that such a simple act could ferment so disquieting a feeling.

We sat before we spoke further. Then he told me of his journey. He had traveled far and if it had not been for heaven's fury on the land, he would have arrived months earlier. Numerous noblemen along the way implored him to stay for extended periods. Unlike myself when I traveled to Chengzhou, he hadn't shared too many roadside meals with peasant farmers.

"At last, I meet someone who truly understands me," he said, nodding towards me. "Though many seek our counsel and wisdom, few know of the rigors of contemplation. Yet we cannot blame heaven, nor can we blame men. We study things on a basic level but our understanding penetrates the higher levels. But for the gods, no one else but our brethren truly fathom us."

Except for his belief in the gods, he spoke a clear truth. There is an unspeakable loneliness in solitary deliberations, one that even the most trusted servant or most loyal companion cannot comprehend. Indeed, most of the other scholars within the Palace paid me little heed. I felt that although Confucius and I would not always share common ground on many ideas, I dearly wanted intellectual companionship, so I decided to assume his words spoke of a mutual understanding and of respect to follow. But there was something about him that I could not wholly embrace.

"Master Confucius, the doctrines of the Way require much reflection to comprehend, but once understood, are simple to practice," I replied. "However, among our rulers, few appreciate the profits of such practice."

"Indeed, Master Lao Tzu. The world's growing obsession with war and materialism dampens the appetite for such knowledge."

He continued to praise my work as though he were my apprentice. I had never required such acclamation, so I redirected our discussion to our respective upbringings, which we shared at length. Both of our fathers were absent during our childhoods, relegating our families to poverty. But they both ensured we received an education. He had received training in the traditional six subjects—rites, music, archery, chariot driving, writing and mathematics—while I had had such privileges only in writing and mathematics. In any event, I demonstrated limited interest in handling either a bow or a horse. Nor would I have been especially successful at them, even though, years before, my cousin Shun did teach me how to use a slingshot. By fifteen, Confucius found work as an administrator, as did I. We developed our own beliefs after witnessing the failures of our rulers. But that was also the area where he would find his most receptive audiences. He traveled through many Royal Courts, slept in many mansions and attracted many loyal followers.

Perhaps it was because his journey was less arduous and he was more coddled than I, that I could not warm to him entirely. Was it envy? Would I have exchanged places with him? True, there were many nights I longed for a greater audience for my thoughts. But now it was he who had come to me.

I showed him around the garden, then the Archives and what was becoming a very presentable collection. We sat to rest and awaited tea as our discussion inevitably moved on to our core beliefs.

He was particularly interested in discussing ancestor worship, music, rituals, social hierarchies and ceremonies, believing them to be keys to stability and continuity in the world. He said there were two poles that balanced order and harmony—ceremonies and music. While social ceremonies reinforced necessary social hierarchies, music unified all hearts in shared enjoyment. They were both embedded within our social world and reinforced in our relationships, as are the five pillars: between father and son, husband and wife, prince and subject, elder and younger, and between friends.

I had heard and read all this before. As I expected, he continued to speak of duties and how they had to be balanced, and how a subject had to obey his ruler.

"But one also has to be able to tell one's ruler when he is wrong," I countered..

"This will not be necessary, Master Lao Tzu. Our rulers will provide good government by providing an example for the people to follow. They will show good character, they will be humane and righteous and provide necessary structures. Humanity needs to be trained and controlled through the strict observation of social rules, rules set forth by our leaders and replicated within families. This is the foundation of order and stability. These are not new ideas. They have been germinating for some time, primarily among the many splinter states."

Just then, as if to contradict Confucius' point, a squad of Royal Guardsmen entered the Archives and began searching the rooms. I remained nonplussed while Confucius shifted uneasily in his seat.

"Some time ago, General Wu ordered regular searches throughout the Palace," I explained. "Apparently spies and dissidents lurk everywhere, even among these centuries-old tablets. The searches are more a show of authority than a real security measure. Nothing or no one has ever been found, at least not since I have been here. But it is a type of controlled agitation that is as perverted and futile as rammed earth walls in keeping out fresh ideas and locking in old ones."

"People need order and good governance, Master Lao Tzu."

"Agreed, but it needn't be an artificial order, nor should we equate nobility and rank with virtue and moral superiority."

"But neither can we assume the ordinary man can both lead and be led without guiding examples."

As my guest, I could not tell him directly that his beliefs were misguided. But I did ask how he expected peasant farmers to enjoy music, the elixir of the elite? To this, he did not reply. Evidently he had forgotten what it was to eat spoiled food, or to not eat at all. And I have yet to meet a nobleman, let alone a Royal, save Prince Meng, who would allow an underling to tell them when they were wrong.

"Perhaps our differences are mere semantics, Master Scholar. For your notion of simplicity and mine of following a social order are not mutually exclusive. If people know their place in the order of the world, it is an uncomplicated existence. Amongst themselves, people may practice and believe whatever they choose so long as they do not disrupt the necessary stability."

"That is an interesting notion, but I have yet to see an order that allows such a choice. People bend best with the wind, not the whip. People are happiest when the simplicity of the heart leads to spontaneity and to balance. And so my path finds resonance among those who lead uncluttered lives, unlike many who dwell among the elite."

Kao Shin interrupted us with a tray of licorice tea and cakes. I nodded my appreciation.

"Your servant pours us tea. I would say he knows his place, would you not agree, Master Lao Tzu?"

"He was found begging and stealing on the streets," I replied. "He was good at neither." Kao Shin flashed an easy smile. "He never knew his parents. Unlike most of those living hand-to-mouth on the streets, he possessed a stillness in his actions, a scarcity of movement, and so I took him in. He has learned to read three hundred characters and shows much promise with a writing brush. Yes, he knows his place, and it is wherever he chooses. He can leave here any time he wishes, for he is no servant. Within the Archives, there are no servants in the manner you infer. We each have our respective roles and duties, but none among us eats more than the other. Although I must admit he is the most devoted person on my staff."

"How just and reasonable it appears to be. And yet you find yourself in a privileged setting, in the spiritual capital of the world, in the Palace of the Son of Heaven. While your work here at the Archives is timeless, it is hardly uncluttered or natural. And the Royal Family, can you truly say they are models of the natural spirit?"

It was an obvious contradiction. I explained that at first, I had hoped the Archives would provide salvation for myself after the tragedy that beset my Academy, and that I could rise from my despair and derive some redemption in such work. I revealed that my hopes lay not only in the dusty collection, but also in Prince Meng finding the Way.

"I do not distinguish between myself and other people in the world, regardless of whether they are of noble or humble stock. One must live in harmony with the world. And one's mind is the world's mind. So I nurture the minds of the world where I can, as a father does his children, but not as a ruler does his subjects. Because the latter is based on coercion not benevolence. I believe Prince Meng is not of this ilk."

"But Prince Chao is?"

He was unexpectedly direct, but then again, I had just disclosed my stake in Prince Meng.

"There is a necessary balance in Nature, a contractive force, and an expansive force. Together they form a continuous cycle of creation and destruction. These are the true poles of all existence, not rituals and music. This balance is no different among men. The Way believes that opposites help us to see the relationships of reality. Without knowing light, you cannot possibly know dark. The Way functions with the understanding that one cannot know what is good without knowing what is bad. All life forces tend to move toward harmony and balance. We are all part of an inseparable whole."

"You mean to say that Prince Chao's potential for destructiveness is a necessary balance to Prince Meng's desire to create? Forgive my forwardness," he continued. "I think we can agree that we share a common hope that the path to our respective vision lies through enlightened rulers."

Though I never would have thought such a route was necessary, Confucius was correct. In chaotic times, social change on a wide scale could not be possible without visible leadership. Individual beliefs, however refined, would be to no avail. I needed Prince Meng.

My silence was finally interrupted when Confucius laid his hand on mine and grinned.

"Did I not say that heaven alone knows us?"

When we retired early the following morning, I found my way to bed and pondered my first audience with Confucius. As a teacher, he had few equals. But as a student, he was unsurpassed. He absorbed everything I said, challenging my thoughts further without any disrespect. We talked through the night and agreed we had only just begun. My weary body was many *li* behind my excited mind, although I should have felt comfort knowing that Confucius and I shared some ideals. We stood together for peace and benevolence in and for all, though he would say such goodness was built on a social, and I on a natural foundation. I had found someone not unlike myself, a self-trained scholar of humble origins, an intellectual equivalent, a visionary if you will. Yet it did not give me the ease I had anticipated and sleep evaded me.

I arranged for Confucius to stay in a small guest house in the Gongyi, a modest district near the Palace favored by minor officials and traveling bureaucrats. I released Kao Shin to be at his disposal for inspections of the Archives as well as of Chengzhou itself. It turned out to be unnecessary, as Confucius had numerous seals of references and was able to call upon several nobles. One of them was a favorite of Prince Chao, who offered up one of his residences to Confucius.

I also made arrangements for him to have a quiet audience with Prince Meng in his private chambers but Confucius, seeing that the Qing Ming festival was approaching, insisted on deferring it until later. He felt there was no more important a date on the calendar than the day on which ancestors and tradition are honored. I was not surprised by this. His views on the power derived from familial rituals spoke to his love of tradition and continuity, and the festival reflected this more than any other celebration.

The custom is said to have originated when corrupt men wanted the Duke of Jin's eldest son Chong'er assassinated. Jie Zitui, Chong'er's loyal servant, dressed his master in peasant's clothing and smuggled him out in the middle of the night. Because Chong'er had shown much concern for his people, Jie cared for and protected him as befit a future King who would be a benevolent and dutiful ruler. Once, when they were on the edge of starvation, Jie cut off a piece of his own flesh and cooked it for his master. Many years later, Chong'er finally became King of Jin and rewarded those who had assisted him during his exile. But he forgot his most loyal servant, Jie. When reminded of this, the new King immediately sent for Jie. But Jie had felt betrayed and had fled with his mother to the mountains to live as a hermit. So hidden was Jie's hermit refuge that the King and all his men could not find them. But someone suggested that to find him, they set fire to the mountain, because Jie would not allow his mother to be in danger. The fire burnt for three days and nights, but still Jie did not appear. After the fire had completely scorched the mountain, they found Jie and his mother under a smoldering willow tree, burnt to death. So heartbroken and sorrowful was the King that he declared that each year on that day, no one was to use fire and everyone had to eat cold food to honor Jie's loyalty. All graves of ancestors were to be swept and cleaned. Families would make offerings of cold meat and fruit to the guardian spirit of the graves, followed by incense offerings to their ancestors.

That the festival originated from Jin territory, one of the breakaway regions, yet was also practiced by the Zhou house was most ironic. Perhaps previous generations of the Zhou house saw it more as homage to loyalty and allegiance, things they felt little of as time went on.

Following the festival, I waited for Confucius in the garden, which had just undergone a small expansion. I had dug a third but smaller pond that connected to the original with a narrow footbridge. Grey flagstones and fine pebbles weaved in and around newly-planted bushes and trees. Plants foreign to the region that had proved hardy beside the vegetable garden were transplanted around a raised pagoda. Within that, stone benches provided reflective views of every angle of the garden.

"Is Master Lao Tzu lost or found in this oasis of quietude he has created?"

I turned at the now-familiar sound of Confucius' voice. "I am neither, Master Confucius. To be either lost or found is to imply that I am unsettled, disquieted. Quite the contrary, my friend."

"Yet this solitude clearly gives forth a natural remedy," Confucius replied.

"Indeed, but I have not constructed it as a retreat of water, stone and wood with the brushes of the air and wind. The Way begets all things. Harmony nurtures them. Nature shapes them. Our use completes them. Each follows the Way and honors harmony. Not by law, but by being. The Way bears, nurtures, shapes, completes, shelters, comforts, and makes a home for them. Bearing without possessing, nurturing without taming, shaping without forcing: this is the harmony I revel in. One cannot construct that which is unbuildable. I could no more shape the winds than I could hold water."

Confucius smiled. "It is pleasing to see a fellow scholar content, or should I say harmonious and not merely preoccupied?"

I returned his smile. "I confess that doubts I once harbored have retreated. I have learned that he who conquers others is strong, but he who conquers himself is mighty. When neither you nor your demons can do harm, you will be at peace with them. And perhaps this oasis serves to embody this harmony. I possess purpose, yet I also possess an acceptance that things will follow their own natural course."

"You speak of our Royal Princes?" he asked.

I hadn't wanted to refer to the quarrelling Princes, but the whispers were loud and unavoidable once inside the Palace walls. I chose to defer answering his query, and instead reminded him that Prince Meng was expecting us. I led Confucius along to the Prince's quarters.

"It is with the highest moral standard that we must all model and lead," Confucius said. "The ancients understood this. Their rulers and their followers lived within a code. It was a balm that bound them to immortality."

I could barely contain my smile. "The ancients did not seek to rule people with knowledge. Instead they sought to help them become unencumbered. It is difficult for knowledgeable people to attain this by contrived means. To use laws to control a nation weakens the nation. But to use Nature to control a nation strengthens the nation. To understand these two paths is to understand subtlety. Subtlety runs deep, ranges wide, resolves confusion and preserves peace."

"I wonder if there is much of an audience for such preachings here, Master Lao Tzu. The Zhou royal house, however troubled, and all the other clans, possess the promise, indeed the hope, of order, of good government and of a just society. Even amidst the endless wars, only our leaders can provide a foundation and purpose."

I stopped. "You misread me, Master Confucius. I do not preach, nor do I counsel. He who understands does not preach. You must reserve your judgments and words. One must accept the world rather than try to regiment it. We must choose when and how to direct our teachings. There are those who will pick words ripe for their occasion and ply them to their advantage."

"A fool despises good counsel, but a wise man takes it to heart," he countered, then added: "It is understood that Prince Meng makes time for your wisdom."

"Prince Meng seeks a contentment that he does not know he already possesses. I merely assist him in refining his focus so that he will be able to see clearer. Having said that, as we enter the inner Palace, I implore you to conduct yourself even more solemnly than you have with previous noblemen and rulers."

I had not previously attended to the Prince's outer chamber and was surprised to see how lavishly decorated it was. Intricately painted beams criss-crossed the ceiling, and the most resplendent furnishings I had seen in the Palace lay before me. But the most stunning objects were two enormous bronze vessels, each with a pair of animal eyes projecting from the bronze surface staring at the viewer with a bewitching force. These protruding eyes, from some imaginary or mystical beasts, were the eyes of fierce predators. They were unsettling at first, although I recognized some of the craftsmanship and guessed them to be perhaps seven hundred years old. Needless to say, it was in contrast with my expectation that his surroundings would reflect the simplicity and austerity he longed for.

We stepped inside his chamber and his personal attendant directed us onto our knees in front of the Prince. I introduced my guest to the Prince, who was far more formal and curt than I had been accustomed to in his presence. No doubt Confucius' presence demanded this. He queried Confucius about his travels, the lands and courts he had visited, and the people he'd spoken with.

I admired Prince Meng's curiosity and also quietly relished his bluntness with Confucius.

"I have heard that you assume one's station in life automatically destines one's role, that duty and virtue guides us all, and that family ties alone would bind people. These are idealized notions, fraught with the pitfalls of reality."

"Your Highness, the reality you speak of is indeed creviced. But to leave it so would doom our world to the instability and upheaval that surrounds us. I believe we must reflect the good and the virtue that is within us. How else can people see otherwise?"

"And suppose people do not value virtue as they should?"

the Prince responded. "Suppose their notion of good does not reconcile with our own? You want order though many people lack such a choice. For those with such a choice, it is often impeded by those with divergent interests."

In the face of such an admonishment, Confucius was silent, and after the necessary formalities, we left Prince Meng. As I returned to my chambers, I wondered how the rest of the court would receive him. I felt an obligation to oversee and host his visit, though I both feared and anticipated the King and Prince Chao mocking and chastising him as they did most scholars.

13

The Royal Hunt

Given that Confucius courted my views so soon after he first arrived, I was somewhat surprised when we subsequently met with less frequency. My introduction of him to the rest of the court was understated, generating little response except from Prince Chao. The Prince queried him about governance practices in other regions, but then soon dismissed him. Soon after, in the autumn of that year, the King and Prince Chao decided that in keeping with their continuing desire to re-establish a credible Royal presence, they would resurrect the Royal hunt in all its grandeur. For generations it had been an event largely confined to members of the Royal Family and its entourage, lacking the scale and pomp of their ancestors' times. Once, when the Zhou dynasty stood for something, the hunt was a vital component of the political and social culture. Royalty and nobility would assert their elite status, the hunts doubling in function as inspection tours of not only the military, but of the entire countryside.

Archive records and some old timers recalled how rulers used it to demonstrate their heavenly dominion over the natural world. Kings from all lands would exchange cheetahs, elephants and exotic birds as diplomatic gifts and as tools. Elite hunting cultures transcended political allegiances. The hunt was an opportunity for the court to ostentatiously display its grandeur while entertaining guests and dignitaries, as well as to bestow favors on subjects.

But I also believe these hunts were crude attempts to master Nature. There are few things more contemptuous of the rhythms of the world than to hunt wild beasts for the purposes of sport, amusement and patronage. The naiveté that humans could wantonly master Nature is a mistake I knew would someday be regretted. How I abhorred the very notion. So when the King ordered his entire Palace to accompany the hunt with no aim other than to engorge the appearance of his splendor, I wished nothing more than to withdraw into my own thoughts. But Prince Meng urged me to come and I could refuse him nothing, nor would I. As a Prince, he was expected to spearhead one of the competing formations of the hunt and requested my moral support.

Despite the dire state of the treasury's coffers, the court spared no expense and showed little fiscal restraint. The Royal kitchens set up temporary quarters on the edge of the hunting grounds. Hundreds of slaves and servants were seconded to supplement the existing Royal staff. Huge numbers of pigs, ducks, swans, goats and cows were slaughtered for the occasion. Fearing a paucity of nobility in the entourage, bribes, gifts, promises and women were pledged to all who attended. It appeared to work. Dozens of nobles and diplomats of all ranks and their followers presented themselves to the King as he left through the south gate.

The hunting grounds stood ten *li* up river from Chengzhou. A prized wild buck had been captured and released within a controlled perimeter. To prevent the beast from escaping, a battalion of soldiers surrounded it on three sides, leaving the hunters to approach from the river. To call it a hunt would be akin to calling a farming implement a sword. It was more of an amusement, a ritual slaughter, than anything else.

The early morning commenced as if the Sun God, as Yi Ban would say, had personally blessed the event. An unseasonal warmth and stillness filled the air, adding a festive atmosphere to the Royal procession. The Guardsmen battalion and guests left Chengzhou in the morning after a brief dawn ceremony at the temple. From my carriage, I could see flocks of birds flying away in haste, as though their instincts foretold of a darkness to come. It took until noon for the procession to thread its way to the hunting grounds.

Prince Chao sat high atop his prized mount Leishan, named after the Thunder God. The beast was a rare beauty with a long arched neck, high tail carriage and finely chiseled bone structure. Having descended from a powerful quarter horse smuggled at great cost from the Kingdom of Ferghana well beyond the barbarians and across the desert sea, Leishan was the last of its kind in Zhou.

Prince Chao joked with his contingent. He was clearly in his element, barely able to contain his enthusiasm. He led one of many groups of hunters and servants. Several other nobles including a Duke from Jin were amongst the regal competition. Prince Meng had few hunting companions so he filled out his group with some of General Wu's aides. Together they rode up to the starting position. His participation was likely aimed at appeasing the King, as I knew the Prince enjoyed hunts and military exercises with the same enthusiasm as his brother did poetry recitals. Since the misfortunes borne during the floods, he had become more involved in affairs of the state and rituals of his station. But I sensed a subtle detachment which I had initially attributed to his brother upstaging him during the relief efforts. Upon reflection, I now better understand his mood and the events that transpired.

There must have been a thousand guests and servants. They

huddled within and around numerous tents, all of which circled the enormous Royal tent, creating a makeshift city with guests entertained by magicians, acrobats and musicians. By then the wind had shifted, and thick clouds swirled in our direction. The Royal banners and flags flew straight. Extra servants were assigned to hold the anchor ropes of our tents.

No one could have known that the soft rain that began to fall portended a much darker day. The King sat crossed-legged on a portable platform as servants scurried about filling his wine vessel and lining up platters of food. He looked down at his subjects with the most jovial façade I had ever seen him display in public. It was the most casual and informal gathering of a Royal I'd ever witnessed. Most of the guests showed little restraint with the Royal feast, wantonly partaking of the free-flowing wine. The King was carried out of his tent in his palanquin to another platform in front of the hunting parties. He struggled to stand as he toasted the hunters and promised a hundred bronze pieces to whomever returned with the head of the beast. The moment the King dropped his hand signifying the start of the hunt, the competitors were off, with Prince Chao and his party at the forefront. As the hunters charged away, clouds black as soot and as thick as porridge whirled towards us, and heaven began releasing a steady drizzle.

The hunters had been told the buck had been funneled into a narrow corridor. However, now there was a report that indicated it had broken clear and had last been seen running north in the direction of the river. A later reported sighting placed the deer ten *li* west of the feast, in the deepest part of the forest. Then a contrary rumor had the buck grazing in a meadow to the south. The fearlessness of the buck and the uncertainty of its whereabouts fueled the hunters' excitement. They galloped in all directions. Prince Chao yanked his reins westward. His entourage and even the most skilled of his horsemen struggled through the drizzle to keep up with him and his steed, Leishan. Yet surprisingly, Prince Meng and his party were never far behind.

The rain intensified. Fine drops became a blanket of showers, and the orgy of feasting and merriment soon became a wind and rain drenched debacle. Thunder and lightning erupted from the skies. Dancers and musicians fell completely out of rhythm, unable to hear one another through the thunder claps and the boisterousness of the guests. Gusts ballooned the tents, then uprooted them. Fire pits with half-cooked pigs were doused. Then the guests scrambled for whatever shelter still remained intact. Many attempted to leave and were immediately ensnarled in an immovable crush of carriages and litters.

Many hunters were lost in the diminishing light of the forest, though some had returned to the chaos of the scattering feast. Prince Chao paid no heed to the deteriorating weather. His entourage would later say the more challenging the hunt, the more focused and determined he became. Other hunters marveled that, although he was born the son of a God on Earth, he had the blood of a hunter and the grit of a warrior. I would learn later from one of his servants that he charged with Leishan deep into the forest, first in one direction, then another. Most of his entourage lost sight of him. The din of the rain and thunder would be to the advantage of the prey, but a seasoned hunter could also make use of it. Soon, Prince Chao had the buck in his sights, barely ten *zhang* away, beneath a canopy of trees where it had found shelter.

Oblivious to the pelting rain and crashing thunder, the Prince transferred the reins to his teeth, reached for his bow and then notched his arrow. His fingers curled around his bowstring and arrow. He drew the bow and aimed. As he was about to release it, an arrow flew by him, grazing Leishan's ear and coming to a rest in a tree trunk just a *zhang* away. Spooked, Leishan reared onto its hind legs and bucked. The Prince had no time to recover and was thrown hard, landing on his head and shoulder. He lay completely motionless. An attendant came to his aid. One of his swifter companions jumped off his horse and gathered up the Prince, and as he cradled his master's limp body, Prince Meng came crashing through the forest. The elder Prince's chest heaved, his eyes bulged, a look of bronze determination in them as he gazed down at his fallen brother. Dangling from his hand was his Royal bow.

Led by Major Huang, Prince Chao was carried out of the forest by a litter of Royal Guardsmen. They returned to the remnants of the feast, which had disintegrated into absolute disorder. I heard the Major's report, which emphasized the accidental nature of Prince Meng's stray arrow. Despite this, the King upon seeing his breathing but unmoving younger Prince, ordered the Prince's attendants to be flogged and Leishan destroyed.

For five days and five nights, Prince Chao remained in darkness. His attendants and Prince Meng took turns at his brother's side, as did the Queen. Her Royal Highness came in frequently and re-did Prince Chao's attire, sometimes even applying make-up as though he were a doll. But the strained expression on her face suggested she was more aware of the situation than her usual madness would suggest. The Son of Heaven could not or would not bear the pain of seeing his son on the edge of death. He made no attempt to hide his grief. I heard stories of wine-fueled rages at his ministers and at Prince Meng. He had his most loyal servants flogged for no reason. He likely heard the whispers—that the elder Prince had seen an opportune moment to eliminate his rival for the throne, and that his arrow had just missed its intended target. As crude and cumbersome as such a plot might have been, many believed there was no better reason for the elder Prince's actions on the hunt.

With only his personal attendants in tow, the King appeared unexpectedly one day while I attended to Prince Meng in his office. The King's face was gaunt and his eyes weary as though he hadn't slept in days. His speech was slurred but remained cutting.

"Until a few days ago your lack of skills with the bow would have merited sentry duty by the latrines. Does the heir now believe he has demonstrated abilities worthy of an heir or a conspirator?"

Prince Meng remained silent, eyes fixed to the ground.

"Speak, or is an arrow behind the back the only courage you can muster?"

"Heavenly Father, if I had but half the courage of my ailing brother…"

"Let alone the Son of Heaven, you could never be half the man he reveals himself to be even now as he fights for his Royal life. If duty and tradition did not dictate my actions, it would be obvious who would succeed me. Heaven help us all if a poet dreamer inherits the throne."

Prince Meng's face reddened. "I am innocent of misdeeds. I beg you to see this. My wish is to serve Zhou and my Heavenly Father however he sees best. My own aspirations are not worthy of your attention."

"Indeed they are not. There is little about you that is worthy of my consideration. If you are fortunate, your mother in her madness still possesses a modicum of thought for you. But this would only further reveal the extent of her insanity." The King continued his diatribe in this vein until finally he ran out of breath. As he departed, Prince Meng's sloping shoulders had collapsed even further.

"No amount of abuse is worth the throne," he muttered. "I

wish another errant arrow had somehow found its way to me."

On the sixth morning, drenched in perspiration and wearing a haggard expression on his face, Prince Chao parted his dry lips and opened his eyes. He asked for water and proceeded to drink as though he'd been parched for days, which indeed he had. He grimaced as he complained of pounding pains in his head, a shoulder and arm he could scarcely move, and a leg that had twisted grotesquely.

When asked if he remembered anything, he shook his head, then asked, "Are we under attack? Have my would-be assassins been captured?"

He listened attentively to his attendants' report of that day. He displayed neither emotion nor bitterness when told of the accident and who was involved. The Queen was the first of the Royal Family to greet him. Even through the thick layers of face paint, she appeared weary and confused, almost as if she had been crying. But soon she was back to her usual self. "Would my Prince care to see a new dance? Or would he prefer a song?" she asked with a giggle.

Before Prince Chao could answer, the King entered. He towered over his ailing son, barely containing his relief.

"The gods smile on Zhou and they send a miracle to me," he declared. "Your Royal Father is most pleased. Zhou remains in good hands and continues to have a warrior Prince."

He proclaimed that offerings to the temple would be made to Shennong, the God of Medicine. He offered to feed one hundred peasant families and free twenty prisoners. Wine flowed freely within the Celestial Hall, and the King prodded the rest of the court to drink and celebrate with him. He even invited the ambassador from Chu to join in the festivities.

The King's relief and gratitude to the gods was boundless. To Prince Chao, he gave one hundred bronze pieces, a stable of horses and three of his newest handpicked maidens. The Prince barely acknowledged the offerings. But his convalescence was swift. Within a month he was on his feet, though his arm remained in a sling and he moved without his usual assuredness. During this time he declined repeated requests from Prince Meng for an audience, a rebuff to the elder Prince that meant a tremendous loss of face. But he did have private meetings with selected generals, ministers, diplomats and scholars. I heard rumors that Confucius was among them. That Confucius would receive such access to the Prince was intriguing. We continued to exchange our views on a range of matters, but he never once mentioned any audiences with Prince Chao.

I had hoped Prince Chao would have returned with a newfound temperateness, perhaps a respect for the frailty and delicate balance of life. Thus, when Prince Meng was finally granted an audience with his brother, I was curious as to what his reception would be. Having long since won Prince Meng's confidence, I was permitted to accompany him, along with Yi Ban.

As we entered Prince Chao's Hall, we were surprised to find the King was also there, sitting comfortably beside him. After the usual formal greetings and felicitations, Prince Chao held little back.

"So, dear brother Prince Meng, have you come to offer blessings at my recovery, or to apologize that your marksmanship was so sadly but predictably found wanting?"

The King interceded. "Chao, we have spoken of this. Today is a joyous occasion. My Princes are together again. It is time to place our differences to one side."

Prince Meng swallowed a heavy sigh. "I agree, Heavenly Father, I too do not wish to quarrel. My brother mistakes my position. The crown is not all that is of value in this world. I am the elder and the heir to the throne, so why would I harbor any other aspirations other than what my birthright has already decreed? Why would I find joy in seeing blood spilled, especially blood so close to my own?"

"Your smug, self-righteous morality tires me more than my wounds," Prince Chao replied. "If you truly have only the most noble of intentions and have little appetite for the throne, why do you not renounce your birthright here and now?"

Prince Meng hesitated. "It is not for me to re-write history and tradition."

Prince Chao laughed. "Ah, how convenient it is to embrace tradition now. But I am not without regard for the dictates put forth by our ancestors. In fact, I have become quite familiar with them through the words of Confucius."

"Confucius is just one of many toadies of the court who need to be reminded of who it is they serve," Prince Meng responded.

"Perhaps you'd care to do so yourself?" Prince Chao beckoned to a darkened corner, from which Confucius emerged, bowing three times in supplication to Prince Meng. Somehow I felt I had been outflanked without even knowing I was in competition for the ears and eyes of the court. Without a formal decree, Prince Meng had made me a de facto advisor and included me in discussions where trusted aides were required. Yet I was disappointed to see that Confucius had achieved a similar status with the other Prince in such a short amount of time. My thoughts began to simmer upon hearing the Prince lavish praise on Confucius.

"Confucius weaves a fabric that binds society. He espouses ideas that are not dismissive of a strong monarchy, unlike your archivist. I suggest you heed his words," Prince Chao said.

Prince Meng glared at Confucius, who remained prostrate on the floor in supplication. "Those who would suggest followers of the Way lack respect towards their masters are themselves lacking in respect," he said. "Does the wandering visitor to our court suggest that the Royal Archivist is not a man of peace and deference? Speak, visitor."

Confucius replied. "Your Highness, I make no suggestion that the Royal Archivist is anything other than a man of peace. That would be the furthest notion from the truth. But peace cannot come without order, and order cannot come without clear social and political roles. Let the ruler be a ruler and the subject a subject. The Son Of Heaven has a divine right to rule, yet for him to rule effectively his virtue must be reflected in all around him."

"Well spoken, scholar," the King called out. "It is time for us to move in a different direction. As the cornerstones of Zhou, I expect you two to weigh some of this scholar's views."

"Indeed," Prince Chao agreed, "Confucius is a modern man. He has seen much of the world, and he confirms what our diplomats and spies tell us. It is changing rapidly." He paused. "Those states around us that have embraced modernity have not gone unrewarded. They now have standing armies and they control their own border regions not with the family relationships but through models of governance founded on functioning administrative units. They possess none of these bloated bureaucracies populated with minions as ministers." Prince Chao glared at Yi Ban then continued. "Instead, officials of merit all report to their king. Laws, measurements, farming—all things have been reorganized in line with idea that the entire land exists to serve the wishes of the king. In return, the king is just and leads by example, ruling with wisdom, authority and morality. All those of noble stock will follow his example, as will the peasantry. Thus social order re-binds the world. That is 'the way' that Zhou also will be. That is the future. That is order, my dear brother. We must adapt if Zhou is to re-claim its place in this world. You may choose to join me on this course, or you may flutter in the wind like soiled linen. Are you prepared for this, dear brother?"

Prince Meng waited but a moment to respond. Then he turned to the King.

"Heavenly Father, perhaps my brother's injuries have affected his thinking. This quest for order is no different from a permanent state of fear and perpetual war, albeit with more efficiency. How this will help to sow morality among the people is incomprehensible to me. Prince Chao's proposal would encourage people to take a perfidious course towards your followers and those with Royal blood. He proposes meritocracy. Is he saying that faithful ministers and followers such as Yi Ban lack competence and are mere sycophants? They are not only loyal subjects, but are also of Royal blood. It is not order that he speaks of, but privilege for a few, servitude for most and chaos for all. This is absurd. I will not be a party to it."

"This is an irreversible course, dear brother," Prince Chao said. "The Son of Heaven can see beyond the horizon. He and I are not without our own philosophical beliefs. I can quote not only Confucius, but also General Sun Wu's book on military tactics, although it is more about spying and deception than war... most useful. You see, we are not naïve idealists such as yourself. Our Heavenly Father sees this and he has empowered me to review all aspects of governance. He listened favorably to my suggestion of retaining a standing army, of proper taxation, of standardization of all elements of commerce and trade and the construction of schools of enlightenment. With these, all lands and regions will be bound not only by blood, but in every aspect of life. In short, we will not simply join the technological revolution, we will overtake it, and in time we will re-unite the empire."

Prince Meng's voice took an uncharacteristically menacing tone. "This is not for you alone to decide."

"Did you not hear me? Our Heavenly Father already has." Prince Chao sighed.

The King made no move to repudiate this statement but shifted uncomfortably as though he realized he had said too much and no longer wished to be present.

"How can you can speak of virtue whilst ignoring me, the future King? How can you expect to pursue this course once I am on the throne? Or does my dear brother believe the throne will be his? Do not provoke me, or..."

"Or you'll hone your archery skills and not miss again?" Prince Chao shot back.

"Enough!" The King commanded.

Prince Meng was silent. Neither Confucius nor I dared to break the tension.

"Do not think, Prince Meng, that you alone stand for virtue and compassion," Prince Chao said, then paused to take a breath. "A strong dynasty means a strong nation, and a contented people with full bellies. We cannot achieve this standing still whilst others ride in circles around us. We must move forward. In time you will see this, regardless of who sits on the throne."

Prince Meng stormed out of Prince Chao's Hall, leaving Yi Ban and I struggling to keep up. The younger Prince had out-maneuvered his elder brother. The hunting incident had swung the King's ear firmly in his direction. And in many respects, Prince Chao spoke correctly. The world had indeed been evolving as Zhou stood by. For generations, the world had only known war, but now the scale and scope of the conflicts had mushroomed. Kingdoms were learning better how to wage it. It had become a conduit for change. Regional lords needed ever-more skilled, literate officials and teachers, the recruitment of whom was based on merit rather than on blood and favors received. Also, commerce was being stimulated through the introduction of coinage and technological improvements. New metals were even replacing bronze, making possible the forging of new weapons. In essence, man was becoming better and more efficient at conducting war.

These advances also benefited society in other ways. The manufacture of sturdier farm implements led to higher yields. My father's methods from forty years ago were no longer new and had been copied widely. Public works on a grand scale meant the digging of canals to move troops and supplies quickly. But they also resulted in better flood control. Enormous walls were being built around other cities and towns, just like the capital's, as well as along broad stretches of the northern frontier.

Confucius seized the moment and capitalized on it. In fact, he likely had a hand in steering the tides of change, as his musings found an eager ear in the younger Prince. I found it objectionable that Confucius had used his position to exacerbate the conflict between the Royals and wanted to tell him so. I arranged a meeting with him at my favorite inn outside the city on the Luo River. It had been many months since I had had an opportunity to relish its quiet surroundings and savor its porridge. The inn was as removed from the Palace as Confucius' ideas were from the daily conversations of the common people. I wanted Confucius to see this.

Yet as I climbed the hill towards the inn, a completely unexpected scene greeted me. A high brick wall had replaced the crumbling low stone wall and the roof of the structure was now peaked with new clay tiles. A large, unmarked door was the only access. I thought I had misjudged my bearings until a guard, the former assistant innkeeper, cracked opened the door. Because I was wearing my work robes, he didn't recognize me at first, but when he did, he flung open the door and greeted me like an old friend. He explained how the inn had been taken over some months ago by General Wu and turned into a bawdy house. I was stunned and speechless as he led me through a haze of incense smoke and a cacophony of drunken laughter and gambling to a small table against a wall where once an open panorama of the river had been framed for customers. A woman in a fine silk gown led a procession of luxuriously dressed young women around the tables. She knew every patron in the room and joked with them like old friends. When they arrived at my table the woman welcomed me with a flourish then offered a choice of any of the women behind her. Stunned, I declined and instead asked for snacks and drinks. She gave me a puzzled look, then smiled and suggested that she also had some precious young men who would soon be available. I re-stated my request for a snack and drink which dampened her smile. She and the young women quickly moved on.

At last Confucius arrived. I studied him as he was escorted to my table. He nodded greetings to several patrons. He appeared more at ease with the establishment than I, and he made no reference to it being a brothel.

We greeted each other with our customary layers of salutations: as friends, as highly-regarded colleagues, fellow members of the intelligentsia, even minor nobility. After some yellow wine and honey cake, I could hold back no longer. I congratulated him on his position within Prince Chao's circle, but expressed disappointment at his not sharing this with me earlier.

"Honorable Lao Tzu, Prince Chao scarcely gave me a moment to catch my breath. The accident has given him the energy and will of a thousand horses."

"A thousand wild horses," I snapped back.

Confucius looked around to ensure no one was within earshot.

"Discretion, Master Scholar. Even here the eyes and ears of

the Palace roam. I feel you may have misunderstood Prince Chao. His desire to seek a path ahead is noble and enlightened."

Prince Meng's frustrations were reflected within me and I could not hold back.

"I see now how dangerous is this path, wholly unnatural and unintuitive to the course of man. You seek order through strict regimes, you foster division where none should exist, you encourage the anointment of privilege under the guise of virtue, as though power and position are incorruptible."

Confucius was momentarily taken aback, but he quickly recovered and revealed no loss of face. He even cracked a slight smile.

"Honorable Lao Tzu, you cannot deny that man is divided so many ways already. This is a given. One of these divisions is virtue. I see that perhaps you under-value virtue and forget the advancement and security that our ancestors gave us. Virtue means more to man than either water or fire. I have seen men die from treading on water and fire, but I have never seen a man die from treading the course of virtue. Surely you cannot find offense in loyalty, reciprocity, dutifulness, filial and fraternal affection, courtesy and good faith?"

"I harbor no qualms about virtue or any of those other attributes. It is rather the unnatural and aberrant ways in which you seek to sow them. You assume that virtue is the purview of nobility, that it is an unnatural creation that can be bought, molded and re-sold as mortar to bind society. But these are not bricks to build for men, but to imprison them."

Confucius' smile faded. "Perhaps Honorable Lao Tzu finds comfort in the primitive ways of men. Perhaps you see beauty in endless wars and conflicts, in humans in conflict, in corruption and malevolence. If this is your way, then there are many barbarians beyond our realm amongst whom you may find followers.

But this is not the way of the world here, and it is not the wish of the Son of Heaven and Prince Chao to continue in such a way."

"My dear Confucius, I once believed that heaven saw through the eyes of men. It heard through the ears of men, and that it inevitably sent down calamities, but that there was always hope of weathering them. But when men bring misfortune upon themselves, there is no hope of escape. I now know that the fate of man rests with the impartiality of the Way. Your ideas, however, deny man's ability to overcome unnatural barriers."

Confucius remained still.

"I fear, Confucius, that your position is much removed from the people. Otherwise you would see that when people have nothing to lose, uprisings will result. Do not take away their land or their livelihood. If their burden is not heavy, they will not shirk it. Scholars such as we must maintain ourselves without accepting tribute, profit or personal glory. We must not forget that it is the interests of the ordinary people that are paramount."

Confucius shook his head and sighed, as though he had just heard the protestations of a child. I could see that further discussion was futile.

More wine and honey cakes arrived. I had no stomach for food but Confucius ate as though a famine was approaching. The manner in which he so ardently and casually devoured his food stirred my discontent even further. Then I remembered a saying I had heard from some soldiers: 'It is easier to lose a yard than take an inch. In this manner one may deploy troops without marshaling them, bring weapons to bear without exposing them, engage the foe without invading them, and exhaust their strength without fighting them. There is no worse disaster than misunderstanding your adversary. To do so endangers all.'

I had miscalculated Confucius and his intentions. Years of contemplation had not prepared me for this, and suddenly I felt very vulnerable. For the first time, my standing in court mattered to me, and I feared it was slipping. I knew I had to arm myself with a new approach to tactics.

I commended Confucius on his thoughts and partook of the lavish treats before me.

14

Royal Defilement

"Captain Yin, Captain Yin!" A corporal rushed into the shelter, interrupting Lao Tzu's story.

"What is it?" The Captain scrutinized the soldier, who was one of the new recruits who often praised Lieutenant Zhang to his face, but demeaned him when he was not present.

"It is Lieutenant Zhang, sir. He took a mount, one of our stronger ones. He aims to meet with the General as soon as possible." "When did he leave?" the Captain asked.

"At mid-day, sir."

"And you waited until now to report?"

The corporal struggled for words. Then the scribe rescued him.

"It's about time someone around here showed some sense. These ramblings are completely unbelievable. It's a waste of good ink and tablets." He dropped his brush and looked defiantly at the Captain and Lao Tzu.

The Captain glared at the scribe. "Your presence here is for one purpose alone." He took a step towards the scribe. "Your opinion has not been requested. Pick up your brush."

The scribe hesitated for a second, then complied.

"Master Scholar, please do not delay," the Captain said to Lao Tzu. "I suspect the Lieutenant may find a sympathetic ear with the General. Our time may be limited. I implore you to continue with your story. But first, tell me how it is you are able to account for events and details for which you could not have been present."

Lao Tzu grinned. "Your query is reasonable, but betrays impatience. The conclusion of my story will reveal all. But I can tell you those parts of the story where I was not present were reliably conveyed to me by those who were. Shall I continue with my ramblings?"

He looked at the Captain and then the scribe.

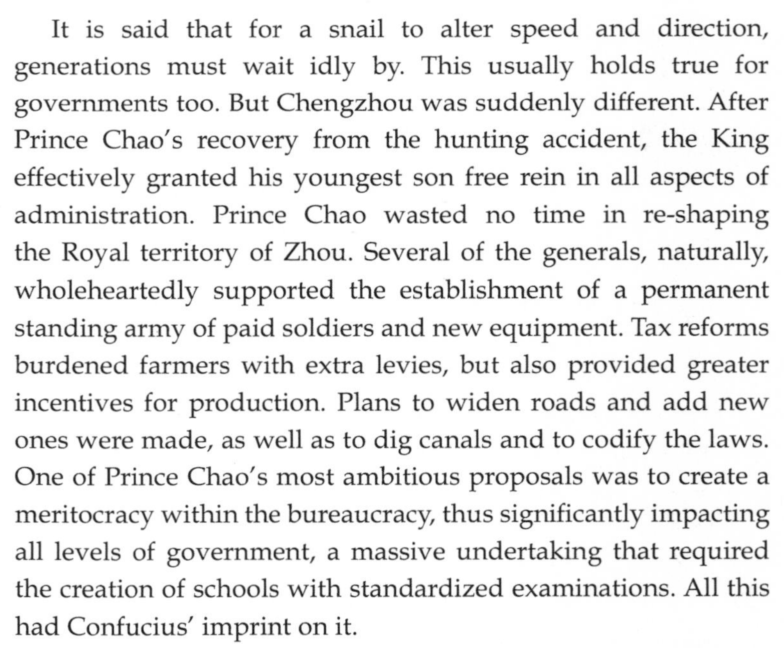

It is said that for a snail to alter speed and direction, generations must wait idly by. This usually holds true for governments too. But Chengzhou was suddenly different. After Prince Chao's recovery from the hunting accident, the King effectively granted his youngest son free rein in all aspects of administration. Prince Chao wasted no time in re-shaping the Royal territory of Zhou. Several of the generals, naturally, wholeheartedly supported the establishment of a permanent standing army of paid soldiers and new equipment. Tax reforms burdened farmers with extra levies, but also provided greater incentives for production. Plans to widen roads and add new ones were made, as well as to dig canals and to codify the laws. One of Prince Chao's most ambitious proposals was to create a meritocracy within the bureaucracy, thus significantly impacting all levels of government, a massive undertaking that required the creation of schools with standardized examinations. All this had Confucius' imprint on it.

All these and many more changes were meant to add to the Royal coffers and leapfrog us into modernity. It was impossible to escape the breadth of the changes, not even within the Archives. I wondered how Zhou would sustain this pace, and how it would be paid for.

During these dizzying times I once encountered the servant girl Mei just outside the Palace walls. She recognized me immediately and bowed.

"Ah, Lord Lao Tzu, the man with compassion for a fortress," she said. "We meet once more. I have heard much of you since we last met, and have seen the fondness that Prince Meng has for you, my Lord."

I motioned her to rise. She was wearing a simple silk robe fashioned with a pattern of stitched chrysanthemums. Yet she carried herself with a grace and dignity untainted by the false perfection of one so close to nobility and privilege. With a discrete but mindful gaze and an airy yet attentive posture, she looked very much like the heroine that all classes and manner of men would gladly claim. Together we walked towards the Central Square.

"I see Mei, that you continue to wander outside the Palace without an escort, even though your garments now are a step above that of a kitchen thief. And that jade hairpin has Royal markings on it."

She smiled. "There was a time that I would have quickly sold such a luxury. This hairpin alone would feed my family and buy seed for the next five seasons."

"But now we are at a different station in our lives. You have done well in a short time, progressing from slave to maiden to one of the Son of Heaven's favorites. I have observed you accompanying him on many occasions."

She glanced at me, betraying not a hint of satisfaction or smugness. It was more a puzzled look that I would state the obvious. The King's established reputation for sexual avarice didn't reconcile with my first image of Mei. Viewing her as such still seemed peculiar. She seemed to read my thoughts, thus confirming my initial impressions of her intelligence.

"You stare at me, scholar, as though I am still that farm girl or kitchen hand, lost in a Palace world that sullies all. It would be well within reason to think so, given where I sleep in the Palace. But as you know, my Lord, there are many legends, myths and secrets within the Palace walls."

She looked around then whispered, "One rumor is the King's voracious love of women. It is true that he jealously protects his women, but his insatiable appetite is a myth. His pleasures with women are not really carnal. And one secret is his, how shall I say it… loss of authority. I believe it has been some time since he has fulfilled his full manhood. I have been told how he treats women with scorn and contempt, rejecting all but a few whose presence he values."

I interrupted her. "This is what many would call idle gossip, and it is dangerous. You should learn discretion, my child."

"That goes without saying, my Lord. Yet much goes on within the palace, much of it unintended for commoners such as myself. Still it would be beneficial to have a trusted and sympathetic ear to guide me."

"Like the Black Serpent who was instrumental in you feeding your family?"

She nodded.

"Was his identity ever revealed to you?"

"Unfortunately not. He was a life-saver when we needed him. I wish I could have thanked him. There are so few one can trust within the Palace."

We each took a nonchalant but careful look at our surroundings.

"Is it necessary for me to once again prove my discretion?" I asked her.

She shook her head. "It is not the Son of Heaven who worries me the most, it is that hot-headed Prince. He has many faces, particularly with women about."

"What do you mean?"

"He presents himself with such chivalry and grace in the court. Yet I suspect there is much beneath that veneer, things untoward ready to happen. Are you surprised, my Lord?"

"Not entirely, though I am curious to know how you came to your understanding."

"Call it a woman's second sight if you will. Since that hunting accident, a foul mood has enveloped him."

I was not surprised to hear this, although I had hoped Prince Chao would heal into a different man. We continued walking through the crowded streets. She told me her position in the Palace had allowed her to support her parents, though it was not sufficient for them to stop working the farm. Before the spring floods, they had had some success with a new rotation of different crops and some new tools, for which she thanked me. But if it was not for her, their survival would be in question. She no longer had to resort to stealing kitchen stock and sneaking it back to them. Now she had Royal Blessing to gift them with supplies, seeds and food.

As we approached Wai Chao Square, a column of Royal Guardsmen came charging down the street, knocking over a fruit vendor's cart and creating a maelstrom of people lunging for the scattering bounty. A Royal Litter and its escort followed. The crowd lowered themselves in supplication. I caught a glimpse of Prince Meng as the carriage passed. He peered out from behind a curtain and saw Mei with me, then gave me an anxious look that suggested that my ear was required.

Mei recognized one of the Guardsmen and asked him why

the litter moved with such haste and urgency. Apparently it was because the Royal Tombs in the northern frontier had been plundered. For the King, nothing more sacred could have been violated, no family humiliation greater. The shame would be on him and he would no doubt be furious. Mei bid me farewell, explaining that when the King was in a foul mood, one did not want to be unavailable to either soothe his anger or absorb his blows. Once he left his formal proceedings, it was his concubines he valued above everything but his own position.

Indeed, when I joined Prince Meng at the Palace, the King was in a rage, sending servants scattering to summon his entire court and then the Chu Ambassador. Confucius stood among Prince Chao's ministers. We had spoken little over the months since our discussion at the inn. He had clearly been busy. But if the truth were to be known, I had been avoiding him, as deep down I knew he had bested me.

The Ambassador of Chu entered the Celestial Hall with all the customary kowtowing and greetings. He appeared oblivious to the tension. There was even a swagger to his gait.

"Son of Heaven," the Ambassador bowed and prostrated himself. "The Royal Tombs lie only two days ride from the closest reaches of the barbarians. Safeguarding them required battalions of heavily-armed soldiers, most of whom normally sit idle. It is a heavy investment of resources for such a task. Thus the garrison was halved and deployed to a more strategic location where they would be better utilized to guard the trade routes that friends of the Royal Court have imperiled."

The King began to speak, but a coughing fit overtook him. Finally it subsided and he started again slowly, though he was clearly seething with anger.

"You speak of strategy, but what of duty? What of obligation? It is a task and responsibility which Chu agreed to uphold in return for trading privileges. You have failed."

"The Son of Heaven is correct, an understanding was in place. Even while the Son of Heaven's emissaries promoted cultural and scientific exchanges and brokered a common trade strategy for all, the Son of Heaven's troops, few as they are, have been re-armed and have been on a war footing for some time. Why? When Zhou had secret meetings with Qin, Jin, Zheng, Chen and those barbarian Wu for the purpose of surrounding Chu, it changed the spirit of our understanding. I trust the Son of Heaven would not attempt to deny this. Nor would I imagine that the Son of Heaven would think we were unaware of this. The garrison that was halved was re-deployed to face an incursion of mysterious marauders who destroyed numerous Chu villages and a district capital. We lost lives, the Son of Heaven lost valued treasures. However it is not through Chu's doing that the tombs were plundered."

Prince Chao challenged the Ambassador. "We have no quarrel with Chu but not all in this world are pleased with it. You have no proof of any such alliances. Zhou is the rightful throne, the spiritual centre of the world. Why would we endanger this standing by fomenting a war?"

The Ambassador responded immediately. "That is not for me to answer, for there can be no logic to such an undertaking. Such provocation comes at a cost. Chu troops have moved to control the eastern bend of the Yellow River, thus assuring safe passage for the trading of goods. No other kingdom can provide such security. And it appears the marauders who attacked us were not bandits at all. Their weaponry and skill suggest they were well-trained soldiers. They appeared to be from various combined territories. Nevertheless, each and every invader was captured, and each one fouled himself as he was beheaded. This took place deep within Qin territory, which we easily penetrated to ferret out those raiders. The Son of Heaven must know it is a dangerous game that is being played. Shall we continue?"

The Yellow River bend was a mere five days' ride from Chengzhou and on the door step of Zhou's allies, the Jin and Qin. It was a bold, audacious move by Chu. The Royal Court was silent until Prince Meng spoke.

"It is most regrettable that our Royal Tombs have become a feasting ground for the most depraved of intentions. Yet Nature says only a few words: high winds do not last long, nor does heavy rain. If Nature's words do not last, why should those of man? What is important is that trust is not lost. Chu loses lives. Qin suffers. Our Tombs are desecrated. But Zhou will endure. There are no victors in such squabbles. Ambassador, there is little cause for anyone to rejoice at these developments, would you not agree?"

Prince Meng's remarks reflected an emerging wisdom and tact. I knew he had the ability, and now he was showing the confidence to use it. I could not have been prouder had I been his father.

"The heir speaks with wisdom beyond his years," the Ambassador said, smiling and nodding, a clear salvo at Prince Chao. Then he continued, "It is refreshing to deal with minds that are not only agreeable, but also able to see beyond their immediate horizon. Perhaps it might be of benefit to all if all future diplomatic maneuvers were framed with such sensibility. And any dalliances with other kingdoms that occur should be far more restrained."

With little more to say, and with the King at a loss for words, the Ambassador was dismissed.

"The fools!" the King spat out. "They moved too quickly, and now our ancestors are nothing more than overturned rubble."

Prince Chao nodded. "Our allies were supposed to send a

small band of troops posing as bandits to probe Chu's reactions. Chu's response suggests one of two things. One, our troops moved too hastily and too deep. Two, Chu's reaction was swift and calculated because there is a spy amongst us."

Several ministers seized the opportunity and accused others of running weak and disloyal departments. One general denounced another for failing to train his troops properly. General Wu promised to ferret out anyone disloyal and personally behead them. The Minister of War suggested a doubling of the guards and a strict search of all those entering and leaving Chengzhou. Finally the King raised a hand, silencing the chatter. He was about to speak when Prince Meng interrupted him.

"Heavenly Father, do you mean that this entire incident was a game? Our Tombs were laid to waste in order to test Chu's reaction? Why was I not made aware of this?"

The elder Prince could barely conceal his anger.

The King snarled back at him. "Prince Meng, you can hardly pretend to be interested in the minutiae of governance. It is not for you to judge our decisions."

A composed Prince Chao joined in. "Our Heavenly Father speaks from wisdom. It is not your place to pronounce, Prince Meng. The effect of such actions were unanticipated. We must investigate the possibility of there being a spy among us."

Prince Meng could restrain himself no longer. "We have spoken of forging new and progressive links in all the lands. We are supposed to be modernizing with a view to binding the territories. And now we have lost face. We stand on a war footing after having been shown to have secret alliances with other territories. Chu flies like a vulture hovering over a wounded rabbit and you call this minutia? Thanks to such foolishness, am I to inherit a throne that is no more than a bedpan to Chu?"

A silence enveloped the hall. Nobody stirred. A moment

before, Prince Meng had demonstrated diplomacy and maturity, and now he was showing a biting edge. I had never heard Prince Meng more lacking in composure with the King.

At first the King sat stunned, then he stood and let the full weight of his anger explode.

"If you could extract yourself from your useless books and pitiful little birds for just an instant you would see there is a real world beyond your walls. This world requires a ruler, a ruler with a warrior's will and a tiger's cunning, not to mention a realistic view of how the world works. Are your precious little fish teaching you the ways of the sword? Do the branches of your garden instill gallantry in your feeble little heart?"

The King's icy gaze cut through Prince Meng and the court. He continued.

"I hear little from my precious scholar prince. Yet now you have the temerity to question your Heavenly Father. You forget your place. And perhaps I should forget yours, for your words and actions do not suggest you are now or will ever be ready to inherit this throne. Zhou deserves better, and as Son of Heaven, I can make this so."

It seemed that the very timbers of the hall shook with the King's tirade. Ministers, generals, guards… all cowered in fear that the King would target them as well. The King looked to continue his tirade when a violent cough overcame him. He stumbled, then motioned for his attendants. They were too slow for his liking so he slapped them. He called for his sedan, which carried him back to his chambers, followed by his entourage.

The hall remained silent, broken only the Queen's whining miniature dogs and her child-like giggles. No one dared to move until the rest of the Royal Family exited the hall: first Prince Meng who looked pale, followed by the Queen, her pets and her maidens, then Prince Chao, looking victorious, followed by

Confucius and the Prince's closest ministers, and Major Huang leading the Royal Guardsmen.

That evening, the sky resembled the darkest ink blot imaginable, blanketing the stars above. Except for the hour drum, the night remained especially still and quiet. I had stayed late in the Archives, partly because I could not remove the bitter taste of foreboding from my mouth. Prince Meng's words in court were poorly chosen and ill-timed. For that, his father had humiliated him. I asked myself, how deep were his wounds? I wanted to offer comfort and solace. I walked through the Celestial Hall. Though the entire building glowed with hundreds of lit candles and torches, it too was eerily silent. I walked briskly towards the inner palace and Prince Meng's quarters, but his attendants said he was not present, nor were his whereabouts known. Having just left the Archives, it occurred to me that the Prince might be in the garden, his one true refuge. But he was not.

Perturbed at not finding him, I intended to leave the Royal residences and the Palace. I doubled back away from the Princes' chambers, through dimly-lit corridors. I heard voices and movement and looked back and I saw two females scurrying in my direction. A troubled-looking Queen and one of her servants were chasing the two Royal shar peis. They were small beasts, yet one of them looked as vicious and savage as any animal I had ever seen. The other dog was bloodied and terrified. It tried to flee from its fierce sibling. I bowed to her Highness as she passed. At first she appeared highly agitated, then her manner suddenly changed. She stopped and spoke to me as though she were suggesting I was no higher than one of her beloved, squirming dogs. But her typical demeanor could not hide the bewildering scene and I wondered what had happened.

Walking further along, I turned a corner only to hear someone panting. I looked around and saw another female figure also hurrying away from the King's residence. She weaved as she walked, stumbled onto the ground, picked herself up, but fell again before finally finding her footing. I stopped, allowing her to reach me.

I recognized her and called out, startling her in the process. "Mei?"

She was about to scream, then recognized me. I grabbed her by the arm. She recoiled.

"No, let me go," she begged me.

"Mei, you must allow me to assist you." I released my grip on her arm, raised her chin and examined her. Her robe had been torn, her face was bruised, her face paint smeared with tears. Blood dripped down her leg onto the porcelain floor.

"Mei, what has happened? You have been harmed. By whom?"

She looked away. "You must not speak of this encounter, not to anyone, not ever."

"But Mei…"

"Promise me!" she said almost breathlessly.

"Before I can give you such assurance, I must know what happened. I must know you will not be further harmed."

She exhaled. "Not here."

She allowed me to escort her to her chambers, avoiding the guards and any attendants. Once we entered her chambers, she began to quietly sob. She said she had been getting ready to leave the King's outer chambers. He had exhausted himself after much drinking and ranting and had finally fallen asleep. She'd heard someone's movements but before she could turn to look, she was knocked down onto her face. A hand muffled her attempt to cry out. With one hand he tore through her robe and under-layers. He forced his member into her from behind as he grunted and cursed her. Those were the only sounds out of his mouth as he pushed himself in and out of her.

When he was done, he collapsed onto her back. Her face never left the floor but she could smell Prince Chao's distinctive jasmine scent, see the fiery red cuffs of the robes he often wore and pointy red silk shoes with rubies hanging off gold tassels. Between gasps for air, he whispered so softly that she could barely hear him. But his message was clear. If she uttered a word of this, he'd see that she and her family would lose their heads.

I poured her some tea and was about to fill her washbasin when Mei's slave entered, startled at seeing any man, let alone myself in the chambers of one of the King's concubines. I implored Mei's attendant to remain and to attend to her mistress. Mei had by then collapsed on the bed, moaning and covering her womanhood.

Stunned, I retreated from Mei's chambers. Prince Chao's reputation for excess was well-known, but to dally with one of the King's mistresses was extreme and risky, even for him. Why would he show such recklessness? By then, I assumed there were few safe secrets within the Palace, except from the blind such as myself. Eventually the King would learn of this. I picked up my pace and once again came upon the Queen. I found her kneeling over her shar peis, now both lying motionless, their open mouths foaming. The Queen looked up at me and told me to be quiet as her dogs were sleeping. Even I knew that such a sleep would never end. They had been poisoned.

It was a disturbing deed, made even more bewildering on the heels of the attack on Mei. I shivered, though sweat was beading off my forehead. An involuntary impulse led me to turn in every direction and scrutinize for any further offenses. But I could not imagine any connection between the two events. The attack on Mei was a brutal act of violence whereas it was possible the death of the dogs had been accidental. Who would want to harm two of the Queen's few pleasures? Perhaps the dogs had ventured somewhere and eaten something foul. I studied the Queen, and felt that on this occasion, her madness was a blessing. I offered to carry one of the dogs for her, but she quietly shooed me away.

I walked back to the Archives with no real sense of purpose. The ink-stained clouds had cleared, revealing a dark sky studded with gleaming stars. But this could not mask the vileness of men below. I stared back at the buildings reserved for the Royals, then towards the Archives in front of me. Both appeared different though neither had changed. Perhaps it was that neither seemed to hold a place in my heart anymore. I was weighed down with thoughts of Mei and worries for Prince Meng.

15

Aura of Doubt

Another bitter winter crawled by, temporarily muting some of the tension of the autumn. It was as though an unstated agreement called for the world to suspend its conflicts. I saw Mei on several occasions following that night, but each time attendants were with her or she was in the presence of the Royals. Always her eyes were in their customary downward position. I felt it was too risky to attempt to reach her for a private meeting. We were unable to converse freely. Yet something about her suggested she had not recovered. There was added weight to her appearance and movements and her manner was stilted, contrasting greatly with the ease and grace I had previously associated with her.

As much as I wanted to avoid Prince Chao, he was everywhere and a part of every aspect of governing. The Prince continued his bureaucratic, social and economic reforms with much vigor. Bureaucrats were already up in arms about their ranks soon opening up to outsiders and commoners. Prince Chao had proposed civil service examinations around an official curriculum based on knowledge of Zhou history, aristocratic etiquette and rituals and rites. These undoubtedly had Confucius' imprints all over them.

I understood the logic behind this, though I found the motivation and practice misguided. The Court wanted scholars and bureaucrats who were objective, competent and who had earned their way into government. Essentially Prince Chao was saying the blood of the aristocracy should not be a guarantor of government positions. As much as I agreed with this, the proposals directed that examinations were open only to those referred by nobles, so the likelihood of a commoner having the knowledge, let alone the connections to such an opportunity, was an illusion.

The King made no apparent attempt to overrule Prince Chao's direction. In fact the King presided over fewer audiences but made it clear to the Court that Prince Chao had the authority in his absence to manage both the more mundane as well as important state matters. When the King did appear, no amount of face paint could hide his pallor and thinning body. He looked as though he slept little, and even in the cool spring air he perspired profusely. I'd heard speculation that the King's drinking had escalated. Meanwhile, Prince Meng had retreated into himself. He had been completely out-maneuvered by his brother and humiliated by his father. His official duties were reduced in number, though the Chu ambassador preferred to deal with him over either Prince Chao or the King.

Prince Meng's visits to the Archives became less frequent and when he did appear, he was not as he had been. He did not lose any of his fine manners or deference towards me, but he lacked the enthusiasm he had once possessed. One early morning on the eve of the lunar new year, I found him waiting for me in the garden hovering over some plants. He looked up and all around before whispering, "The natural world finds its own course, however contemptuous and ignorant others are towards it."

"Does your Highness speak of cultivation?"

"There are natural laws, and the laws of man. Neither should be cast aside."

He noted that the stalks of the rhubarb would soon be ripe. "Yes, a product of nature with multiple dimensions. Bitterly tart if left alone, but heavenly when boiled with something sweet," he said. He then changed the subject again.

"I come with a specific purpose. Your colleague Confucius has made quite a place for himself. He is my brother's favorite scholar, and either a bane or a beacon among many of the gentry. He has the Prince's ear, and much say in the proposed reorganization of our bureaucracy. I trust you too find this objectionable?"

It had been some time since Prince Meng had directly asked my opinion. I hesitated before replying. I wanted to freely join in his frequent denouncements of his brother and I wanted to speak of Prince Chao forcing himself on Mei. Instead, I responded as Prince Meng would have expected me to.

"I foresee a sea of change disguising a mountain of mud. It is naïve to believe that anything as disingenuous a form as strict social expectations will either bind man or build him. Quite the opposite."

The Prince brushed some dirt off his shoes. "It is a strange world we inhabit, where hearts and souls matter less than rules and order."

It pleased me to hear the Prince speak with authority and maturity.

"Your Highness, all things unnatural will find a natural conclusion. Perhaps not now, nor soon, but inevitably so. Until then, living the Way within what we can direct, can be our solace."

"Is that it? You accept the influence of Confucius with little protest. Moreover, is this just? Can you not spare more resolve to preserve all that you have taught? Surely you scholars have more fortitude than that."

It was an unexpected strike, both in tone and content. I could only muster a feeble response. "Your Highness, as the Royal Archivist I do not make policy. I am here to serve you and the Court as it pleases."

He smirked. "My dear Lao Tzu, has the Way ever enjoyed such favor? Has it ever been as close to the centre of the world as it is now? Will your Way ever again have such an opportunity to spread its influence? Once society becomes permanently locked into artificial divisions, can you co-exist with such a new social order?"

"Your Highness, the path I follow works harmoniously according to its own course. When someone exerts their will against the world, they disrupt that harmony. The Way does not identify the person's will as the root problem. Rather, it asserts that he must place his will in harmony with the natural universe."

"Yes, yes. Action without action, empty our minds of bodily awareness and thought and our minds shall be cleansed. How could I forget? While we sit in oblivion to all that unravels about us, others prepare for endless and repetitive conflict. Are you prepared to wait idly through this while my brother, Confucius and their sycophants reshape the world into disharmony?"

"Your Highness, it is not my place to direct or advise on government policy. I only wish to serve..."

Prince Meng abruptly cut me off. "I shall speak bluntly. I did not come here to discuss policy or the natural world. Master Scholar, you have done much for the court. Zhou's place in the annals of the world is more secure than it was. And you have taught me a great deal. For this, I am grateful. But I feel I must warn you. Once the civil service examinations are done, my brother aims to create a new and powerful sub-Ministry, the Ministry of Scholars and Education. All scholars will answer to this post. Your Royal Archives, the civil service examinations and schools will fall under its command. I have little doubt this will be Confucius' official new post."

I was dumbfounded to hear this and wondered why Yi Ban had not warned me.

"There is more, Master Scholar. There are suspicions that treason emanates from within the Royal Archives. Your frequent trips into the country have been cast in a dubious light. You are thought to be a spy. Your Archives and your work will be cast aside and your staff executed or banished. All that you have done, all that you have created will be gutted."

I was speechless. Me a spy—the absolute absurdity. I knew I was no favorite of Prince Chao but I had no sense that my place had even been questioned, let alone placed in such danger.

"Your Highness, I must ask the source of such allegations. Surely anyone who has had even the slightest encounter with me could not form suspicions. I beg your Highness to allow me to speak to those who might harbor such ill thoughts. Surely they will listen to reason and I can undo any misunderstanding."

"It matters little how such suspicions were cast or whether they are just," Prince Meng responded. "The mere aura of doubt is enough to ruin you. But consider this, scholar. If Confucius benefits the most from your removal, you must deduce that he is behind this. It is a clever ruse he has constructed. You must know that I have been protecting you for some time. There will be limits now to how much I can shield you and the Archives. From this moment on, your fate is in your own hands. I realize you have a disdain for subterfuge. However, now is not a time for contemplation. It will be up to you to act, to divert such uncertainties before you are destroyed. I suspect they will start with members of your staff. They will be questioned. Before long they will be tortured to create a case against you."

"Your Highness, my staff and I have been nothing but completely loyal to Zhou. I personally selected and trained each of them myself. I would just as soon cast myself into a raging river than engage in disloyal…"

"Venerable teacher, you needn't prove yourself to me. I am the rightful heir," Prince Meng said with a thinly guarded trace of bitterness. "I can restore a harmonious order and balance. You have been more than loyal. We both know this. But you must deflect the accusations before they become unstoppable."

"Your Highness…I do not understand what you are saying."

"I am saying that if you fail to take some initiative now, all will be lost."

I could not accept the incredulity of his words and looked away.

"Lao Tzu, in order to save yourself and all you have done, you must discredit Confucius. He must be humiliated. He must be neutralized. The allegations against you will then crumble. And perhaps then my father may poke his head out of his shell and come to his senses."

Neutralize Confucius. I felt like I'd awakened from an uneasy dream into an even darker world. The elder Prince was asking me to become a full and complicit member in the rot and decay against which I had so often declaimed.

"But your Highness, how could I possibly do this? I would not even know how to begin."

My words were barely audible, as though I did not want them uttered or heard.

The Prince looked around then drew me closer. "You will denounce Confucius."

I paused while my mind raced. I was at a complete loss for words.

"There must be another option, your Highness?"

The Prince shook his head. "I would have preferred it if this had not come to pass. I have contemplated other options, but there are none. You must denounce him."

I stared into the pond, tracking the movements of one of the newer fish. "But how?"

"I have learned that one of the King's consorts is pregnant. He will be furious. His women are nothing more than an illusion of manhood for the world. He has not been able to make seed in years. You will get that woman to denounce Confucius as having forced himself upon the King's property."

"Your Highness, can this be true? Who is she?" I thought of Mei and my heart sank.

"I have seen you conversing with her. She is the one my father calls his white peony. Her name is Mei."

"But this is false. Mei was forced upon by..." I barely stopped myself from making an accusation against a member of the Royal Family.

"What do you know of this?" Prince Meng eyed me carefully.

I skirted a complete response. "Your Highness, I am aware that the woman you named was violated. But I am certain it was not Confucius. He would not be so vile."

"How can you know this of him, as well as her?"

I paused, hating the half truth I had to utter. "I had heard she has grown. I felt there could have been no other explanation. Try as I might your Highness, even I cannot close my ears to the sounds of scandal. However, I heard no mention of Confucius."

"Yet are you certain he is not part of those accusing you? For I am not. Once he is gone, there will be less compunction to slander you, I am certain of this. Furthermore the King will be disinclined to denounce and condemn someone who has stood up for him."

I quietly ruminated. The Prince filled in our silence.

"I implore you, do not be deceived by his supposed virtue and disposition towards women. Regardless, it matters not who planted the seed. For all I care it was likely one of the guards or a bureaucrat unaccustomed to keeping his member under control. She was one of the King's favorites. You will speak to her and convince her to accuse Confucius. You must convince her. It is the only way she can save herself and her family. I will arrange an eyewitness, one above reproach who will corroborate her. The time to act is now while both Prince Chao and Confucius are on a diplomatic mission to Qin. They cannot muster a defense until it is too late. There will not be another opportunity."

"Your Highness, it is not in my character to act in such a way. I must consider this further."

He stood with hands on his hips, looking more warrior-like than I had ever seen him.

"You have little time to toy with, scholar. But I understand this is a grave decision. I will allow until tomorrow to ponder this, but no longer. I shall meet you again here at midday."

After the Prince left, I was able to re-consider all that had just been said. It occurred to me that even were Prince Chao present, he would not quash any accusation against Confucius because his scholar could conveniently provide him with a scapegoat for Mei's pregnancy. If I were to help Prince Meng, I would be responsible for Prince Chao escaping all consequences of his actions against Mei and the King. Yet these were not the only issues at hand. I felt naïve and betrayed. Could there possibly be a spy working under me? How could I stand idly by while my reputation and all I had worked for came crumbling down? And then there was Mei. I felt obligated to her. Like myself, she was an outsider who had learned to survive and thrive here. I knew her, felt somewhat akin to her. She was a victim and a pawn. I would make her even more so in asking her to bear false witness and protect her real attacker from justice.

I walked through the Archives, discreetly examining each

staff member as they worked. No one appeared to act differently, no one appeared tense or suspicious. That is, except for myself. Once I realized this, I left the Archives, telling my staff that I felt unwell. I made my way to my quarters located just outside of the Palace. Along the way, I cast suspicious looks at other travelers, imagining that they were potential spies, and carried hidden weapons at the ready. By the time I arrived at my quarters I was doused with perspiration. My thoughts flitted everywhere. I remembered my academy burning down years before—the sense of guilt associated with the death of my colleagues and students had never left me, the helplessness and hopelessness nearly consumed me. Was I prepared to be passive again? Could I live with myself if Mei and my staff paid with their lives while I dithered?

It was serendipitous that Kao Shin who shared my quarters, had earlier requested leave of several days. I did not wish for any contact with anyone. So when he appeared that evening with head bowed and face strained, I was startled but also wary. He said he had finished attending to his business sooner than expected. He attempted to smile and nod but I could see his movements were a struggle.

"Kao Shin, what has happened?"

He looked away. "Nothing, Master. May I prepare you some dinner?"

I agreed, though I was not at all hungry. As he bent down to light a fire, he could not conceal the pain he was obviously in. I looked closely at his tunic. It had been torn and I could see bruising on his stomach.

"Kao Shin, stop what you are doing at once. What has happened?"

He tried to deny any pain and discomfort. I took him by the arm and he put up a feeble struggle before he collapsed into my arms.

"They came for me, Master," he whispered into my ear. "They took me into the Palace. They asked many questions about you. Then they said you were a spy. They even accused me of helping you spy."

"Who? Who said this to you?"

"Soldiers. They said shielding a spy would cost me my head. But I explained that you were no spy. They wouldn't listen and they beat me. They said I could live but only by watching you and reporting back to them. Master, you must run. I will not be spared, but perhaps I can convince them that you have disappeared. You might still have a chance. Go, Master."

Kao Shin shook and heaved. I prepared a wet cloth for him and wiped him down. Regardless of what happened to me, I knew his admission to me would cost him his life. He was ready to sacrifice himself for me. I looked at him and felt shame for not having his courage and conviction.

"Kao Shin," I said stroking his back, "I have done nothing treasonous. The accusations are completely false. If that was not the case I would not be here now, would you not agree?"

He looked at me and half-nodded.

"There is nothing further to fear. I shall speak to Prince Meng. He will see that this misunderstanding is corrected. Please think no more of this."

With that he seemed to calm down. But I instructed him to remain inside until I sorted the matter out.

The following midday Prince Meng appeared in the Archives garden. "Master Scholar appears worn, tired. Have you eaten?"

"Your Highness honors me with his concern for his humble servant. But it is the welfare of another that concerns me. One of my staff was detained yesterday. He was beaten and questioned about me and my activities."

The Prince shook his head. "It is as I feared. It has begun. I suspect the perpetrators were Royal Guardsmen under Prince Chao's control. We have little time. Have you made a decision?"

"What will become of Confucius should he be accused?"

"The King will be enraged. He will likely have Confucius tortured and executed."

"Your Highness, I cannot remain passive. However I will not have a colleague's blood on my hand, regardless of how deceitful he is."

"You are forever a gentleman and a scholar Lao Tzu, showing concern for the welfare of all others, including your enemy. Very well, I will persuade my Heavenly Father to banish Confucius, and to have his name and teachings expunged. I too have no desire for blood. So, you will act?"

Once again I contemplated the complexity of the situation. How could I stand idly by while my reputation and all I had worked for came crumbling down?

"Yes....yes your Highness, I shall act as you prescribed."

"Excellent. I suggest you begin at once by engaging Mei."

From the shy, indifferent dreamer I had met when I arrived, Prince Meng had become a decisive and calculating thinker, and quite possibly the next King. Prince Chao might have more of a struggle for the throne than he realized.

I did as Prince Meng directed and risked an opportunity to speak privately with Mei. Through a message from a trusted staff member, I asked her to meet with me in a quiet tea house just south of the Sheji Temple.

I carefully locked the door and shuttered the window. Kao Shin was ordered to remain at our residence where he would be safe while he healed. My mind could no longer attend to matters at the Archives except to carefully watch each of my staff with a distrustful eye that I never knew I possessed. It was startling how quickly and easily I was able to get myself to act with such willfulness. I slept little that night.

The next afternoon I arrived at the tea house much earlier than necessary. I played with my food while carefully watching each and every patron. Finally Mei arrived in simple forest green trousers and a plain but matching tunic, easily the most humble attire I had seen her wear in some time. She stood tall and stoic, yet her eyes avoided mine. I asked her how she was. She thanked me for my concern and replied that she was well, though her tone was not convincing.

"I have heard you are with child," I said in a quiet tone.

She did not so much as blink. "There are neither safe secrets nor trustworthy people in the Palace or anywhere else," she replied.

"This is not entirely true. For my part I have respected your place, admired your loyalty to your parents, and fretted about your safety."

Her eyes met mine and she nodded.

"I assume the Son of Heaven has not yet learned of your condition?" I asked.

Again she nodded. "It is but a matter of time."

"And what will you do?"

She looked around the tea house. "I can wait. I can flee. I can take poison to kill my child, though the risk will be great. These all lead to the same fate. Eventually the Son of Heaven will learn that I am no longer his white peony."

"I have a proposal."

She scoffed. "Excuse me my Lord, but what could you or anybody possibly do for me? A Prince takes his King's mistress. By force or whatever means, it matters not to the Son of Heaven. She becomes with child. How could this possibly end except with death? If you are proposing that I accuse the Prince, poison would be a better option. At least then I could choose the manner of my death and perhaps save my family."

"But what if you had a witness?"

"There was none. And even if there were a witness, they would not sacrifice their life for mine."

"I agree. But it would not be the Prince who would be accused."

She stopped and looked directly at me.

"Mei, I suggest you accuse Confucius of violating you. He has no power over you."

She laughed. "You are asking me to accuse an innocent man. He will be condemned along with me. Regardless, who will believe a woman over the Prince's respected scholar? You forget he is among Prince Chao's favorites."

"It can be arranged that a witness will come forth on your behalf." I paused and added: "The Prince might also welcome a false allegation and his defense of Confucius would likely be muted."

Mei looked directly at me. "Who is this scholar across from me who would do such a thing? My Lord, I would not have taken you for one to engage in such duplicity. Why?"

I could not answer her right away, for I did not have an answer, either for her or myself. At last I responded, "I have few options, Mei. In addition to you and your family members, other lives may also be imperiled."

She pondered this, then said, "This is a flawed strategy. I will be tortured as will any witness."

"No. I have support within the Palace. No blood will be shed. Confucius will be banished. No one will be harmed, I have been assured of this."

"By whom, Prince Meng?"

I did not need to reply. It was self-evident. She agreed to consider the proposal, then to find me and give an answer within two days, well before Prince Chao and Confucius were due back. I heard myself sounding like Prince Meng had only days earlier—forcing an argument onto an unsuspecting and blameless mind. It was then that I knew that nothing would ever again be as it had once been.

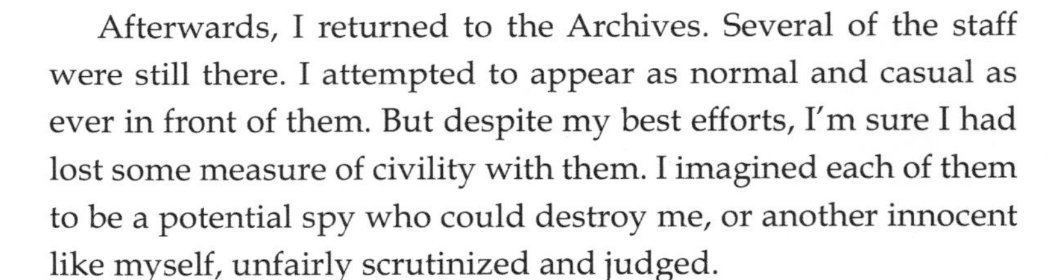

Afterwards, I returned to the Archives. Several of the staff were still there. I attempted to appear as normal and casual as ever in front of them. But despite my best efforts, I'm sure I had lost some measure of civility with them. I imagined each of them to be a potential spy who could destroy me, or another innocent like myself, unfairly scrutinized and judged.

I returned to my residence. Mercifully Kao Shin was asleep. Unfortunately I could not, as I spent much of the night admonishing myself for my naïveté and ignorance for believing I could remain disengaged from the politics and maneuvering within the Palace. Then I began to seethe at both myself and at Confucius. I had come to Chengzhou with the hope of leaving my past behind, and of building a foundation for the Way. With Prince Meng, this was possible in that he was someone who could weave the Way into corridors previously inaccessible to me. Then Confucius arrived full of reverence for me, extolling my wisdom and seeking my opinion on all manners of etiquette. As colleagues, we agreed and sometimes disagreed. But we spoke with a rigor few others understood. Regrettably it had come to this. I never anticipated that the stakes were this high, that such a game was in progress.

He had won Prince Chao's favor, and by extension the King's. The path he had chosen was neither harmonious nor natural and far from open. Confucius' teachings and actions would close the doors on people already shunned, forever affixing the world into artificial roles and servitude. And he would succeed in destroying me, and destroying the Way.

Then there was Prince Meng, who had now revealed a side of his character I had not seen before. Was it desperation or was it decisiveness? That I could not distinguish between the two further showed that my trust was too easily dispensed. I had been a dullard in this game. Patiently awaiting a natural course was not an option when all around me Nature was being violated. Confucius and Prince Chao likely had snickered at my very thoughts, my very being. They saw me as weak and irresolute. I would reveal myself to be otherwise, even if I had to momentarily set aside all I had espoused. They would see that the Way was not to be ridiculed.

Prince Meng had worked hard to convince me to be a fellow conspirator, but I no longer needed his voice to move me. I wanted Mei to side with us, I wanted her to accuse Confucius. I wanted her to disgrace him and his teachings. He may have been an innocent in terms of Mei, but his very presence had stoked this game, and for that his removal would be just.

The next day, the lunar new year provided a momentary reprieve. The occasion called for the Royal Family's visit to the Temple of Heavenly Worship. As the Son of Heaven, the King led the praying and incantations, offering sacrifices to the sun and the moon. Hours later, they rode through the freshly-swept streets in their carriages, inspecting the many hanging peach wood tablets inscribed with auspicious sayings. The next day the King would be offered gifts and tributes from across the land, ensuring that he would be in a pleasant mood.

I stood outside the Palace gates as the Royal procession returned. Each Royal, save Prince Chao who was in Qin with Confucius, rode in their own carriage. The festival parade was poorly choreographed and the whole occasion lacked any sense of celebration or grandeur. In fact there was an emptiness to it, as though it forebode something foul. I walked away from the Palace, intending to purchase some fresh blocks of ink, then slowed my step. I felt eyes on me. I studied the milling crowds, the fruit vendors, the medicine hawkers, and the fortune tellers. Nothing appeared unusual, no one seemed to notice me. I quickened my pace, then took detours. Glances over my shoulder revealed nothing. But still I felt studied. I found my ink, then took a different route back towards the Palace gate. I rounded a corner when a hand quickly pulled me into an opening between buildings.

Mei put her fingers to my lips, looked around, and then nudged me further into the opening.

"Venerable Master, could you appear any more suspicious?" she said with a grin. "You scurry about as though you carry treasonous secrets "

I took a deep breath, not sharing in her humor. "Was I that conspicuous?"

She nodded. "The eyes of the Palace are everywhere."

"What say you, Mei? Are you prepared to stand with us?"

"I have little choice. If this is to work, it must be soon. I am expected to attend to the King's painful muscles in two evenings. And if I do so he will surely notice I am with child. I could be ready. But who will stand by me? Who will be my witness?"

"That is being arranged."

"By whom? Prince Meng?"

"I cannot say, but he is to be trusted and he has the means to follow through."

"My life depends on whoever it is. I must know him. We must meet. How else can our stories support one another?"

She was correct and I agreed to ensure this. I should have been pleased with her agreement to the arrangement. I should also have been pleased that I would be advancing my own cause. Yet nothing felt settled, nothing felt certain. Everything appeared still out of reach.

Prince Meng arrived at the Archives appearing tired and distracted. Lines creased his forehead and bags hung beneath his eyes. He had aged. The idealist had grown, though not into the leader I had wished him to be. Not that it was my place to judge. No longer a young man searching for a path, he appeared to have finally found one, however diverted from his more romantic days when we had first met. While his path had largely been constructed by his station, and chiseled with the blunt instrument and savagery of Palace life, he would make as virtuous a ruler as would be possible. Perhaps his plan was credible. Perhaps it would arrest the misguided direction Prince Chao and Confucius were taking.

When I told him of Mei's decision he was pleased and his disposition altered. Very quickly he seemed to find more energy. He said that once this was done, we would have an opportunity to truly create a society on a course of its own design, unfettered with misfortune and manmade struggles. I nodded.

"Your silence speaks loudly, Lao Tzu."

"Your Highness, it is not power I seek. For now I would be

pleased to have my name and my work vindicated, and Mei left in peace. In you, my Highness, I believe the world has the best chance of uniting the estranged kingdoms into something more purposeful than war and conquest, that you could define our world by something other than artificial walls and titles."

"All this is possible. But a consort with a child not belonging to the Son of Heaven cannot return to her original standing. This is obvious, Lao Tzu. As for you, I believe much of the court will come to reconsider your teachings and view you with more respect."

"But your Highness, would that be respect earned through good deeds or through a new approach within the political machinations of the court?"

"You think too much, Lao Tzu. If in the Way one must accept the natural course of the world, perhaps we must also see that people and politics also have their own inevitable bent."

Was the young Prince speaking with a wisdom beyond which I had foreseen? My discomfort in this deception clouded my judgment. This game was as foreign to me as it would have been for Prince Chao to walk away willingly from the throne.

I conveyed Mei's request to meet with the witness. Prince Meng said he had arranged for a very credible person, one intimately connected to and trusted by the King. He would meet her tomorrow. He then arranged for himself and her to have a private audience with the King. But until that audience, his involvement would best be kept secret.

I started to walk away when Prince Meng asked a final question.

"Did she speak of who violated her?"

I held my breath. I would have been simple to bring forth Prince Chao's name. The brutality of his actions would surprise few, and it would bring favor to Prince Meng in his father's eyes. But Mei made it clear she understood the repercussions of accusing Prince Chao. Prince Meng might disclose his brother's brutality for his own gain, but there would be severe repercussions for Mei and her family if she were to do so. In the end, I felt there was little to be gained by disclosing all and my reply to the heir was the least of all evils.

"Your Highness, it is as you said. It matters not by whom."

The Prince nodded and a glint of a smile emerged as he walked away. And so it was done. I had stepped onto a crooked path. It disturbed me that I could live with this.

16

Pawns of War

I had delivered Prince Meng's instructions to Mei. She received them with the same glee that a condemned man might reveal had he been told his manner of execution had been changed from beheading to poisoning. I explained that once the King was in a good mood, likely after receiving tributes, Prince Meng would gather Mei and the witness in one of the King's small chambers. He had instructed that I remain in my own quarters, away from the Palace so that my presence would not lead some to question the credibility of the allegations. I heartily agreed.

That was the plan as I anticipated. But the day began poorly and nothing went as plotted. The Temple ceremonies dragged on, to the point where it sapped the King of his strength, for he was alarmingly weak during the reception of the tributes. His pallor continued to appear ghostly. When he wasn't trying to shout at his supplicants, he was doubled over with severe coughing fits, prompting the Royal Physician, who had become a regular member of his entourage, to attend to him.

The dull festivities might have been forgivable and quickly forgotten, except that very few tributes arrived, far fewer than ever before. And the absence of so many lords and ambassadors was glaring. The King demanded explanations but was offered only weak excuses. The entire court shook with fear before the King's rage and humiliation. He had lost face yet again, this time on an auspicious occasion. The King, the Queen and their entourage along with several ministers and their attendants were the first to leave the Celestial Hall. As the only Prince in attendance, Meng would leave next. The plan was for the elder Prince to have Mei and the witness brought to the King immediately afterwards. However, the King was in no mood for more bad news. I would have expected Prince Meng to see this, but he did not appear to consider it as he instead followed the King closely as he exited the hall. I wanted to tell him to abort our scheme for the moment. There was no telling what the King's judgment would be, given his state of mind. As soon as the Royals left, I attempted to make my way to the King's complex, but the guards stopped me. They said that all the Royal residences had been sealed. I implored them to grant me an immediate audience with Prince Meng, but they paid me no heed.

With few options, I sought out Yi Ban. I learned that he had left the Hall in a hurry. I found him in his Palace office, head down and massaging his temples with his fingers.

"Yi Ban, there is something of concern I must share."

"Yes, yes I know of what you speak."

"You do?"

"Of course, is it not obvious? This festival was a disaster. The King is outraged, and he will be looking to me."

As the Minister who oversaw the festival and the paying of tributes, it was one of his moments to shine publicly and in front of the King. Yet now, with the King humiliated, he too had lost face.

"Minister, my concern is far greater and of a different matter. It concerns allegations about myself, and separate accusations that may involve Prince Chao and one of the King's consorts."

Yi Ban chortled. "Lao Tzu, since when do you allow yourself

to be troubled by such talk? Truly, I thought you valued yourself as being above that. I suspect Prince Meng is the source of your discontent, am I correct?"

I nodded. "But the consort…"

"Is the King's business." He shook his head in dismay. "This is not the time to upset him further. I will bear the brunt of today's debacle. My best hope, indeed yours as well, is that his ill-health will expunge this from his memory quickly. In any event, why distress yourself and me when we have genuine matters to attend to?"

It was clear he knew nothing of this affair, which made it impossible for me to seek his support in at least delaying an audience between Mei and the King. I considered speaking of his failure to forewarn me of Confucius' expected appointment to the new sub-Ministry. But it was clear the timing was inappropriate. I walked out of his chambers despondent and completely unprepared for the events that transpired. The only consolation for the horrid deed to follow was that salvation came from the most unlikely ears and eyes within the Palace.

This and much of what you are about to hear came from the most noble and trustworthy source, whose identity will soon be apparent. Prince Meng did arrange for an audience with the King, heedless of his father's mood. However, it was not a private audience with him, the King, Mei and the witness alone. At first she remained outside his outer chamber while those present included the King's Royal Physician, the highest-ranking Ministers, the Queen and Major Huang with a phalanx of Royal Guardsmen. Prince Meng had planted a different seed than we had agreed.

"Heavenly Father, it is with a heavy heart that I must bring such news as you sit in poor health, and with the bitterness of our humiliation still scalding," Prince Meng said.

At first, the King barely acknowledged his son, then spoke in a voice not much louder than a whisper.

"How many times have I had to endure your squabbles and disagreements with your brother? Why must you still bother me so? Do you assume that the more you criticize the more I shall give favor?"

Prince Meng remained kowtowing on the floor. "Father, it is because of my love for you and respect for the throne that I must share this despicable news with you." He paused. "One of your concubines is with child."

Prince Meng glanced at the Queen who played with her jade hairpiece, then continued.

"It is Mei, the one you refer to as your white peony. She will claim that she was taken by Confucius, Prince Chao's favored scholar. She will claim to have a witness, but this is a deception. She hides the truth. She protects her true assailant for fear of death. I believe she shields… Prince Chao."

The King looked ready to laugh, but all that came out at first were deep coughs, then copious amounts of phlegm.

"No man is to have passage to the King's women, regardless of their station—in this you are correct. But this is an absurd accusation, well beyond the level of pettiness I have witnessed you two engage in."

"Your Highness, I too scoffed at first. Yet my source is impeccable. But do not take my word alone. Have that consort brought in. If she accuses Confucius as I believe she will, have her present her witness. If she fails to do so, have her tortured. The truth shall not be far behind. If she continues with her story, then I shall pledge allegiance to Prince Chao as your heir, if that is your choosing. I will serve him as my King. However, if she speaks the truth and accuses Prince Chao, I am to be officially named heir. My brother is to be cast aside. The honorable history of Zhou deserves a just and upstanding continuance. I do not wish for it to be tainted with a continuing odor. The King's virtues must be beyond reproach. Should you do otherwise, and not attend to this matter I will leave Chengzhou. I will not defile our ancestors by remaining a part of a court that respects its Son of Heaven so little."

The King's breathing became even more erratic. His physician opened a small jar and handed the King some pills, which he waved off. He leaned forward.

"You propose to roll the dice and stake your future on this? Do you truly believe your insolence can move me so?"

"This is not about me, Heavenly Father."

"I must say Prince Meng, I hadn't expected such brazenness. Your entire inheritance..."

"It is not for my inheritance that I stand, Heavenly Father. Our mandate from heaven sanctions our rule. Yet we have recently suffered a natural calamity unknown in human history. Our ancestral tombs have been plundered. Our neighboring regions treat us like latrine cleaners as Chu sits on our doorstep, waiting for an opportunity to usurp our authority and enslave the world. And your health is a prolonged battle with which even your greatness struggles. We must ask if these four bad portents are to be feared or fought. If they are to be fought, we cannot allow a moral lapse and an unscrupulous act to taint the court's name amongst the nobility and masses, least of all the wayward territories. No, Heavenly Father. As the son of the true ruler of all of Zhou, I fear not and stand for thee."

The King sat back. His eyes glossed over. He slumped into his seat, retreated into his weary pallor. Several of the Ministers shifted uneasily, quietly whispering among themselves. Even the Queen seemed to pause and reflect.

"Bring her to me," the King commanded.

Within moments, the King's most trusted Royal Guardsman dragged Mei in by her hair. Even with her clothing torn, Mei neither whimpered nor begged for mercy, showing a dignity and fearlessness seldom seen before an enraged King.

Prince Meng took a seat beside his father and offered to speak on their behalf. "Do not even attempt to deny the truth. You are with child," the Prince thundered.

At first Mei did not respond, but continued to remain kneeling with arms outstretched. Prince Meng then shouted at her, as if he not only spoke for the King but had effortlessly assumed his father's persona.

"There are vermin in this world, and then there are low life, lying, deceitful scum who could only aspire to be vermin. You are one of them." He paused to give his denunciation more weight. "Do you take our generosity for granted? Do you play us for fools? Speak, and do not dare to utter another lie or you and every member of your clan will pay with their heads. Did you think you could conceal this trickery from us?"

Mei was silent at first, then responded. "No your Highness, the allegations are true. I beg the Son of Heaven's forgiveness."

"Who is the father?" Prince Meng snapped. Mei did not respond. Prince Meng repeated himself. Again she did not respond. He left his seat and signaled to a Guardsmen to slap her across her cheek. She took the blow silently.

She hesitated at first. "Your Highness, it is the scholar Confucius."

Prince Meng laughed. "You expect the court to believe that a woman who is known to wander the town without escort was taken by a man no more interested in lying with a woman than a farmer is in reading?"

Mei repeated the allegation and apologized again to the King, but denied any wrongdoing.

Prince Meng stood up and slowly walked around Mei. He paused then calmly asked the next question. "How did this happen?"

"The scholar... Confucius... he took me by force. I tried to resist but could not."

Prince Meng asked if she had a witness.

She nodded. "Your Highness, the Royal Physician saw Confucius and I that evening. He saw Confucius drag me into one of the King's outer chambers where he had his way with me."

Prince Meng asked the physician to step forward.

"This is the King's Royal Physician. Look at him!" Prince Meng ordered Mei. "Is this your witness?"

Mei lifted her head from her bowed position and looked at the physician.

"Yes, your Highness. He witnessed Confucius' actions upon me."

Prince Meng turned to the physician. "Is this true? Have you ever seen this woman with Confucius or with any other man?"

"Your Highness," the physician looked at her, then at the King and spoke with alacrity.

"I have never seen this woman except in the service of our Son of Heaven. Nor did I see her with Confucius or any other man. If I may be permitted to add, the suggestion by a woman that I would be drawn into such vulgarity is reprehensible. I humbly ask that this court severely chastise such insolence."

Betrayed, Mei lost her stoic composure. The life seemed to drain from her body. But she knew better than to plead her case further. To do so would have cemented the perception of her corruption and impertinence, and likely would evoke an even more severe response.

Prince Meng turned to the King. "It is as I feared, Heavenly Father. This woman's loyalties are not to you."

Prince Meng nodded at the guard who slapped her in the face, knocking her over. She got up and resumed her kowtowing position, panting heavily.

The Prince continued.

"She has deceived our Heavenly Father, but she is not alone. The father of her child may be a Prince, but no man should dare mock the King. We must send a clear message. This low-life should be executed. More importantly, we must also discuss the actions of my brother and the large shadow it casts on his suitability as heir. You have already heard my thoughts on this, and I cannot imagine that we would not agree that the heir must possess absolute reverence for the throne and whomever sits on it."

The King's nod was barely perceptible. He did not look at Mei. He appeared more exhausted and disappointed than angry.

Prince Meng signaled to a guard, who grabbed Mei by one arm.

"Ensure it is a swift death," the elder Prince told the guard.

"Wait!" the King commanded. "Prince Meng, you have made accusations of Prince Chao. But your word alone is not enough to condemn him. Prince Chao will be allowed to answer. Furthermore, if Prince Chao is innocent, she must confess the name of the true father."

He looked down upon her with a trace of pity.

"I also cannot believe she alone would attempt this deception unless aided by another."

Prince Meng paused and briefly glanced at the King. "I beseech our Heavenly Father to note that my dear brother has chosen this time to be absent. I would also further remind you which of your sons stands by you while you are ill. As for this low-life, the ways of women can be ever so deceitful and treacherous. I am not convinced that she did not act alone. Nevertheless, we will break her." Prince Meng lowered himself and spoke within inches of her. "Whom did you open your vileness to? Who else is involved with your treachery?"

Mei glanced at his pointy, red shoes with rubies hanging on gold tassels. A moment of recognition is all it took. She stopped panting and remained still.

Prince Meng returned to his seat. "We will make you speak. However, the court can be merciful. When you give us the name of whomever conspired with you and defiled you, we will spare your family. I suspect you will do the sensible thing and give us but the one name we already suspect. Take her," Prince Meng commanded the guards. "I'm sure you'll find your next accommodations rather sparse compared to what you've become accustomed."

She must have been stunned. She had anticipated a different audience and an entirely different outcome, with support that I, in my deepest naïveté, had helped convince her to accept. For all the times I bemoaned having to stand through the tedium of court affairs, I wished I had borne witness to that moment. If events hadn't so quickly unfolded after that, I would never have believed Prince Meng could have acted so.

While Mei suffered through her unexpected fate, I paced in my garden, trying to calm my nerves. To an observer unaware of the unfolding drama, that day would have appeared to be one of the most remarkably serene autumn days in memory. A golden sun swathed Chengzhou while bursts of colors blanketed lush forests. Wafts of burnt sugar teased the air as several of my katsura trees' heart-shaped apricot colored leaves unleashed their splendor. Further afield and beyond the northern wall of Chengzhou, a grove of towering bamboo swayed gently in a warm southern breeze. Unbeknownst to me at the time, making their way through the bamboo were six of General Wu's soldiers and two of his officers—a chiseled-faced colonel and a sergeant whose glistening leather armor was improperly cut for his svelte, wiry physique. General Wu was an ambitious and rising flatterer in court. In a short amount of time he had endeared himself to Prince Meng and several other Ministers opposed to Prince Chao's many proposed reforms.

The soldiers dragged Mei to a clearing among the bamboo where three prison interrogators were playing dice. The sergeant debriefed the interrogators and gave them their instructions. The interrogators strung each of Mei's limbs to a separate post, thus suspending her face up and horizontally above the ground. That alone would have been excruciatingly painful. But the real agony would occur more slowly. Beneath her grew young bamboo stalks, known for their incredible strength and near unbreakable firmness. The interrogators had sharpened the tips of the stalks to fine, arrow-like points. Each plant would mature half an arm's length a day, thus inching towards her. The first tips would feel like a crude arrow prick at first, then slowly pierce her skin, and drip the life out of her.

Once she was strung up, the three interrogators returned to their dice game. Their leader dusted off his tattered prison guard tunic, revealing crusted blood and weeks of spilled food and drink. He was a stout, broad-shouldered man who had lost one ear in battle when he served in the army. His other ear had been hideously chewed up by a dog, hence his nickname Gou, or dog. Gou cast a disapproving eye at the colonel's finely-tailored army uniform, then returned his attention to Mei as she lay suspended. Gou watched while his two underlings groped her body and laughed.

"Enough," the colonel commanded the interrogators. "You are here to extract information, not to amuse yourselves."

Gou reared his head and cocked his remaining ear like a dog that had been caught with its head in his master's rice bowl. "What?" Gou asked, forcing the colonel to repeat himself.

"Why hurry, sir? You know them stalks will do their job soon enough, guaranteed."

The colonel shook his head at Gou. "Enough now."

Gou sighed in disappointment then turned back to Mei.

"Okay you scum, who did ya open your whorish legs to, huh?"

Then he leaned into her ear and added, "If you can tell this prissy colonel whose bastard child you is carrying, I promise you won't suffer no more."

The colonel stiffened but remained silent. Mei named Confucius. At first Gou could not hear so he slapped her. When she named Confucius again, he slapped her once more.

"Wrong answer, you filth. You be saying his name again and you get a bamboo stalk directly up your asshole."

From then on Mei refused to utter another word, nor did she even close her eyes. The interrogators didn't seem to care. They warned her that soon the pain would be so unbearable that her screams would be heard for many *li* around. Her kidneys would burst, her liver would explode poison all over her body, and her intestines would be skewered like meat on a stick. She would talk. Everybody did, Gou told her. The interrogators chuckled before returning to their dice game.

In just over an hour the first stalks reached her buttocks, then the back of her head. She gasped. Her eyes bulged as she struggled to arch her body upwards. Soon another stalk had touched her shoulder, followed by another on her lower back, then her calves. Still she refused to answer the interrogators' questions. Straining to keep her head up, her eyes welled.

"Don't be holding out. Tell us whose little stalk did you invite in and your death will be quick. You won't be feeling this no more. I can guarantee you that. And better not be saying it was that shrivel-dick scholar."

Before Mei could reply, fast-moving footsteps could be heard trampling through the forest. While Mei was unable to turn her head, the men all stood at the sound, as Major Huang with two other Royal Guardsmen appeared in the bamboo clearing. He quickly surveyed the scene. He squared himself before the colonel and saluted him.

"You and your men are being relieved."

"Relieved? On whose orders?"

"It is not you I answer to, Colonel."

"Need I remind you of your rank, Major?" the colonel said.

"Perhaps that would be wise. You may recall that I serve directly under the Son of Heaven."

"We have direct orders from the court," the sergeant standing by the colonel interjected.

"Over which the Son of Heaven presides."

"We are questioning a spy engaged in treasonous activities, yet you dare obstruct us?" the colonel asked.

"She will be questioned, indeed, but by me."

"You claim that the King has sent you, but I doubt this. Regardless, he can barely recall what he had for breakfast, let alone what orders he may have given. So you must realize, Major, that disobeying a superior officer is something that no one of rank tolerates. Sooner or later your back will need to be covered. Fellow officers and friends might suddenly forget you.

You will never be safe. Wherever you stand, you will lose. Turn around now, and I will try and forget I had to tolerate your insubordination."

The Major stood tall and firm, his right hand tightened around his halberd.

"How very bold," the colonel said, his own hand moving to his sword. "You Royal Guardsmen have always had a brashness and arrogance. It is time you learned some respect. Perhaps we should resolve this now."

"I have been threatened with worse and by more."

The colonel signaled to the sergeant and his six men who started to ready their weapons. Before they had done so, the Major brandished his weapon, Thunderclap, spun it around his head, and struck three of the soldiers, stripping two of their swords which flew into the bushes. Another soldier drew his sword and lunged towards the Major who jabbed the butt end of his halberd into the soldier's stomach, knocking him back several feet and onto two of his comrades, bowling all three over. The final soldier came at the Major from behind. He gripped his sword with both hands and chopped down towards the back of the Major's head. The Major spun around and ducked, spread his hands apart on the halberd held horizontally, blocking the oncoming sword.

The soldier shifted his stance and attacked again, making a low sweeping ankle kick which the Major deflected by ramming the blade end of his halberd into the ground. Then he swung the butt into the soldier's face, knocking his teeth out as he fell motionless to the ground.

The Major's two Guardsmen had meanwhile surrounded the colonel, who drew a rare two-handed long sword decorated with a winged hilt and gems. The colonel swung it at the Guardsmen but he was slow, and the bejeweled sword was clumsy. Unable to fend off the Guardsmen, he desperately hacked away at nothing as he exhausted himself. The Guardsmen were content to give the colonel some distance and backed him out of the clearing, away from Mei and the Major.

That left the sergeant standing alone, but grinning in amusement. He also held a halberd and wielded it as though it were an extension of his arm. He thrust it at the Major, probing his defenses. The Major threw back each attack, barely escaping the blade as he stepped backwards. Just as the Major planted a firm foot and prepared to counterattack, the sergeant changed tactics, lengthened the reach of his halberd by gripping the end of its shaft, and jabbed with it again and again, coming within inches of the Major's face. The Major managed to deflect each stab, but the sergeant was fast and he was forced to retreat further and further until he was backed into a stand of bamboo.

The sergeant spun himself around holding the halberd horizontally, easily slicing through several bamboo trees. In one motion, the Major raised his own blade and chopped downwards, slicing the shaft of the sergeant's halberd in two.

"Your movements are quick but wasteful. Predictable, even," the Major said matter of factly.

The sergeant spat, reached into his waist belt and pulled out several three-sided darts. He was about to throw them when the colonel shouted for him to stop.

"Once again, you are all relieved," the Major calmly ordered.

"The General will have your head," the colonel pronounced before he and his men staggered off. "And if he doesn't, others will."

Gou had followed the confrontation and let out a laugh, then some flatulence. Major Huang nodded at the trio of dice players standing before him, then examined Mei. The stalks had penetrated into her left shoulder, her buttocks and calves. Blood dripped slowly at first. But her weight was slowly stretching the slackening ropes and her body sank further onto the points.

"I assume, Gou, that you have learned nothing," Huang asked.

"What?" Gou's head leaned towards the Major. The Major repeated himself with greater volume.

Gou nodded and turned to Mei, leaning over her.

"Tell me now who you opened your legs for!"

She moaned and writhed, gulping for air. The longer she remained silent to his questions, the louder and more frustrated Gou became.

He threatened to bring her family in for questioning if she continued to resist. He warned that her mother would be raped, as would all the women in her clan. The children would be sold to the Qin. Hearing this, Mei struggled further, impaling herself more deeply in the process. The ground beneath her had became a thick pool of blood. Her eyes pleaded and at last she looked ready to talk. The Major extended his hand to halt the interrogators.

Gou was exasperated. "Major, let us do our job why don't you? What do you care about a low-life whore?"

"I didn't say I did. But there are to be no mistakes, and I want answers."

"We don't make mistakes. She's ready to sing and scream, I'll have you know."

"Really? And how will you know if it's anything resembling the truth? The last suspected spy died after giving you false information. If not for me, you would have been whipped for that."

"You did only what I would do for you, dear cousin."

"Be that as it may, Gou, you don't want to answer to the King this time," the Major said.

Gou held his hands open. "Then be my guest, Major. Just don't get too close. The blood will splatter out all over that fresh uniform of yours."

The Major glared at Gou, who backed away but lingered nearby. He leaned over Mei.

"You already know who I am. And I already know more about you than you realize." He bent his head closer to her ear. "I know you did nothing wrong. I know you were taken by force, perhaps several times over."

Gou and the interrogators moved closer, straining to catch what he was saying.

"I suspect it is not your assailant you are protecting, but your family," Major Huang continued.

Mei's eyes brimmed over, and tears streamed down both sides of her face. She squeezed her eyes shut tightly but her breathing was labored. She lost control of her bladder and could no longer keep her head above the daggers below. Her weight was now partially supported by the numerous fast-growing stalks piercing into her.

"Just as I suspected. Then it is a person of great position who is responsible, am I not correct?"

"Yes," she whispered.

"And you were either bribed, coerced or manipulated into accusing Confucius, correct?"

Her whisper was only barely, understood. "Yes."

"Prince Chao has already been accused by his brother before the King. So your struggle now is only for your family. You naming Prince Chao merely serves to validate Prince Meng's accusation. Your death will tie up one of his loose ends."

Gou chortled. "Why are you wasting time with this talk, Major?"

The Major peered up at Gou. "We have the same purpose,

but differ in our approach. She is too strong for you. She will not break. She is not afraid of death or of pain. But she fears for her family."

The Major returned to Mei. His pace quickened.

"When did this occur?"

Her reply could barely be heard. "The night... the court learned... learned of... the desecration of tombs."

"Was it in the Palace?"

"Yes," she said as though it was her dying breath.

"Untie her, now!" the Major shouted. He slid his arms between the bamboo stalks to prop up her bloodied, limp body.

"What? She have given us nothing. She's playing with you, Major," Gou said.

"Do it now and I'll explain later. Otherwise you will have to justify why you let your prisoner die when she is the only witness who can point to the man who betrayed the King."

The three interrogators stood by while the Guardsmen untied Mei and carefully laid her on the ground on her stomach. The Major ripped off part of his tunic and those of the other Guardsmen and wrapped them around her many wounds as makeshift bandages, working feverishly to stop the bleeding. Then he sent for a physician from the armory.

All this time, I continued to wait in the Archives, unaware of the outcome of Mei's meeting in the Palace. However, I unexpectedly received a message on a tablet with a map and instructions urging me to go to the bamboo grove. At first, I assumed it was from Prince Meng, then noticed the insignia of a small Black Serpent on the corner of the tablet. The Black Serpent—Mei's silent ally. I wasted no time considering its origins and rushed out immediately. I exited the Palace through the little-used north gate. I noticed a physician and one of the Guardsmen ahead of me on the same path. I chose to follow them discretely at a distance.

They walked just over a *li* into the forest and stopped in a small clearing. I hid behind a cluster of bamboo and peered out cautiously. At first, I could only hear rapid whisperings. I edged closer until I saw Major Huang and the armory physician bent over an apparently lifeless body. I recognized it as that of Mei on her stomach, back reddened with blood. At first I thought it was an illusion of some sort, that my fatigue and worry were playing tricks with my mind. I blinked to re-focus and realized my eyes did not deceive me. I stuffed my fist into my mouth to stop from crying out and dropped to my knees, fighting back tears. I buried my head between my knees and asked myself, why and how this had come to pass. I was tempted to present myself to these men, to implore them to make me their prisoner instead. I wanted to tell them that Mei was defiled by Prince Chao, and it was only through my meddling that she had been further entrapped in the web of Palace intrigue. It was I who should have been there, not her. Despite having armored myself with all my beliefs, with the Way, suddenly I felt paralyzed with fear. I could not move. The truth was that I was not then, nor have I ever been, very heroic.

The physician worked quickly and began dressing the wounds. I could now see that Mei was still breathing, but only barely, and that she had lost consciousness. It was a few moments before I realized that they were trying to save her.

"We won't be answering for this one, Major, I can guarantee you that," I heard a guard with a deformed ear say.

"You won't have to, but you may soon have to choose sides. She did not give us a name, but she gave us the means of determining it. Why would she refuse to tell us the name? Think about it. Only a crown prince could command such fear so that she would rather die under extreme pain. Who else but a crown prince would benefit more from the defamation and scandal mongering of another prince? "

The guard looked puzzled. "Accuse a prince and you might as well say your goodbyes."

"Correct. She likely knew this and had no intention of doing so, not even when under such intense pressure. Nor would she have accused Confucius without having been persuaded somehow. Whoever arranged this played her and knew she would be tortured but also expected her to break. Though she likely knew the identity of her attacker, she was expected to name a false assailant, someone far more believable than the scholar."

"What? Slow this down for me."

"Think, my dear cousin. In the darkness of the Palace, with her eyes downcast or gazing elsewhere, or bowing on the floor, a man in disguise could easily overpower her. He could be dressed in royal garments, he could sound and smell and act like another. She would know no better, at least not at first. That she became with child was unfortunate for her, but perhaps presented a new opportunity for the attacker."

"But how can you know this for sure, Major?"

The Major stared off. "I do not. But I think she knew the true identity of her attacker. She could not name him with Wu's men about. She could not bear witness that one of the Princes in particular was in the Palace that night. Prince Chao is innocent of this attack. He will want to defend his name."

His words struck me like a blow and I almost cried out. It came to me then, all too late. Prince Meng had played each and every step of this game, and no one was more duped than I. The sudden realization that I had contributed to a most odious of plans became clear. What a complete and utter imbecile I felt myself to be.

I stepped out of the bamboo cluster.

"And I can bear witness that Mei was indeed coerced into

accusing Confucius, knowing full well that her accusation of Prince Chao would cost her and her family their lives."

The Major raised his halberd and the Guardsmen rushed towards me, throwing me to the ground.

"Lao Tzu?" exclaimed the Major. He lowered his halberd and motioned for the Guardsmen to release me.

"It is I, Lao Tzu, the dupe. I am the one who deserves to be there." I nodded to the bamboo where Mei had been hung. I went to her and fell to my knees beside her. I could not even touch her at first, so mortified was I. Then I assisted the physician in wrapping the rest of her wounds. The physician explained that the loss of blood was grave, perhaps fatal, but that her major organs were fortunately still intact.

I then turned to face the Major. I explained that I had been told that Prince Chao suspected myself and my staff of treason, that he believed a spy was nestled within the Archives. I shared how I had been told that Confucius was to be given a new Ministry with wide powers. One of my staff had already been questioned and beaten. He was told under threat of death that he had to spy on me. By persuading Mei to accuse Confucius, I was able to discredit him as well as the younger Prince, thereby also ensuring that the right Prince would assume the throne. More importantly, neither my staff nor Mei would be harmed.

The Major chuckled. "Forgive me Master Scholar, but for all your lofty ideals and your proximity to Prince Meng, neither Prince Chao nor anyone could suspect you of being a spy any more than they could a child of mastering a twelve foot halberd in battle. Prince Chao's search for spies never even paid a cursory glance your way."

Confused, I looked at him. "But Kao Shin was beaten. He urged me to run."

"I don't doubt that, but it is I who oversees investigations into spies. I neither sanctioned nor oversaw any activity related to you or the Archives. There is little that I do not know."

"Then tell me this, Major. How is it that you speak so assuredly that Prince Chao was not the attacker?"

The Major drew me away from the physician and explained that as Commander of the Guardsmen, he made sure always to know the whereabouts of each member of the King's family and when they left the Palace, even if they disapproved of such shadowing. It was also customary to follow all those new to the Palace until it was determined that they were not a threat to the Royal Family. This included myself, he explained. On the day in question, Prince Chao left the Palace soon after the King's tirade. The Prince shed his Royal garb for one of the Guardsmen's uniforms. I rode with him to an inn on a small hill outside of Chengzhou, overlooking the river. The Prince drank there quietly for much of the night. It was unlikely many could identify the Prince out of his customary garb. But he was definitely not in the Palace until much later that evening. It was someone disguised as him.

It sounded like the same inn where I once had met Mei and later sat with Confucius. It was then that I felt old and most unwise, as though I had thought myself riding the currents of existence only to suddenly realize that I'd been lodged on the beach the whole time, watching the tide ebb away.

"Major, I too have been taken for a fool. Betrayed and played like a child. I persuaded her to accuse an innocent man. How contemptuous I am."

The Major sighed. "You were not alone. Nor do I believe you engineered this." He raised an eyebrow. "Prince Meng is now the clear adversary. We have all underestimated his strength and guile. For such a miscalculation, it may be too late."

I nodded, and the interrogators gasped at the implications of what the Major had said. "Clearly subterfuge is not my strength."

I shook my head. "But I suspect that as long as Mei lives, she is a loose end for Prince Meng. Therefore we are all in danger."

"For you, that may depend. You played your part for Prince Meng," the Major said. "If you continue to support his moves he may protect you from what follows. But you too are a loose end. Your other option is to be truthful, which may engender a positive response from Prince Chao. For the rest of us, keeping Mei alive risks our own lives. But attempts at virtue may be all we have left as the Palace is thrown into chaos."

"It is the Son of Heaven who will have the final word," I said.

"The Son of Heaven? He has not been far from his final words for some time. If he is to have any bearing on this, it will have to be soon."

"What do you mean," I asked.

"Do you not know?" The Major shook his head. "How anyone can suspect you of anything but that which you are, is beyond me. Our Son of Heaven has the consumption disease. We have been awaiting his last breath for months. Thus I am not surprised Prince Meng is making such a desperate last attempt. He would be among the first to know that our Son of Heaven's time and judgment is limited. But there are other voices within the inner court. One of them diverted me here after I unsuccessfully searched for Mei in the Royal Dungeons."

"Of whom do you speak?" I asked.

"How trustworthy would I be if I were to divulge my source to you? But to be perfectly honest, I know not the origins of this information. I was given this." The Major pulled a small tablet from his tunic, similar to the one given to me, carrying the seal of a Black Serpent.

I paused. "This is indeed the case with me as well. I was sent instructions from this Black Serpent urging me to this spot. But what are we to do now?"

"Did anyone see you come here?"

I shook my head. "I may not have the swiftness of the young, but neither do I create their disturbance."

"You could risk a return to the Palace. Perhaps your innocence may afford you some time to decide where you stand. But that is a perilous route. Prince Meng may see your integrity as a danger, one he may not wish to leave dangling."

The Major turned towards Mei. His face softened. "If I had a battalion of men with her courage and determination.... Her wounds are severe. She should not be moved far. But her life depends on leaving this place as quickly as possible. Wu's men will soon be swarming all over this area."

He ordered his Guardsmen and interrogators to construct a litter, and to shelter her amongst millet farmers whom he trusted, across the river where it bent just west of the bridge. He looked at me. "Come with us scholar," he said. "There is nothing you can do by returning. I cannot imagine Prince Meng tolerating your presence."

I was torn. I wanted to confront Prince Meng and hold him to account for what had happened. Yet I also wished to accompany Mei, not only to do what little I could to help her, but because the prospect of returning to the Palace and facing the advancing storm also greatly distressed me. To flee at that moment would have branded me a traitor. I had little doubt that my work and my Archives would also be discredited.

"I do not disagree with you Major. But I cannot join you just yet. There is someone I left behind. I will find you across the river."

The Major looked incredulous. I bade him farewell and took the path back, not towards the Palace, but to my quarters where Kao Shin remained. If I was to flee, I owed it to him to take him with me.

17

Madness Revealed

It was early evening when I returned in haste through the north gate, back into Chengzhou. The guards cast a wary look at me. Only then did I realize that Mei's blood was smeared on my robe. I deserved that mark of stupidity. In hindsight, I saw much too late that Mei had seen through Prince Meng before any of us. She had said her woman's instinct saw past the Prince's chivalry and grace and sensed what was beneath that veneer. I did not realize she had been referring to Prince Meng, not Chao.

I changed direction towards my residence, taking the quickest route to Kao Shin, dodging vendors hoping to do end of day sales and ignoring the cacophony of people milling about. I had hoped Kao Shin had heeded my instructions and remained there. As I approached I could see that our front door had been smashed in. I entered with much caution, searching for evidence of undesirables.

I stepped inside and called out for Kao Shin. A stool had been overturned, clay pots were shattered on the ground and heavy blotches of blood led to a dark corner. I called his name out again, then almost stumbled upon a motionless form in the dark. It was Kao Shin. I reached for a lantern and lit it.

He rested on his back, his hands open with palms by his side. His stomach had gushed blood all over his tunic, spilling onto the ground into two small pools. Despite his injuries, his bruised face and youthful eyes appeared at peace. Or perhaps that is what I wanted to believe, for his death was on my hands and guilt has never been something I swallowed easily.

The dissonance of the outside world lapsed into silence and restfulness descended. A thin shaft of the dusk's last glow streamed in through the door, illuminating columns of dust dancing in every direction. I sat on the ground, closed Kao Shin's eyes and placed his hands together on his chest.

I leaned against the wall to clear my head. The past few days had whirled out of control. I scarcely recognized myself, let alone others I had trusted, in particular Prince Meng. I had managed to avoid thoughts of him, not wishing to face my anger and disappointment. I had taken to him like a father to a son. In him, hope and innocence had seemed to spring. I could not bring myself to call this a betrayal. Betrayal occurs when men are flush with want and desire, when they strive to control and conquer that which should not be governed nor hoarded. I could not admit to myself that the Prince who was closer to my soul than any other person, or had seemed to be, would prove to be thus.

I was jolted out of my thoughts when soldiers stormed in and yanked me onto my feet. I tried to kick them off me but I was quickly held down.

"Force is the choice weapon of the weak and insecure," I declared. "This isn't necessary. Nor was that." I nodded towards Kao Shin.

The smaller of the soldiers was a sergeant who backhanded me across the cheek.

"Traitor! You will speak only when told to do so."

The blow awakened me from a corporeal lethargy. "Unhand me. What manner of cowardice did it take for armed soldiers to slay one so recently removed from boyhood?"

"Slay?" the sergeant asked. "That's a fancy word for slicing up that little peach of yours."

They dragged me through the streets as curious onlookers gawked from partially-closed doors and windows. I raised my voice at the soldiers. At every step I tried biting, kicking and pulling away. They laughed at me but I shook inside, seething with anger at Kao Shin's death. I was taken back to the Palace where most of the Royal Guardsmen appeared to be scrambling. Orders were being shouted, torches were lit, weapons were distributed, horses saddled.

I was led towards a small shed with a heavy wooden door into which I was pushed. The door slammed shut, muffling the sounds of the outside world. The darkened shed reeked of fresh urine and feces. A single candle in a alcove gave off a dim light. As my eyes acclimatized, I saw that there was only the one room and no windows. In the shadows sat a soldier and two others behind him. Judging by the markings on the seated soldier's tunic, he was a Captain under General Wu. He untangled some rope as he quietly hummed a tune about harvesting fish and drying them in the warmth of the sun. He did not acknowledge his fellow soldiers or me. Instead he continued to uncoil the thick bundle of hemp rope. He stood on the stool, and then looked back at me, as if he were taking my measure. He threw one end of the rope over a ceiling beam, caught it as it came down and used the end to create a noose. Stepping off the stool he secured the other end of the rope to a corner post.

"Where is she?" he whispered.

I studied his face and his expression as best as I could in the dim light. It was weary, detached, almost pessimistic.

"To whom are you referring?"

"If you want respect in your last moments, you will need to give some in return. Do you understand?"

My 'last moments.' The Captain said it with such indifference that it removed any fear I might have felt. "Yes, indeed I do," I replied.

"Good, then where is she?"

"She is innocent, let her be." I said.

"I thought we had an understanding?" He nodded to the Guardsman holding me. He punched me in the stomach, knocking the wind out of me, and I collapsed onto the dirt floor. When my breathing returned, the questioning continued, as did the kicks and blows.

"You rushed out of the Palace this afternoon. You somehow managed to elude the eyes and ears of those within and outside the Palace. Major Huang has also disappeared, but not before he attacked those who oversaw the questioning of the King's consort. All very suspicious. Explain."

I struggled to speak at first. "What is there to explain? Why are the innocent most likely to suffer? Why do the most cunning seemingly profit the most?"

"These words are pointless, scholar. There is no escape, there is no hiding and there will be no games. The only choice you have is how much you will suffer before you die."

If that was the case, I wanted to know my executioner. "You handle rope with the deftness of one who has fished. And your words are accented with a lilt I encountered among the Donyue in the Kingdom of Yue who live by the Eastern Sea. They are very honest people, hard working, gentle in fact. They lived their lives in harmony. And then the Wu invaded their homelands and enslaved or conscripted many innocents. Many others fled with nothing left but their dignity."

The Captain paused, as did those around him. He slackened his grip on the rope. A soldier rushed into the shed and muttered something to the Captain. The Captain quietly cursed, then ordered my hands bound behind me. I was forced to stand and balance myself on the short stool previously occupied by the Captain. The rope was coiled around my neck, jolting my head upwards. I was left with just enough slack to remain standing. The Captain stood straight, his eyes looked up to mine.

"Be still. If you move suddenly, or slip, you will hang yourself. Beware."

His words were almost whispered, almost as though he was pleading. Then he promptly left. The remaining guards spoke with one another, wondering how long it would take for the General to arrive, if he came at all this evening.

My mind raced at an unprecedented speed. Their questioning of me suggested that Mei had survived. Why else would they have kept me alive? But who had betrayed me yet again? Did the King and Prince Chao learn of my role in the false accusations? Was the King even aware of what was happening? Perhaps one of my staff really was a spy and I had been tricked. Had Prince Meng learned of my presence in the bamboo grove and ordered my arrest? Or was he protecting me? My head saw conspirators behind every door and my body as a mat beneath every foot.

I told myself that if exhaustion overcame me, the guards would not let me die. I was there for a purpose. Nevertheless I did not wish to test their resolve. I fought the fatigue, even though my muscles were stretched and aflame, ready to snap. I took long slow deep breaths, expanding and then contracting my muscles where I could. A glint of light shone through cracks in the door, falling on the wall in front of me. I stared at it, imagining the path of the moon, and awaited the light of dawn. For an old fool, I prided myself on possessing vestiges of resilience.

Some time before dawn, one of the guards stepped outside. I could hear him urinating. He was quickly admonished but told to remain outside. I recognized the voice of the Captain, and I sensed the presence of several others. Then I heard another voice.

"My, how the foolish dreamer has fallen!"

I recognized General Wu's acerbic tone as he entered the shed along with someone else.

"It is by the grace and benevolence of Prince Meng, our future Son of Heaven, that you still live," he said to me. "If it were up to me, you would have died quickly but painfully hours ago."

To emphasize his point he dug his finger into my abdomen, pushing me just enough to almost tip me off the stool.

"It is futile, scholar. All is lost. The bamboo field was searched. One of the interrogators tried to hide. We captured him immediately. He played innocent. So we strung him up. He offered little resistance after that. That he crumbled so easily by his own handiwork is what I believe you intellectuals might call poetic justice. Nevertheless he revealed what we needed to hear, that the woman was defiled by Prince Chao. Then he spoke of friends of Major Huang, millet farmers across the river. He assured us that we would find the woman there, as well as the Major. For his cooperation, a swift death was promised once he had repeated his confession to the court. However, it turns out he is a cousin of the Major. So after his confession he will indeed die slowly and with much pain. The woman has likely bled to death already. The Major's death will be no less painful. My guards should be upon the farm at this moment. Her head and that of the Major's will be forthcoming."

General Wu ordered the guards to untie the noose so I could stand and speak. I inhaled deeply and limped to one side, supported from falling by one of the guards.

"Life is a precarious balance, is it not?" spoke another voice that I recognized as Prince Meng's. "You taught me that."

Strange as it may have seemed, I was relieved he was there. He was not accountable to me, but I hoped he came to provide me with some answers. More importantly, I wanted to see if I could still inspire in him some humanity.

Prince Meng stepped forward, removing the hood that covered his head and much of his face. He was grinning but his expression also revealed a hardness I had never before seen in him. He dismissed the guards and General Wu, who tried to protest, but a glare from the Prince sent the General off.

"You chose a treasonous, perilous route, all under the guise of moral righteousness," he said. "That you acted against me surprises me. That you threw your hand in with Prince Chao disappoints me. It must be a bitter pill you are swallowing. The meritorious scholar gambles for once in his life. He loses, and is completely abandoned. It is my men who will now ease your final struggle."

I tried to speak and gagged for a moment. "Life is not so much precarious, as it is the guise by which certain brands of morality are imposed."

"It is rather late to be philosophizing, Master Scholar," Prince Meng said. "Sit."

I landed heavily on the stool. He reached for a cup, scooped water from a nearby barrel and held it to my eager, parched mouth. As I gulped the water, he spoke.

"You did teach me well, Master Scholar. But it was I who worked out that an erudite's value is multiplied many times over when strategy and opportunity are maximized."

Evidently he had absorbed Sun Wu's artful treatise on war and deception rather well.

"Is that all I was to your Highness? Erudite value?"

He shrugged.

"But why, your Highness? I cannot believe what I saw in you was a complete illusion."

"That was your vision, Master Scholar. At first it resonated for me as well. It gave me respites of acceptance and peace when the court was nothing more than a crushing burden. The Way lit my world, it gave me clarity. I tried, Lao Tzu, I really did. And for a while, seeing the world in this manner might have been enough, throne or not. But in time the Way began to weigh me down like sacks of worthless currency. It gave cause for others to mock me, to ignore me. Then after my brother's recovery, I was increasingly overlooked. I could see my throne and my standing slipping away. You cannot possibly imagine the humiliation. In a world decided by metal and might, there is little respect for thoughts and actions, or shall I say, inactions. Eventually the Way merely reinforced this for me.

"But there is much to thank you for. Your garden introduced me to the idea of using poison. Your Archives gave me Sun Tzu's illuminating strategies. It appears he also was one with the Way. He taught me that one must be flexible and adaptable to ever-changing conditions. I proved this when my initial plan to deal with my Heavenly Father was inadvertently thwarted by my mother's dogs. Admittedly, it was a sloppy plan, crude in fact. I'm new at this, you see. But one must be ready to take advantage of opportunities that suddenly emerge. I have just done so again with my father's rapid deterioration, which coincided so wonderfully with that woman being with child. All while my brother is out saving the world. Fortunately for me, he and Confucius chose this moment to play the hero-diplomats."

I looked at him silently for a moment.

"Your Highness, you still might have found the contentment you had always lacked," I said. "Instead, something unnatural befell you and you have chosen a path paved with deceit, treachery and blood. This is not you, my Lord. I cannot believe that what I saw in you was a complete illusion. You had such clarity, such conviction. You alone possessed the nobility and means to choose a different path. You could have been a beacon that led others to pause and reflect. You have now made grievous errors but it is not too late. Your father will no longer be able to stir your conflict with your brother. You can unite with Prince Chao, you can create a destiny and a world that has never before been witnessed, one filled with enlightenment, justness and prosperity for all. You can be remembered for greatness, not treachery."

Prince Meng hesitated. His face softened. "You always believed this about me."

"Yes. Yes."

"You saw in me things no one else imagined. But surely it is too late."

I shook my head. "You can choose the path which only you are capable of treading."

Prince Meng slowly paced the room. "And what of my brother?"

"Your Highness, he will come to see you in a different light, I am sure."

General Wu re-entered the cell. I overheard him whispering that forces loyal to Prince Chao had begun to marshal against them. Prince Meng's face hardened once again. He dismissed the General.

"Never, never will we unite. He will indeed see a different brother now, one that he will fear and recoil from. You did not appreciate, you could not have appreciated, that I also learned to stand with those of like mind such as General Wu, who find nothing but idiocy in Prince Chao's actions. Isn't it ironic, Master Scholar, that my dear brother happens to be an even bigger dreamer than I once was?"

"There is ample room in the court for two dreamers, provided their aspirations speak of a common good, not a vainglorious quest for power," I said.

"And miss out on such an opportunity? How could I have remained a student of the Way? Eventually my brother would have banished me to some backwater territory. No, never. The Way is a path that resonates for individuals such as yourself who already have little to lose and can afford impracticalities. Perhaps in another time and place, if enough of you had stood together, the world's cadence could have been harnessed. But for me, in the grander scheme of the world, there is now no place for such luxuries."

"Your Highness, it is still possible to avert further bloodshed. I urge you to choose wisely."

"I already have. As for you, I did not mean for this to unfold in such a way, Master Scholar. My instructions to you were clear and simple. Had you remained in your quarters and not conspired with other traitors, you would have remained free."

"Traitors?"

"The Major surprised me. He had always performed his duties with honor, as the Commander of all the Royal Guardsmen should. He had been above and beyond the fray of shifting loyalties, much like you, Master Scholar. I'm curious to know who informed him that Wu's men took our little whore to the bamboo field instead of this shed, where a proper interrogation might have been carried out undisturbed. At first, I presumed it was Yi Ban. You were seen rushing to him immediately after she was dragged off. But I was wrong. The stench in here is Yi Ban's, by the way. He fouled himself as he begged for mercy before he was hanged."

I gasped. Prince Meng continued.

"We would have preferred him to have left us a confession. So I am left to wonder how the Major found out about the interrogation in the forest, and why he shunned his duty and turned against me."

"You just answered your own question, your Highness. The man is honorable. As was Yi Ban, who did not deserve such a fate. The Major saw through your plotting some time ago." I also thought of the Black Serpent, but was not prepared to reveal the presence of the one person who might still be standing against Prince Meng. "He likely remained neutral and silent as he was duty-bound. Yet it would appear his duty in the end was to his conscience above all else."

"Ah, yet another dreamer. I still consider myself to be one. There is a place for us all. Your place, however, is here, and the Major and the whore and all those who would oppose me will follow. It is men of action, not ideas, who shall rule. It is not possible to reconcile this chasm any other way."

"Reconciliation is only impossible because hard feelings abound. This is what is dangerous, your Highness. A sage accepts less than is due, and does not blame or punish. It appears to be you who cannot accept reconciliation. Alas, I believe that is now of little consequence to you."

"Bold words coming from one so near to death. But then again, I expected righteous indignation and demands for me to be just. I also had hoped for some groveling and pleas for mercy. But that just would not have been you."

"Justice seeks payment and retribution. Harmony seeks agreement and accordance. The Way is impartial. It serves those who serve all. There is much to be learned still, your Highness."

"You would not speak to me in this way had I not spoiled you by granting such proximity to me. You have forgotten your place."

"I have always known my place was to serve, and have done my best to do so nobly and honorably. But leaders also fail when they forget whom they serve. There will be few who regret my passing out of this world, and whoever passes judgment on me will do so justly. Can your Highness say the same?"

"Such impertinence!" Prince Meng threw the remaining water into my face. I licked the few drops dripping from my upper lip.

"No regrets you say? Have you forgotten those who died at your precious Academy? And your servant Kao Shin, whose loyalty to you cost him his life? Even as he bled to death he tried to protect you. He even confessed that he was the spy." The Prince chuckled. "And let us not forget Yi Ban who recruited you, and now Mei and the Major. In fact, everyone who has had the folly to pursue your ideals has had a tragic end. That is, until I came to see that where decisiveness and strength are required, one must be practical and shed precious ideals. Where I have spilled blood, it was for a cause, not a foolish dream. Still no regrets, truly, Master Scholar?"

I had no answer for him and looked away.

He lowered himself until our faces were only an arm's length apart.

"Do not despair Master Scholar, I still have the nobility you spoke of. I can offer you life, but that will be cruel. For you will spend your remaining days wandering the world, and self-recriminating in a manner far more painful and lasting than a quick, merciful death. No, I will grant you death with your precious honor, your noble ideas, and your Way, however tinged with the bitter hue that your failure in every way aided me. Your passing will happen unbeknownst, undocumented and unnoticed. Whereas I, the soon-to-be new Son of Heaven, will live on in history." He paused to give me an opportunity to refute.

"What say you, Scholar?"

Again I could not respond.

"And now the man of ideas is speechless."

Prince Meng turned and left without another word.

I remained still, almost lifeless. He was correct. I would die with nothing but blood to show for my ideals and a lifetime of work. The guards re-entered, and once again stood me on the stool where my balance was precarious. They re-wrapped the rope around my neck. It would only take a moment before I would hang myself, they said to each other.

I struggled to breath and remain motionless. Where the blows had landed, sharp pains punctuated my body. The ropes slowly dug into my neck and wrists, leaving scores of burning itches I was unable to soothe. I could feel my cold sweat against the brisk autumn night air. I lost all notion of time. My legs stiffened and cramped. A searing thirst further labored my breathing. What was left to struggle for? What had my enlightenment brought me? I had attempted to nurture and cultivate my fellow man. I had lived the life of my choosing. I had followed the Way. Where I had failed, it was not for lack of endeavor.

A slight shift in either direction could end it all swiftly. If I could not choose the manner of my departure, I could choose the precise moment. More than anything else I felt profound sorrow. I thought of my father. I had known him less than I would have liked. I'd learned the ways of the world first by his hand, then my own. A scholar's life was not an existence of toil, but it was unspeakably solitary and lonely at times. Ironically Confucius was perhaps the only other one who understood this. I had neither the comforts nor the demands of family. Perhaps that was why I had taken to mentoring. I knew how very crucial it was for unformed minds. I wondered if Father would have been proud of me, if he would have forgiven me for my simplicity, for my incessant romanticism. But I could not forgive the abject failures of a dreamer such as myself. The Way had given me cause and hope for most of my life, but it could not shield me any further.

I realized that with the absence of pretense, the veil of any ruse lifted and an unexpected quietude befell me. I had been a complete knave. It was easier to live with a fatal truth than to dance around denial and a conspicuous lie. Yet I would not die feeling any animosity towards Prince Meng. Instead, I would die blaming myself for my blindness, and for my part in the deaths of all those Prince Meng had mentioned. I had not followed the intuitive path that Father and even cousin Shun had lived. Whereas I philosophized about the Way, they breathed life into it in a manner I only spoke of. And as for what little harmony that remained, I would wear it until my last breath. I had no strength remaining to fight the pain and fatigue. My body would decide the next step, naturally.

Then I heard shouting. It came from every direction. The voices sounded fearful. The guards attending to me began to panic as they too wondered what the commotion was about. "Water!" I heard the voices cry out. Then, "fire!" Soon the smell of smoke seeped into the little room in which I was imprisoned.

The door opened. A blazing torch lit the room.

"The Palace is on fire! Quickly get over there!" I recognized the voice of an officer from the inner court. After the guards left, several others entered.

"I believe he still lives," the officer said. They untied the rope around my wrists, then lifted the noose from around my neck. I collapsed, knocking someone to the ground as I did so. A woman's voice ordered me off. I rolled to one side and struggled to stand. The Queen lay beneath me on the dirt floor.

She waved off a guard's hand of assistance and stood up. "There is little time," she said. "You must get up and follow them." She gestured to her bodyguard standing by the door and several Royal Guardsmen. She wore a plain silk dress and was bereft of her usual bejeweled adornments and make-up, save for a gold phoenix hair pin.

I could barely move and was speechless. "But what... how?" I stammered.

"Master Scholar, you may believe that learned ways open the mind, but sometimes feigned madness achieves more."

She and the guard steadied me. I beckoned for some water, which they obliged. I gulped it down as though it would be my last.

"What has happened?" I gasped.

"The Celestial Hall is aflame. It will not survive such a blaze. The entire Palace is at risk and is being emptied. The Son of Heaven has been evacuated. A more fortuitous opportunity could not have presented itself. Go, now."

I stared at her. I recognized the face, and even the child-like intonations of her voice, but I could not reconcile them with what I was seeing. Despite the dim light I could see that her manner was different. There was assuredness in her tone and a confidence I had never before witnessed. "But I thought..."

"Master Scholar, if one does not masquerade insanity here, it will soon befall them anyway. I have survived all manner of vices, wickedness and misdeeds. I have seen and heard more of my court than anyone should. I could not have done so if others did not see me as a simpleton."

Her revelation stupefied me.

"What manner of subterfuge is this now? How can I..."

"Trust me?" she cut me off. "You have little choice. But on the night Mei was attacked, you were outside the King's residence, as was I. I was chasing my poor dogs when they ran into Meng, dressed to appear like his younger brother."

"Your Highness, how can you be sure?" I asked.

She looked at me as though I were an imbecile. "You are asking how a mother can distinguish between her two sons?"

I nodded sheepishly before she continued.

"My dogs' accidental meeting with the Prince likely caused him to drop a vial, which shattered on the floor. This was in the corridor leading to the King's residence. My dogs happily licked up the contents. The Prince avoided my gaze, but I could tell he was furious. He continued onwards and spotted Mei. Unable to complete what I believe was his initial plan, he saw another opportunity to unleash his anger. He defiled her. It was well after my dogs enjoyed the contents of that vial that you came upon us. The dogs had begun to behave erratically and shortly afterwards they suffered an agonizing death. I believe Meng had intended to poison the Son of Heaven in his brother's guise."

It was as Prince Meng boasted. I knew he had taken an interest in one particular plant, the poisonous rhubarb.

"Your Highness, it is not my place to question your actions. But did you inform the Son of Heaven? That might have prevented Mei from having to make a false allegation and suffering so greatly."

"It might have. I have stood silently for many years, waiting for the right moment. At times I have discretely lent a benevolent hand. But a mad woman suddenly stepping forward with such a story would have sounded even more mad, do you not agree?"

"I suppose that was a foolish question, your Highness. But somehow I doubt you stood silent. Are you not the Black Serpent who sent Major Huang and I to the bamboo forest, and who aided Mei and her family?"

She nodded. "And it was I who has alerted Chao to return to prevent his brother's attempt to seize the throne in this fashion. I could see Meng's bitterness over the King's decision to leave the throne to our younger son. But there are too many questions, my dear scholar. You must leave before Meng consolidates his power."

"Your Highness, is this too late?"

The Queen sighed. "I suspect so. The King's judgment has waned considerably in the past week, and he is no longer standing up to Meng's depiction of Chao as a traitor. Chao's absence was a strategic error. He meant well, as he was en route to the Chu encampment along with Confucius. They had planned to negotiate a withdrawal of Chu's troops, and to seek political unification of all states, thus ending this ruinous path of continuous wars."

The Queen commanded the guards to check if the area was clear. Then she continued. "Regrettably Meng has convinced his father that Chao is meeting with the King of Chu on the frontier in order to seek support for him as the Son of Heaven, and that Prince Chao is the spy."

"The defilement of Mei is akin to salt on the wound of a fragile, dying man," I said. "Meng will twist this to make his brother appear opportunistic, conniving and insensitive to his father's health."

"I agree, Master Scholar. I would not be surprised if Meng has compounded this by torching the Celestial Hall and has witnesses ready to swear that Prince Chao's men were seen doing it. He has already bought off many of the Royal Guardsmen with land. Those Guardsmen who have sided with Meng have sealed off the Son of Heaven from all but myself and Meng's most trusted Ministers. They, along with Wu's men, are already fighting against those loyal to the Major and Chao. It grieves my heart to see this."

I looked northward, towards where Mei had originally been taken. Then I looked back at the Queen. "What a fool I have been."

The Queen gave me a sympathetic look. "Does the Way you espouse not see rulers as inherently nefarious?"

I nodded. "Yes, your Highness."

"Then I beseech you, Master Scholar, to see that the closer they are to our hearts, the blinder we are to their faults. For I too could not see the obvious for some time."

"Your words may one day soothe another misguided character. But for now, I have few options. Prince Meng won't let me live, and I have little purpose in running and hiding. I have failed all who trusted me."

"Perhaps their trust was not only in you, but in what you embraced. Think, Scholar. Are your ideas so weak that they cannot withstand dissent?"

"False hopes and fanciful dreams, your Highness, that is all I have to offer."

"No, Master Scholar. You have much to offer to the right receiver. I must believe this, for I myself have waited years to end my silence. Doing so now can have real meaning and no higher purpose. I believe I can deaden Meng's interest in you. I can offer him my continued silence in exchange for four lives—yours, Major Huang's, and Mei's, assuming she lives. I doubt Meng will keep his word, yet it may buy you some time. But you must leave at once. Stay hidden, stay quiet. I forewarned the Major earlier that a trap was about to be sprung. He and Mei have been moved. They are safe, but not for long."

"Your Highness, the Captain, and Mei… they live?"

The Queen nodded. "I am told that she is near death. But she possesses a strength one should not underestimate. I have studied her well. She will live. The Major will provide her with ample protection."

"But your Highness, you said your silence would be exchanged for four lives."

She nodded. "My grandchild will need a teacher."

"Grandchild, your Highness?"

I gaped at her like the innocent I must have appeared to be.

Only then did I realize she was referring to the child Mei was carrying, potentially Prince Meng's offspring and living evidence of his duplicity.

One of the guards returned. He indicated that for now, the immediate area was safe and a clear path existed to a secret exit leading out of the Forbidden Yellow Palace into Chengzhou proper. He opened the door and led me and then the Queen out. The Celestial Hall was ablaze as if the God of Fire himself had spat at the Royals. Around the Celestial Hall, shouting and confusion reigned as soldiers carried water in one direction and precious Palace belongings in the other.

I stopped to glance towards my Archives to see if it still stood. But smoke obscured any clear view.

"Make haste, Master Scholar. My trusted guards will guide you to the Major," the Queen said. "Then show them the Way."

18

Finding the Way

Prince Chao returned while the ruins of the Celestial Hall still smoldered. By then, the Son of Heaven had been convinced that the fire was Prince Chao's doing, and that he was in league with Chu. Broken-hearted and near death, the Son of Heaven ordered his youngest son banished. Prince Chao remained steadfast and denied the charges, setting the stage for civil war within the Palace itself. This may have been the mortal wound for the King, for he died before he could witness the impending battle between his sons.

In a final attempt to avoid bloodshed, Prince Chao invited his brother to tea after their father's funeral. Prince Meng accepted and offered his brother an opportunity to be his most trusted advisor and anything else he desired. But that too was a ruse which Prince Chao saw through. He did not, however, see through the poison he had drunk. He immediately took ill and died painfully the next day. In that respect, some rumors were true. Just as I did not see who Meng was, nor did I see the true character of Chao. Unfortunately their mother the Queen, the Black Serpent, did not survive the transfer of power and supposedly died of a broken heart. Having witnessed her strength, I have always wondered about this.

It is well known that Chu's troops moved into the capital

shortly afterwards, raping and pillaging targeted areas all known to contain Prince Chao supporters. The Royal Guardsmen stood down, awaiting orders that never came from the new Son of Heaven. All voices of moderation and action such as Yi Ban's had been silenced forever. For his cooperation, Chu allowed Prince Meng to rule as a puppet until he too was assassinated, only one year later. I had mixed feelings upon hearing this. The idea of him once gave me such hope. Yet he revealed himself to be an odious being. Among others, he was neither loved nor respected. He had made many enemies.

As for Confucius, he did not return with Prince Chao to court. Had he done so, Prince Meng might have included him in his purge of all things and people associated with his brother. However, our paths did cross again for one final, fleeting moment, many years after we had both fled Chengzhou. It was at a roadside inn where he was holding court with several other scholars and noblemen. I remained in the shadows, listening to him speak, as he always did, about duty, moral obligation and piety. His words stirred up old feelings, and I almost lost all sense of myself. I was about to step forward and exact some cutting words about the ill-advised entanglements caused by him and his advice. Of course, I could have rebuked myself for the same reasons, but at that moment I had lost all perspective. Then Confucius switched to some new thoughts on character that I had not heard him utter before.

"When you meet someone better than yourself, turn your thoughts to becoming his equal. When you meet someone not as good as you are, look within and examine your own self. When you see a good person, think of becoming like him. When you see someone not so good, reflect on your own weak points. And where doubt exists, personal cultivation is insufficient. For when one cultivates to the utmost the principles of his nature, and exercises them on the principle of reciprocity, he is not far from the way which he treads. What you do not like when done to yourself, do not do to others."

Upon hearing such words it became clear to me he was a scholar unlike most others. He was as grand a romantic as I had been accused of being. His ideas and beliefs were as rooted as mine in a principled world that could be as easily supplanted. We roamed among people blinded by too much color, deafened by too much music, whose palates were dulled by too many tastes, and whose hearts were torn asunder by too much desire.

After our tumultuous time in court, there was little more we had to say to each other. As fellow scholars, it was time to look to the next tablet.

As for myself, the Queen's guards smuggled me out of Chengzhou that fateful night to where Major Huang and Mei waited for me. Along with two other Guardsmen, the Major had kept vigil over Mei, protecting her like she was his own. She was not well enough to travel, but we had no choice. I could not begin to describe the joy I felt at seeing her alive. The Guardsmen carried her in a litter as we moved from hiding place to hiding place in the nearby hills until the Major directed us towards Jin territory. The Major was very cautious and we were able to evade detection from Prince Meng's men, from bounty hunters and from the lawlessness by staying north of the Yellow. We walked for weeks. The country was rich but uncultivated and far from any civilization. The landscape, so similar to what I grew up in, evoked memories—some pleasant, others sad. The further we ventured into unknown territory, the more unsettled I became. At times I felt like we were being watched. Other times it seemed as though we had cast ourselves into the fringes of the world. I attributed these foolish thoughts to exhaustion and hunger, for we ran out of food. Then we let our guard down ever so briefly and a patrol of soldiers came upon us as we slept.

One Guardsman was slain before he was able to draw his sword. The Major and the remaining Guardsman retrieved their weapons and fought off the soldiers. The Major fought like a demon. He and Thunderclap were able to keep most of them at a distance, impaling several attackers and knocking several others off their feet. Even I took up a sword and slashed at whatever bodies the Major cast aside. But they were heavily armed and we were vastly outnumbered. Our remaining Guardsman took a sword stroke behind his head and collapsed. The Major and I were cornered, defending Mei who brandished a dagger but struggled to stand. We were doomed.

"The woman is with child, spare her," I pleaded with their commanding officer.

"Oh, most definitely she will be spared, for a better purpose," he replied as he and the others advanced.

A small rock flew by, hitting the commanding officer between the eyes and knocking him flat. Another rock felled another soldier. Then out of the bushes charged a score of sword-wielding, ragtag-looking men. They easily tore through the few remaining soldiers who hadn't already scattered.

I was stunned by our reprieve and looked about with shock. One figure emerged from the bush and approached me.

"There's considerably more respect for swords, but slingshots still have a romantic appeal for me, would you not agree, dear cousin?"

I recognized the voice from long ago. Cousin Shun stepped forward, a slingshot dangling from his waist belt. He commanded his men to lower their arms. His warm chestnut colored eyes lit up. He seemed shorter than I remembered. His hair had receded, but he had a thick, long mane of white hair, adding to an air of self-assurance. Large hands grasped my forearms in greeting.

"Did I not say, dear cousin, that we would be together? Though I never suspected that it would take forty years."

At first I was speechless, and shocked at the sight of my cousin appearing in such a manner. Ignoring the hundreds of questions crowding my mind like gnats, I stammered out a reply, "Believe me, it is a reunion long since overdue and at this moment sorely required. We have not eaten in days, the woman can barely move. Can you assist us?"

He studied Mei and directed his men to dispense food and water. Then he cast a wary look at the Major. "You fight like a whole army all by yourself. I suspect even we would have been challenged."

"You suspect?" The Major asked gruffly as he checked on his fallen comrades.

"Those blades are forged by Royal artisans," Shun said. "I recognize the craftsmanship. Could you possibly be the bounty agent I have heard about?"

The Major reached for his halberd.

"Relax, we are no friends of the King, or whomever purports to rule us,"' Shun said. "These were General Wu's men. There will be others. We must move deeper into Jin territory. Wu will not antagonize the Jin by following, but there will be other bounty hunters, bandits and renegades."

"You mean outlaws such as yourselves?" the Major said, looking over at Shun's men who were emptying the soldiers' pockets and picking through their weapons.

Shun shrugged, "Outlaws we may be, though we take only what we need, rather than what is easily taken."

As Mei was being attended to, Shun told his tale. He had been conscripted by one of the Wu armies and even served closely with Sun Wu as a spy, then deserted after refusing to participate in the slaughtering of yet another defenseless village. He had been on the move for years. He apprenticed in forging metals, took up fishing, and even farmed at one point. But peace was never with him for long. He had been drifting for years but had learned that living day-to-day, hand-to-mouth, fists-to-foes came easily for him. Over the years he recruited a band of outcasts and renegades, honing them into a disciplined and skilled hunting and thieving force. They had never been subdued, nor bested. They identified strongly with the weak and the powerless, and prided themselves on their clandestine skills.

"Then the tale of the White Renegade is true?" I asked Shun.

He chuckled. "Yes, but like all tales, it is heavily seasoned. We bleed like all other men. But what of the great philosopher, Lao Tzu?"

"Like you said, all tales are heavily seasoned."

Over the next several weeks we shared our journeys as the men escorted us, evading patrols of mercenaries working for the Chu and Prince Meng, as well as parties of other bandits.

"We part here, dear cousin," Shun said without a hint of sentiment. "Beyond this river crossing you will be in Qi. There are no known perils here for good, honest men."

"Then why don't you cross with us?" I asked of him.

"Did I not say honest?" he said with a twinkle in his eyes. "It has been years since any of us did an honest day's labor. To do so now would invite an uneasy restlessness. No, I leave it for you and your companions to sow the seeds of humanity."

Shun and his men departed. This time there was little doubt that it would be final. A sense of loss for Shun and the years we hadn't shared together struck me. I almost begged for the steady hand and mind he would have provided, but knew better.

With some nourishment and fresh supplies, the Major kept us moving for another week or so, taking a long but careful route to a quiet corner of Qi.

Captain Yin leaned on a wall, staring off into the distance. His entire platoon had gravitated into the guardhouse. All stood silently, heads bowed, spellbound by the Old Master whose eyes had suddenly rediscovered their vigor.

"And so it was. I hope your curiosity is satisfied."

Lao Tzu stretched his back, and as he stopped talking, the first crickets of the evening could be heard. Otherwise an unruffled calm permeated the guardhouse and the world around it.

"That was forty springs ago. Since I left Mei and her son, not once did I share these experiences with anyone."

Lao Tzu begged for more tea and a moment's rest.

"You too are from Qi originally, are you not, Captain Yin? I recognize your accent."

The Captain nodded.

"Perhaps near Linzi, west of it in fact, in a little bay off the river?" Lao Tzu asked.

The Captain answered, "Yes, how did you know?"

"Do you recall a family named Tang? Their patriarch was a former soldier named Tang Dengjie. I spoke of him earlier. He would have died before you were born. But they were a special family. They took me in on my way to Chengzhou for the very first time. If you lived anywhere in that area, you could not miss them."

The Captain nodded and with a puzzled look said, "Yes."

"And your grandfather; he was likely the tallest man you've ever laid eyes on. He often lost his balance. An injury caused by an arrow which grazed the side of his head during a raid by bandits. Your grandmother, she had a diamond-shaped face, and small, dark inquisitive eyes as shiny as the finest lacquer."

The Captain stiffened. "What are you saying?"

"After we fled Chengzhou, we eventually settled west of Linzi, where Mei begat a son. A miracle, really. There we heard of Prince Meng's assassination but rumors of him having had a son was a threat to any other claimants to the throne. So we kept a low profile. Eventually, I felt it was safest, though most regrettable, for me to leave the Major, Mei and her son. That Major was as loyal and proud a soldier and father-figure as could be. And as it turned out, he was both a fine husband and grandfather."

Lao Tzu paused, allowing his words to sink in, then continued: "I assume you have memories of the man who called himself your grandfather?"

The Captain gave a hesitant nod. "What do you mean, 'the man who called himself my grandfather'?"

Lao looked squarely at the Captain. "It was your true grandfather who defiled Mei, your grandmother, some forty-five years ago. The man you believe to be your grandfather was in fact, Major Huang."

The Captain stifled a nervous guffaw, then stood transfixed. "You are mistaken. My grandfather was named Yin Lu. You must be thinking of someone else."

But the Captain's protests lacked strength. Lao Tzu held a hand up, then in a soft voice and with a slight bow said, "Yin Lu was the name the Major assumed. Your father was named Yin Song. I know this because I was present at his miracle birth and for his first five years. It is all true, Captain. Prince Meng, Mei, your father… and now you… your Highness. I never thought it would be possible to ever meet you. One may easily lose hope when the path meanders endlessly along no apparent track. But the Way has its own direction. It sets its own course. If there is anything to be learned, it is that Nature's course should not be questioned or altered."

Several of the Captain's troops gasped. Then a moment of

complete silence befell the shelter and all around it. It was as though Lao Tzu's soft voice had halted everything in existence.

The stillness was broken by a growing clamor outside and a determined voice called for the Captain. His men investigated. The Captain reluctantly pried himself away from Lao Tzu.

Lieutenant Zhang and their General rode in with a platoon of heavily-armed troops. The General dismounted, as did the Lieutenant. The Captain bowed and greeted his commanding officer. The General wasted little time: "Your Lieutenant reports that your command is slovenly, and your troops lack discipline. I might have ignored such troublemaking had you not shown the audacity to commandeer my scribe without my knowledge. Even worse, you shelter a suspicious traveler."

The Captain looked at his men. "Sir, that these men would serve nobly and loyally in battle I have no doubt. But I will not deny that extreme boredom has made them more slovenly than is desirable, and a lack of training has imbued them with erratic discipline. I make no excuses and take full responsibility. But I was sent farmers and peasants who would best serve Zhou by feeding it. As for your scribe, he will impart a previously untold story that speaks for itself. Hear it out. Then do with it as you wish."

"The spy, General… the spy," the Lieutenant interrupted. "The Captain has not answered to this. There is an old man here who has fled the Royal Court. Only a sympathizer would protect a spy."

The General approached the Captain, stopping only an arm's distance away. "What say you, Captain?"

The Captain didn't hesitate. "If a sympathizer is one who protects and cherishes truth and virtue, then that is I. If a spy is an individual of upstanding moral character, then indeed, it is a spy that I sympathize with."

The General glared at the Captain. "It is as I feared. As of now, you are relieved of your command. Follow me. And bring this mysterious traveler. The Lieutenant shall be the commanding officer until this matter is investigated."

The General began to turn away, but the Captain's group of ragtag farmer and peasant soldiers fell into a tight battle formation behind their Captain, rusty swords, and halberds at the ready. Even the scribe stepped forward wielding a fallen tree branch.

The General stepped back, as did the Lieutenant. The General addressed the Captain's men.

"This is a mutinous act. As your General, I command you to stand down. Your commanding officer has been relieved. He will be taken in for questioning, no more."

The corporal shouted back: "Sir, the rightful heir of Zhou stands before us. He is your leader and mine."

Lieutenant Zhang laughed nervously then gave the corporal and the other soldiers an exasperated look.

The Captain looked behind him, astonished at his troops' new found spirit.

The General signaled for his men to assume a battle formation. They drew their weapons and stepped forward. The Captain's troops responded in kind. Both sides carried an equal number of troops. For a brief moment the only sound was that of the evening crickets. The only thing that stirred was a gentle breeze.

"Enough," a soft but authoritative voice called out.

Everyone looked back at the shelter from which Lao Tzu had emerged, half bent over, hands resting on his walking stick.

"General I beseech you, blood will not irrigate our parched land, nor will my head satisfy the insatiable cravings of power mongers. I have spent an innumerable number of years wandering the earth, reliving lost opportunities, castigating myself and trying to repent my errors. It has taken me this long to accept the natural consequences of my actions and inactions. But these have all passed, and I am prepared to go, however ill-at-ease I remain. Take me if you so wish. I shall come freely if it averts more suffering. I fear you not, for my end is already at hand."

The General looked at Lao Tzu, then at the Lieutenant Zhang. "This is the spy you speak of?"

"Sir, the Captain behaves as though this spy has scoured his mind," Lieutenant Zhang shouted. "The old man gives every indication of having escaped from the court. A reward and favors might follow his capture."

"Sir, I would have arrested him myself if treason and sedition had been suspected," the Captain responded. "But there is no evidence of this, for he poses no more a threat than a sparrow does to a tiger."

"What then of you, whom your men say is the rightful heir to Zhou?" the General asked the Captain. "Such a claim, together with your insubordination, demands severe consequences. Perhaps you will invoke your heavenly powers as the Son of Heaven-in-waiting?"

The Captain let those words hang for a moment. He turned towards his men. His eyes met each one of theirs. He looked back towards the General. He removed his officer's tunic and dropped his sword.

"Sir, you know that I have served Zhou since I was able to lift a sword. But it is not the fabricated divisions of man I wish to conquer. What I seek is the manner and knowledge by which the natural world flows. You may take me as well. Or release us and I give you my word you will never hear of us again."

The General chortled. "To do so would be to endorse desertion."

"Sir, leadership is not the exertion of power and control alone. Rather it is the strategic use of enlightened thought and well-intentioned actions."

Lao Tzu stepped towards the General and spoke softly to him.

"Perhaps the Lieutenant is partially correct. The Captain has indeed lost his mind. Who else under your command but a madman would willingly remove his uniform? He is not a deserter. You can just discharge a harmless madman who believes he is the rightful heir to the throne. Then you will not have to answer as to why your own men have turned on each other."

The General looked at Lao Tzu, then again at the Captain. Lieutenant Zhang called out to the General, but the General shot back with a look that silenced him. The General stepped aside and signaled his men to withdraw. He then ordered the scribe to follow. The scribe reluctantly did so, but not until he gingerly wrapped the many bamboo slips and nodded at Lao Tzu as if to say, his work was safe.

The Captain watched them depart, then unhitched the rope attached to Lao Tzu's water buffalo before handing it to him.

"Do you not tire of loneliness, Master?" asked the Captain.

Lao Tzu threw his few possessions back onto the water buffalo.

"Loneliness foments lucidity. If you offer music and food, strangers may stop for you; but if you offer…"

"… the Way, then all the people of the world will keep you in safety, health, community and peace," the Captain interjected. "The Way lacks art and flavor, it can neither be seen nor heard, but its virtues cannot be exhausted. What was once discounted by me as confusing chatter by my grandfather was in fact a precursor of a future path, one that until now I did not realize I was on. Take me with you, Master."

"No," Lao Tzu said. "I cannot allow you to do this. There is nothing left I can offer anyone." He hesitated. "The Way has run its course, and so have I."

The Captain held Lao Tzu's arm.

"It may be ironic, but Prince Meng, my grandfather, was correct. The Way can have its place for individuals, and it can resonate further if enough people stand together and someday harness the cadence of the natural world. I do not need to be convinced of this, I already live it. I simply was not aware of the balance it had given me. And so it must begin somehow. Just as your father's idea saw the betterment of the world one plot of land at a time, so too can the Way make a difference. These ideas were passed down over the generations, eventually to me. Do you not see that it is possible that many others have come to live and see the world as such?"

Lao Tzu remained silent.

The Captain continued. "I believe so. And I believe this is your legacy, which you cannot deny. Nor should you. How else can you explain how the gnarled path of the Way brought us together? It has its own design, it sets its own course."

Lao Tzu weighed this as he studied the Captain. He saw a naïve and innocent man for whom a fondness of birds, of all things natural and unhindered, superseded all else. But he also saw a man at peace, one who was calm but whose hunger was infectious. And through him Lao Tzu saw possibilities, which made him smile like he had not in many years. The Way in it's infinite capacity to bend, had taken him through innumerable lows and disappointments. Yet perhaps his journey had not reached its end, but had arrived at yet another turn. Perhaps he had one final pupil. It pleased him that he could still dream.

With the soldiers at attention, the Captain eased Lao Tzu onto his beast. It was much too late in the day to begin a long journey, yet neither appeared concerned. The Old Master and his new follower walked towards the Han Gu Pass, oblivious of the waning sun in their eyes. Together they passed through the gate and left the Royal territory. Neither looked back.

ACKNOWLEDGEMENTS

Thank you to Chris Crowder, Amy Tector and Alette Willis — my writing group of many years. They define superb critiquing with an eye for the finer details and a vision for the bigger picture.

Alice Poon for recognizing a diamond in the rough.

Graham Earnshaw for promoting stories of China with a rare enthusiasm.

Melanie Fogel, my writing instructor whose no-nonsense approach and attention to craft launched many a good writer.

Doreen Arnoni, Marc Brown and Mary Gelner for their discerning eyes during my last edits.

And especially my wife Trish Lucy, for her unwavering support throughout and for making me read her favourite book, *The Tao of Pooh* by Benjamin Hoff, which led the way to the Master Scholar.

About the Author

Wayne Ng was born in downtown Toronto to Chinese immigrants who fed him a steady diet of bitter melons and kung fu movies. Like Lao Tzu, his romantic, idealist protagonist in *Finding the Way,* he dreams of a just society, of worlds far from his doorstep, and of tastes, sensations and experiences beyond his imagination.

Wayne works as a school social worker in Ottawa but lives to write, travel, eat and play, preferably all at the same time. He is an award-winning short story and travel writer who has twice backpacked through China. Wayne continues to push his boundaries from the Arctic to the Antarctic, blogging and photographing along the way.

www.WayneNgWrites.com